P9-DGY-718

DOWN & DEAD IN DIXIE

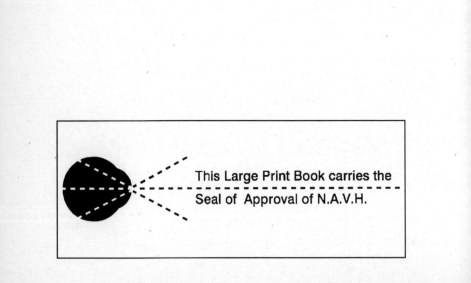

This Large Print Book carries the
Seal of Approval of N.A.V.H.

DOWN & DEAD, INC.

DOWN & DEAD IN DIXIE

VICKI HINZE

THORNDIKE PRESS
A part of Gale, Cengage Learning

GALE
CENGAGE Learning·

Farmington Hills, Mich • San Francisco • New York • Waterville, Maine
Meriden, Conn • Mason, Ohio • Chicago

GALE
CENGAGE Learning

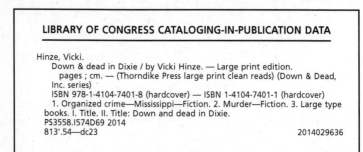

LIBRARY OF CONGRESS CATALOGING-IN-PUBLICATION DATA

Hinze, Vicki.
   Down & dead in Dixie / by Vicki Hinze. — Large print edition.
     pages ; cm. — (Thorndike Press large print clean reads) (Down & Dead, Inc. series)
     ISBN 978-1-4104-7401-8 (hardcover) — ISBN 1-4104-7401-1 (hardcover)
     1. Organized crime—Mississippi—Fiction. 2. Murder—Fiction. 3. Large type books. I. Title. II. Title: Down and dead in Dixie.
   PS3558.I574D69 2014
   813'.54—dc23   2014029636

Published in 2014 by arrangement with MacGregor Literary, Inc.

Printed in Mexico
1 2 3 4 5 6 7 18 17 16 15 14

DOWN & DEAD IN DIXIE

PROLOGUE

Wednesday, October 22nd
Biloxi, Mississippi

If I'd known I was going to die today, I'd have worn more comfortable shoes.

I'm not fond of heels, but I have to wear them, and knee-length black dresses for my job. I'm a hostess at Biloxi, Mississippi's best four-star restaurant, *The Summer House,* and believe me, I'm not a whiner and I'm not complaining about the black dress. If I hadn't been wearing it, and I hadn't bumped into the garbage Dumpster left behind after Hurricane Katrina, and my dress hadn't snagged on the rusty sucker (which probably had me flashing anyone caring to look), then the two jerks in the dark sedan who shot Edward Marcello dead on the street probably would have seen and shot me, too, and I'd have died then with him.

As it was, catching my hem was catching

a break — odd for me, because my standard requirement to catch-a-break is to need both hands and a net to just miss out on any luck at all. I guess I was saving it all up for tonight.

So my dress snagged on the Dumpster, I stepped back to keep it from ripping and hit a crack in the concrete. My heel sank and wedged in the crack — ruined my brand new shoe — I turned my ankle and went down hard, face first and kissed the dirt. Well, actually, I kissed the concrete. So I'm also sporting raspberry scrapes on my face, arm and knee. The ankle is shot.

That was *the fall* by Daisy Grant, Star Klutz (though usually I'm at least a little bit more graceful), which kept me from getting my chest blown open.

As it turns out, all I managed on the being murdered front was a short-term reprieve. Instead of dying on the street, I'll apparently die elsewhere. But at least I get to pick the spot the second time, and for an orphan who's been on her own since her sixteenth birthday (I'd maxed out on foster care and being forcibly separated from my only living relative, a baby brother, Jackson) getting to choose anything is pretty special. Even if it is something most people consider morbid like where you die.

Before you judge me, remember that this morning I had no idea I'd die at all. And I didn't bring this on myself. I was just leaving work and walking to my car, minding my own business and not bothering anyone. Now listen, I work, I pay taxes, and since Jackson moved to Dallas last year, I call and check on him at least three times a week. I feed stray cats because I can't stand the thought of anything being hungry (been there, done that, it sucked) and I don't even gripe about Lester, the old man in the apartment next door who stomps around at three in the morning — he's an insomniac; what's he *supposed* to do at 3:00 a.m.?

Lester forgets his pants half the time but I don't complain about that, either. Nobody's perfect. So he's forgetful; he can't help it. I just bought him some new boxers. His briefs were kind of ratty anyway, and he's pretty fond of dollar bills, so I figured he might remember to wear money-print boxers and, so far, it's working out. The cops haven't hauled him in for indecent exposure in almost two weeks — pretty harsh consequences for walking to the mailbox — and that means I haven't had to go bail him out in almost two weeks. That's progress, but it's all beside the point. The point is I'm a reasonably good person. I didn't ask for this fate twist. I didn't *want* my fate twisted, and I sure don't deserve it. Trust me, I've had a bellyful of that business already.

The thing is we don't always get what we deserve, do we? More often than not we get what other people, who might or might not be good people, shove in our faces. They make us choose either to suck it up and take whatever they dish out or to kick up dust. Unfortunately, I'm not much good at sucking it up, and when I kicked up dust this time, I didn't know who would be standing in the cloud.

Okay, I'll take the hit for that. I should've looked first and I didn't. I didn't, and done is done. Now I know, but now it's too late and there's no sense whining about something you can't change. All it does is make you sick inside and it doesn't fix a thing. The bottom line is this dust cloud won't settle . . . not so long as I'm breathing.

Some things you just never see coming. I mean, who could have expected something like this to happen at all, much less twice — in one day?

Yeah, if I'd known I was going to die today, I'd have worn more comfortable shoes.

Probably flats.

CHAPTER 1

"Miss Grant."

Clasping my shoe, I looked up at Detective Keller. In his mid-fifties, he stood leaning against the door-frame, a little stoop-shouldered and rumpled, though there wasn't a wrinkle in his white shirt or crease-pressed slacks — definitely married to sport those kind of creases — and ruffled his gray, thinning hair. Parted just above his ear, it swept over his reddened pate. The expression on his face was suck-lemon bitter, warning me the coming news was suck-lemon bad.

"The shoes are a total loss," I said, deliberately delaying so I had time to prepare myself for hearing it. Keller was a seasoned detective and if he dreaded telling me, the news had to be the kind that knocks you to your knees and keeps you on them for the duration. "The whole heel cracked off." I flicked it with a fingertip. It swung, dangling by a jagged piece of leather.

"Your ankle doesn't look much better," he said, glancing down at it. "Sure you don't want to run over to the hospital for x-rays? It could be broken, bruising up so bad so quick. Hard to tell with all the swelling."

It was swollen and black-and-blue and it hurt like the dickens. So did my arm and knee, and the scrape on my face burned like fire, but I had to choose: x-rays or groceries; I couldn't afford both. Being kind of fond of eating regularly, I chose groceries. "It's okay. But the shoes really tick me off. I worked double shifts for two weeks to buy them." Tonight was the first shift I'd worn them, and adding insult to injury, they pinched and gave me blisters.

He nodded seeming genuinely empathetic and walked into the cramped office doing double duty as an interview room. With a muffled grunt, he sat down across from me at the scarred table. "Miss Grant, I hate to say this, but right now, you've got a lot bigger problems than your shoes."

I lowered my throbbing foot to the floor. "You've identified those men." I'd pulled two photos from a grouping in no time flat and told the officer, *These are the shooters.*

"Yes, we have," Keller said with a tense sigh. He seemed to age right before my eyes.

"You don't know who Edward Marcello is, do you?"

"He's the guy who got shot, right?" I was nearly certain Keller had given me the same name earlier by the Dumpster at the scene. "Isn't he a local businessman?" Used cars. Pawn shops — something like that. I'd definitely heard his name, but I couldn't recall where. I was still pretty shaken up. Seeing someone mowed down on purpose . . . well, it's not something an everyday-average woman like me sees, you know?

"Miss Grant . . . Daisy," Keller said, softening his voice. "Edward Marcello is Victor Marcello's only son."

"Okay." This *should* mean something to me. I knew it should, but I stumbled, lost and blindly seeking. Understandable under the best of circumstances, and these couldn't in any manner qualify as the best. I'd only lived in Biloxi for a little over a year. Jackson and I had been in New Orleans when Hurricane Katrina hit and we'd been evacuated to Houston. It didn't suit either of us. Jackson got a job in Dallas through Craig Parker, a friend he had made at chef's school, and that left me at loose ends. Nothing to keep me in Houston, so I came to Biloxi. It was struggling for normalcy but the scars from Hurricane Katrina ran as deep here as in New Orleans. That storm turned everything on its ear. Years now, and the whole gulf coast still seemed pretty much a mess. "What's your point?"

"Victor is the head of the Marcello family. Edward was being groomed to take over." Keller talked slowly, as if I was dimwitted. "Don't you watch the news?"

"I don't have a TV. Well, I did have one until last Christmas Eve when some jerk ransacked my apartment and stole it. But I gave up cable months before then — I needed new tires — and we only get one local channel." Lester complains about the thirty-year-old programming on it, but I'm not sure of what we even get. Honestly, I hadn't turned the TV on after daybreak for a couple months before the set was stolen and I have no idea what local programming is on at night. I work three to eleven six days a week and pull extra shifts anytime I can get them. One day, I'm going to buy me a house. I've never had one of my own — a real home, I mean, and I've always wanted one. It's a big dream, and big dreams take hard work. Who has time for TV?

"Organized crime." Keller leaned forward and laced his hands on the tabletop. The lines in his face deepened. "You have heard the term before, right?"

"Of course, but what does it have —" The bottom dropped out of my stomach. "Edward's murder was a mob hit?" Oh, man. This I did not need. This no one needed.

Keller nodded. "The two men you identified are Lou Boudin and Tony Adriano. They're members of the Adriano family."

"More mob people?" I couldn't believe it. A bad situation just nose-dived straight into the bowels of hell.

"Rival mob families," Keller said, a quiver in his deep voice. "Boudin is a suspected hit man. Tony is higher up on the family food chain. Third in line to take over the Adriano family."

"Oh, no." What had I done? I'd fingered the mob on a family turf-war hit? This situation ranked a lot worse than just kicking up a little dust. I'd kicked up a whole storm. What was I going to do? "Forget it," I told Keller, and reached for my handbag on the floor beside me. "I — I've been thinking and I'm not at all sure those two men were the shooters."

My hand shook so hard I dropped the strap and had to stretch again for my purse. I hauled it into my lap, reached into my wallet and grabbed my Grant half-dollar. It'd soothed me through hard times since I was six, and just rubbing its shiny gold surface now helped calm my insides down to a bellowing roar. Any comfort beyond that was hopeless. "Actually, I'm sure now I was mistaken."

Keller pinched his lips together. "A short while ago, you were sure it was them. *Definitely sure,* I believe, were your exact words."

They had been. A lump lodged in my throat. I couldn't swallow it so I croaked around it. "Adrenaline. You know how it is. Terror messes with your mind." I palmed the coin, stood up and checked my watch. "Look, we were shorthanded tonight and I've been on my feet since before noon. I — I don't know who I saw. I'm not even sure the car was a sedan. Really."

"Miss Grant . . . Daisy, sit down." Detective Keller waited until I did, then closed the door. "I don't want to be overheard, and I'll deny having said anything I'm about to tell you. You understand me?"

The inside scoop. *Definitely worse than suck-lemon bad.* Bracing, I nodded.

"It's too late to change your mind."

"I'm not changing my mind," I lied. "I was a little tied up falling and wrecking my shoes and hitting the concrete." I lightly rubbed the burning raspberry scrape on my face. "Edward was across the street and it

16

was dark. I didn't have a clear look, you know?" I had seen perfectly. Edward had stood right under a streetlight, but I didn't want any part of this situation.

No doubt my denial would supremely tick off Edward's dad, Victor. Ticking off the head honcho of a mob family could *not* be a good thing. But ticking off the Marcellos *and* the Adrianos had to be even worse. This mess absolutely called for ignorance and distance. Lots and lots of distance.

Worried and more than a little annoyed, Keller frowned. "You don't get it, Daisy. These families have connections everywhere, including inside this police station. If it took five minutes for Victor Marcello *and* the Adrianos to find out you'd identified Boudin and Tony as Edward's shooters, I'd be shocked. Honestly, they probably heard it within fifteen seconds of the words leaving your mouth."

Fear and dread slammed into me. Acid churned in my stomach and the irritating smell of pine cleaner intensified, making me nauseated. "Well, what am I supposed to do?" Before Keller could say anything, I held up a finger. "Don't tell me to testify and everything will be fine, because I really am not that stupid. If I talk, Boudin and the Adrianos will want me dead to shut me

17

up. If I don't talk, Victor Marcello will want me dead to punish me. Either way, I'm dead, Keller."

"Either way, you're in jeopardy, but we've got a plan," he said, trying to stave off the hysterics hinted at in my shrill voice. "The FBI is on board because of the organized crime ties. I talked with a friend of mine, Special Agent Ted Johnson. He's deeply concerned about your safety."

"I'm not feeling too confident about it myself." I swiped at a dust smudge on my dress at the thigh and anger rose with the sting on my skin. "If you and Johnson know these jokers are mob members, then why are they still on the loose?"

Keller looked me straight in the eye. "Because every time we nail them, the evidence disappears or the witnesses do, or else they end up dead before the trial."

I slumped back in my seat. *Daisy Grant's death warrants numbers two and three, right there.* Boudin or Adriano or Victor Marcello — one of them would do the deed. No way around it. This was the mob honcho's son, no less. The Marcellos and Adrianos obviously were already rivals, but now the Adrianos had declared war. Murder isn't a subtle hostility that passes unnoticed. And, lucky me, I don't have to mess with one mob family. No, not me. I have to tick-off two of them — at the same time.

"Don't panic, okay?" Keller glanced back at the door. His eyes darted and his hand shook. He wasn't happy to be stuck in the middle of this mess, either. "Like I told you, we've got a plan."

I grunted. "No offense, Detective, but if all your witnesses are missing in action or dead before trial, I'd say, your plans aren't working out very well." I squeezed my Grant coin. "Have these families killed cops, too, or just witnesses?"

My question irked him and stung his pride, but he chose to ignore it. "Special Agent Johnson is coming to get you. He'll hold you in protective custody until —"

"Protective custody?" Keller had to be kidding. "I can't do protective custody. I have to work or I don't eat. Understand? I can't hide out — and from what you've said, there is nowhere to hide, anyway." Some plan. They might as well paint a bulls-eye on my forehead.

"You'll be safe with Johnson," Keller said, then softened his voice. "Miss Grant, I know this is hard. You've built yourself a life and it hasn't been easy, being on your own. But if you were my own daughter, I'd be making this same suggestion, okay?"

"What suggestion?" I hadn't heard any suggestion.

"You need to enter the Federal Witness Security Program. It was created for witnesses needing protection. Organized crime, drug traffickers, terrorists. You'll get a new identity and be relocated — everything you need to start fresh somewhere else." He talked fast, then added, "Johnson's setting it all up with the U.S. Marshals."

New identity? Moving? Starting fresh? "No." I couldn't believe it. "You can't just kick my whole life to the curb like it's a piece of trash. I won't let you do it."

"You need to run."

I need to run. "Why am I being treated like the criminal here? If you guys would do your job, then I wouldn't be in prison — and don't think just because your Witness Security Program doesn't have walls it isn't a prison because it is."

"I *am* doing my job, okay?" Keller stood up, leaned toward me over the table. "Listen to me, Daisy. This is serious."

"No joke." He did think I was stupid.

"I didn't mean it like that," he said, and had the grace to flush. "It's just . . . well, you have no idea what these people are capable of doing."

"They're going to kill me, Keller. That

clear enough?" I frowned at him. "I'm not stupid, and I'd appreciate it if you'd stop treating me like I am."

"I didn't intend . . ." He sighed and gave up. "I'm sorry," he said, and then started again. "Your best shot is protective custody and then to go straight into witness security. Seriously."

"No, that's what's best for your friend, Johnson. He needs a witness. I don't need any of this."

"Okay, look. Johnson does need you. Without you, he has no case. But you need him and his protection, too."

I'd end up dead like his other witnesses. "I don't believe this." I stood up then hobbled a short path alongside the table, dragging my cracked heel. "My life isn't much compared to most, I'll admit. But it is mine. I've made it from scratch by myself, and I want to keep it. What you're suggesting isn't fair, and I'm not catching a whiff of justice in any of this. I lose everything, Keller. How can a witness losing everything be right?"

"Who says it's right? Or fair? Or just, for that matter?" Keller raked a hand through his hair. Its tips spiked and caught the light. "It's not any of those things. But this isn't a lip-service warning to get you to testify, okay?" He cut to the chase. "If you enter the program, at least you'll have a life."

"Will I?" Always looking over my shoulder. Expecting them to find me every second of every day. What kind of life is that? None. And — I gasped, looked at Keller. "What about Jackson?" I asked.

Lost, Keller cocked his head. "Is he your boyfriend?"

"He's my baby brother," I said. "Well, he's not a baby. He's only two years younger than me, but if I did your witness security thing, I'd never see him again, right? Or is that just how it is in the movies?"

"No, I'm afraid that's how it is in real life." Regret scratched through Keller's voice, turned his tone gruff. "You wouldn't be able to have any contact whatsoever with Jackson or anyone else currently in your life."

No Jackson. No bailing out Lester. Alone. Totally and completely alone. Again. Everything in me rebelled. "No. Thank you, but no. I won't do it." My knees threatened to give out and the pain shooting through my ankle had me seeing stars. I stopped and leaned against the chair. "I — I can't . . ."

Keller stood up, stuffed his hands in his pants pockets. "You don't have any choice."

Something in his eyes scared me in a way I hadn't been scared since I was six and

Mom gave me the two Grant coins then dumped Jackson and me out of the car at the front door of the Piggly Wiggly. She went to park her car and never came back. "Why not?"

Keller looked at my neck. He tried but couldn't meet my eyes. "Because if you don't agree to witness security and protective custody, you're going to be held here anyway — as a person of interest in Edward Marcello's homicide."

Shock pumped through my body. I planted my hands on my hips and glared at him. "You're gonna arrest me?"

"Technically, no." He blinked hard. "We can hold you forty-eight hours without arresting you."

Oh, no. Two mob families and a professional hitman after me and I'm taken prisoner by cops in a police station full of moles. *Great. Anything else? Through now, or do You think I need a couple more body slams?*

"Daisy, I don't want to do this. But if we cut you loose, you'll be dead in an hour." Keller motioned outside. "We can't protect you out there."

Too rattled to care about manners, I snorted. "You can't protect me in here, either."

23

He frowned, then stilled. "Your odds in here are a lot better."

I stared at Keller a long minute. My highly-honed BS detector swore he was being straight with me. At least he wasn't one of the moles. But his being straight about this also meant he'd been straight about my odds. Stay or go, it was just a matter of time before one of them got to me and I started my toe-tag stint. While being off my feet sounded really good, being laid out on a slab in the morgue held no appeal. What I needed was a plan. *My* plan.

My success record might not be great, but I had kept myself and Jackson alive and out of trouble. Their witnesses were all dead. I couldn't do worse. So the time had come to shift tactics. "Well." I sucked in a sharp breath. "I guess that's it, then."

"You agree to protective custody and witness security?" Keller sounded surprised.

"You said it yourself. I don't have any choice. If I somehow managed to elude them, they'd go after Jackson, and I can't have that." My eyes burned and I blinked hard, clenched the half-dollar until it dented my palm. "But I have to at least tell him good-bye. I'm —" I swallowed hard to get the crack out of my voice "— I'm all he's got."

"I'm sorry, Daisy." Keller said and meant it; the truth shone in his eyes. He might not be alone now but he had been. I saw it in the lines grooving down his face. "We can arrange a final conversation with Jackson. It'll have to be on the phone, though. We can't risk a face-to-face meeting."

"No. It'd put him in too much jeopardy. A phone call will have to do." I sniffed, looked down at the scuffed tile floor. "If you'll excuse me, Detective, I need a minute alone." I shuddered and crossed my chest with my arms. "Where is the ladies' room?"

He seemed torn. Surely he wouldn't refuse me even restroom privileges to pre-serve my dignity. "Detective?"

"Right this way."

He led me down a short dimly lit hallway, took a right and then pointed. "Second door," he said, stopping. His shoe squeaked on the worn white floor. "I'll wait for you right here."

"Thanks." He truly was afraid the families would kill me even in police headquarters. *Not good. So majorly not good.*

I went in and closed the door behind me. Two stalls. Both empty and painted a garish blue. One window — small but I could fit through it in a pinch. And two sinks with the crooked silver pipes sticking out underneath. I limped over, still wearing my cracked-heel shoe. Forget going barefoot in a public restroom. I'd seen a bacteria-and-germ segment on *Oprah* . . . or was it on the Health Channel? Whatever. Even restrooms that looked clean were infested. I took a closer look at the window. If I got out, Keller would likely have someone outside waiting to snag me the second my feet hit the ground. But even if he didn't, where could I go? Home?

Not bloody likely. I didn't even have my car here; I'd ridden in with Keller. That should have warned me, right there. Normally, it would have. But I don't see people blown wide-open everyday, you know? Edward Marcello's death rattled me; I admit it. I didn't think.

"Miss Grant, you okay?" Keller called to me through the door.

Nice of him to worry. Sweet, actually. Not that I was crazy enough to think he really was worried about me. He wanted to nail his case. That's what Keller was about. Special Agent Johnson, too. Not me. I provided the means to an end. That's it. They were all about the case. Likely had been trying to nail both of the mob families for years.

"I'm fine. Thank you." I turned on the tap

and tried to think through this witness security program business. Never see Jackson again? *Ever?* I couldn't do it. I wouldn't. Because I really was about to cry and I didn't want to humiliate myself by blubbering like an idiot, I washed my face and then ripped off some paper towels and patted my skin dry in front of the mirror above the sink. My hair had fallen out of its neat chignon and shot out in blonde streaks in all directions. I plunked street grime out of it, tread lightly over a sore spot, and knew I'd be fighting embedded sidewalk grit for a week. Dabbing the streaked mascara from my face, I avoided the raspberry but nicked its edge anyway. Pain seared my jaw. Cringing, I glimpsed the ceiling in the mirror. Those big tiles . . .

One of my old foster parents, Mr. Venier, had crawled all over the ceiling in the attic once. He hid pot up above those big tiles, too. I looked at these tiles more closely.

The police couldn't protect me. The FBI or U.S. Marshals couldn't, either. I had to protect me. And I needed to buy a little time to figure out how to do it.

I opened the window and left it cracked. Inside the first stall, I stood on the stool then lifted the ceiling tile and slid it aside. I walked up the sides of the stall like I'd seen

Bear Grylls walk up sheer-faced cliffs back when I'd had a TV and watched it. Scaling the wall looked easier than it was, especially with a bad ankle. Pain shot through my foot and up my leg. The whole mess throbbed. By the time I hoisted myself up into the dead space and straddled the rafters, I was in a cold sweat and my muscles burned so badly I shook like somebody half-frozen. Biting my lip to keep from groaning, I slid the tile back into its slot.

"Miss Grant?" Keller's voice carried up to me. "Miss Grant?"

I didn't dare answer. Crawling on hands and knees across and down the wooden beams, I made it to the other side of the building. Lifting the corner of a tile, I peeked down.

Keller was going nuts; he'd discovered I was gone, and he and half the force were looking for me, inside and outside the police station.

A younger man with a flat nose and short brown hair wearing a black suit and a bad attitude hooked up with Keller near the door. "Are you sure they didn't take her?"

"No, I'm not sure, Johnson." Keller shouted back. "I wasn't in the john with her. I was in the hallway. I'm not Superman. I can't see through walls, okay?"

"But the window was open, so they could've taken her," Johnson pushed.

"Yeah, the window was open." Johnson whipped out his phone and barked orders into it.

Special Agent Ted Johnson. The FBI guy Keller had said was coming for me. I hunkered down and stayed put. Once the dust settled, I could get out of here, get some money, and then get out of Biloxi.

They'll just hunt you down, Daisy. You know they will . . .

They would. Fear blew up inside me crowding into so much space I could barely breathe. Doubt crept in and took up the rest. Could I do anything to protect myself better than Keller and Johnson could protect me? They had training, I didn't. They had a track record — a bad one, yeah, but they did know what hadn't worked. I knew nothing.

You can't afford this kind of thinking, Daisy . . .

I couldn't. So okay, I wasn't formally trained, and I didn't have their kind of track record, and I didn't know what hadn't worked. And — just to not delude myself, rationalizing my situation — I was scared spit-less, which isn't the best condition to be in when you're making life-and-death decisions. The cops, FBI, and Victor Marcello wanted me alive to testify. Lou Boudin and Tony Adriano wanted me dead so I couldn't testify. Both groups would undoubtedly go to *any* lengths to get what they wanted. That left me with no choice but to be willing to go to *any* lengths to get what I wanted.

Well, I thought. I do have one thing the families, the police, the FBI and the U.S. Marshals lack, and it's nothing to sneeze at. Actually, it could be pretty powerful — and on several occasions in the past, it had been powerful enough to save my backside. I have a personal, vested interest in the outcome of this situation that is bigger and stronger and runs deeper than their interest or investment — singularly or even combined.

This is *my* life on the proverbial chopping block, and I want to survive to live it.

CHAPTER 2

The hustle inside the police station dulled to a quiet roar, and then fell to silence.

Except for a skeleton crew left to man the station, the cops on duty had hit the streets, looking for me. Between the underside of the roof and the backside of the musty ceiling, I'd crawled all over the building, rafter to rafter, and while my tights and skirt were now in about as good a shape as my once-white shirt and torn-up shoe, I had finally pegged a way out of the station — the side exit door I now watched through a hiked corner of ceiling tile.

Problem was the keypad on the wall beside the door. It had a four-digit code; I'd counted the beeps. But until now, I hadn't been in position to see the numbers the officers exiting the building punched into it. Straddling two wooden beams like a contortionist on crack, I had a clear view and only hoped my left hipbone held out. The constant pain in it had me dripping sweat and seeing spots, but I didn't dare move. The exit had been fairly active. It wouldn't be long . . .

A uniformed officer approached the door, lifted a hand to the keypad and tapped in the numbers. *Three, seven, three, seven.* The door opened, and he walked outside.

I waited a couple minutes, then slid back the tile just enough to drop down to the floor. I landed with a thud. My ankle gave out, and I crashed on my butt. Grunting and groaning, I scrambled to my feet. To me the racket sounded like a small explosion, but no one entered the hallway so I guess the real uproar was inside my head. I punched in the code and shoved the door hard.

Seconds later, the night swallowed me. I ran two blocks on the battered ankle with pain screeching up my leg before I slowed down, then standing on the side of the dark road, I wondered. *What do I do now?* I had my mobile phone, but the police would be monitoring it — I'd given Keller the number, for crying out loud.

Near a streetlamp, I twisted my wrist to check my watch. Finally, it caught the light — 3:20 a.m. I had no one to call. Nowhere to go. I'd heard the FBI guy, Johnson, tell

Keller to put an APB out on my car, so retrieving it was out. The beach and Highway 90 intersected about 2 blocks south. It'd be dense with traffic and people even in the wee hours before dawn, but some of those people would be cops. I walked another block north and noticed headlights on the road. Glancing back, I watched an old clunker pass by and the driver hit the brakes.

Spinning around, I took off south. It wasn't a good idea to cut across lawns — people had gotten itchy trigger fingers since the hurricane because of looters — but better that possibility than — a man in a ski mask grabbed my shoulder.

I gasped and struck out. "Get off —"

"Spitwads and fudgesicles. Don't kill me, Daisy girl."

Mid-swing on a big roundhouse, the man's words penetrated my mind and I stilled, dropped my arm and relaxed my fist. Only one person said *spitwads and fudgesicles*. "Lester?"

He nodded. The ski mask tugged down over his head bobbed and the eye slit crept over his right eye. "Get in the car."

I hustled over and got in. When he slid onto the seat behind the wheel, I asked, "Lester, what are you doing here? Whose

33

car is this — and why are you wearing a mask?"

He slapped at the gearshift with a bony hand and punched the accelerator. "You didn't come home tonight. I got worried. I was sort of waiting for you."

"There was some trouble outside of work."

He grunted. "There was some trouble at home, too."

"What kind of trouble?" Could be anything. *A raccoon in the garbage, teens hanging on the corner.* "And whose car is this?"

"Emily's," he said, talking about the elderly woman two apartments down from him.

"Emily's blind. Why does she need a car?" Did she even have a car? I couldn't recall ever seeing one, and this clunker, I wouldn't miss.

"She ain't blind. She's got cataracts," he corrected me.

"But they can fix cataracts."

"Yep, if you got surgery money. She ain't, and she ain't old enough for Medicare. She's keeping the car for when she gets her eyes back."

Money. Always money. I sighed inside and shifted the topic. "Well, what are you doing with her car?" It did smell musty and like mothballs. Like it'd been closed up a hunter's moon or two.

"I borrowed it after the two men left your apartment."

My heart jackknifed. "There were two men at my apartment?"

"Nope, not *at* it. *In* it." Lester braked for a red light then hooked a right on Highway 90 and passed by my bank.

"Pull in there." Wagging a fingertip, I added, "I need to withdraw some money from the ATM."

"They pretty much tore the place up, Daisy." Lester made the corner and then doubled back to the bank.

Violated to the bone, I swallowed a knot of outrage. "Cops?"

"Thugs," he countered. "I called your work to tell you, and Gilbert told me what had happened with the shooting and all." Lester heaved a sigh and pulled into the drive-thru. "Are you crazy, girl? Why did you call the cops?"

"When I called them, I didn't know who the victim was, okay?" I fished out my bank card and gave Lester my pin number. "Get the max they'll let me get."

He adjusted his mask then stepped in front of the camera, inserted the card, and then punched in the first digit. "What's the number again?"

I repeated it, realizing how this would look to anyone watching — but maybe the false impression was a good thing. They'd think the unidentified masked man was forcing me to withdraw the money and give it to him. This could be helpful in the way of a plan — as soon as I came up with a solid one, anyway — and it wouldn't jeopardize Lester. He had a history of vacant rooms in his personal mansion of a head.

Lester got the money, the card, and then pulled away from the bank machine and its camera. "Here you go."

"Hang onto the card," I said, taking the receipt and money. "And head for another bank branch."

"You're cleaning out the account and getting out of Dodge, eh?"

"No choice."

"None," he agreed. "There's another ATM just this side of the Ocean Springs bridge."

"Hit it." I stuffed the money into my wallet, then looked over at him. "Why are you wearing a ski mask?"

"I was coming to get you before you went home. The thugs are watching your place. Couldn't let you walk into that nasty business unaware."

"Thanks, Lester." Touched, I patted his

arm and took a shot at diplomacy. "Didn't you think they'd consider your mask a little odd?"

"They surely would, if they saw it. But I waited until I was out of the neighborhood to put it on," he said, clearly proud of himself for his foresight and cunning.

"Ah." I didn't know a spitting bit more now than I had before I'd asked. "So if not to hide your identity from the thugs, then why are you wearing it?"

"I was coming to the jail to get you," he explained. "If I showed up like I was, it'd be awfully convenient for them to arrest me, and who'd bail me out? You were being held. I'd a had to rot and you'd a walked in on the thugs at your place."

"Oh." We drove under a streetlamp and it fanned light over his lap. Dollar-bill boxers. Vintage Lester. "Forgot your pants, huh?"

"I remembered 'em — honest, Daisy. But I was scared the thugs'd stop me if I went back to get 'em, so I just grabbed the mask at Emily's."

In some weird and twisted way, he and his actions made perfect sense. For Lester, that is — and if you didn't look too closely and wonder what Emily was doing with a ski mask or how Lester expected the cops to react when a man walked into headquarters

37

wearing a ski mask and money-print boxers. Having enough trouble already, I was perfectly content not to look at all.

We hit three more bank branches, then headed to Gulfport and withdrew the maximum from the two branches there. Unfortunately there was a $250 limit between midnight and dawn everywhere except the casinos, so we made a second trip to one of them. In the parking lot, Lester stopped but he didn't seek an open slot.

"You're going to have to do this one inside Daisy. It ain't a good idea for me to walk in wearing this, you know?"

"I agree." My conscience was nagging at me. "You realize they're going to think you abducted me or something and forced me to use the ATM, right?"

"Course, I do." He tugged at the mask. "Get moving now. The machine is just inside the hallway to your right. Don't linger — I figure we're on borrowed time 'til you're spotted. That's the trouble with firing up half the county, girl. Can't hide in plain sight, you know?"

"I'm learning. This is new to me." I left the car and about two-thirds of the way to the door it dawned on me that this didn't seem new to Lester. Had he been hiding in plain sight? I wondered, but then that crawling-flesh feeling snagged me. You know, the kind of feeling you get when your internal radar has picked up on something you're not yet really aware of and it shoots off an alarm in your gut. My gut-alarm blared. So I turned right around and headed back to the car.

Lester hadn't even moved away from the curb yet; maybe his radar had gone haywire, too. I tugged open the creaky door, got in and slammed it shut. "Something's wrong. Go."

A black van a few slots down chose that moment to back out of its parking place and blocked the road. We were sitting ducks.

"This ain't good, Daisy girl." Lester whipped off his ski mask. His thin hair standing straight on end, he shot a frantic look into the rearview mirror.

I hunched down in the seat and looked around but didn't see a thing that didn't fit. Was it my imagination? Fear making me jump at shadows that just weren't there? Maybe it was . . .

The casino door I'd been about to enter slid open and a man walked out. "Oh, no." I ducked fast, huddling on the floorboard in the wedge between the dash and seat.

"Who is he?" Lester asked, picking up on my fear.

"Lou Boudin." My heart slammed into my backbone. "One of the shooters."

CHAPTER 3

Boudin didn't spot me. The black van moved, and Lester, bless him, took off normally to not draw notice. He pulled out on to Highway 90 and drove west. "Maybe you better start at the beginning," he said.

For the first time since I'd known him, all the lights were currently on in Lester's personal head-mansion. I spilled out the story and ended with, "What am I going to do?"

Lester pulled over at the harbor and parked facing the boat slips. "It's a sorry situation. Sorry situation." He tapped his blunt fingertips on the steering wheel and then suddenly stopped. "Well, no help for it. Ain't but one thing you can do, Daisy girl."

"What?"

"Die."

Shock rippled through me. "I'm not ready to die."

"It's your only choice." Lester turned off the engine and killed the lights. "If Keller and Johnson don't get you killed, Marcello or Adriano will — and they'll all go after Jackson, too. Make no mistake about it."

I frowned. "This isn't exactly being helpful, Lester." He was right, of course, but what I needed was a solution not more worry heaped on the pile. It was plenty high already.

"Just making sure you got a realistic fix on your situation."

"Oh, I've got a realistic fix, all right. The question is what am I supposed to do about it? How can I keep Jackson safe and stay alive?"

"I told you. Ain't but one way." Lester shot her a sharp look. "To live, sometimes ya gotta die."

Bless his heart, he was trying to be helpful, but —

"Don't be looking at me like I got a half-baked brain. I ain't." He grunted and turned toward me on his seat. "If you're dead, and you ain't contacted Jackson, they'll leave him alone and you'll be safe. You'll have to stay away from him, though. They'll watch for contact."

Speaking from experience. Shocked, I swerved my gaze from the docked boats in the harbor back to Lester. "If I'm dead, I can't hardly hang around him or anybody else, Lester."

"That's right." He sighed. "Ain't what I'd a wanted for you, Daisy girl, but you got no other options."

We were on two different wave lengths. No surprise there, but he had something specific going on in his head and I didn't. Grasping for any straw, I asked, "What do you mean?"

He twisted and draped his arm over the steering wheel, then lifted a single crooked finger. "Beyond those boats is a big gulf. I suggest we get you lost in it."

"You want me to drown myself?" *No straw there. Definitely vacant rooms in his head-mansion, after all.*

"*Pretend* to drown," he amended then added, "Don't have to find a body if you're seen falling into the drink."

A plan to fake my death. Lights were on in there! "Okay, I drown. Then what?"

"Then you use some of the money to change your appearance and name, and you make your way over to Dixie, Florida. I got a friend runs a funeral home over there, Paul Perini. He can help you. Now, you head straight there and you tell him I sent you or he won't even talk to you."

A cold chill streaked up my spine. Lester wasn't at all vacant and apparently he never had been. He'd done this death-faking business before. Why had he had to die? Who was looking for him?

Safer not to ask, or to know. About to gag, I cracked open the window. The smell of salt water mingled with the pungent sting of mothballs. "So I go for a swim and drown."

"Nope. Ya gotta be seen and remembered. First, stash your cash and some dry clothes down the beach someplace safe. Then come back here and rent a boat. Any of the charters will do. Take the first one where a captain shows up. Go for a boat ride, hit the drink, and disappear. Then retrieve your cash and get to Paul Perini — no rental cars or public transportation, just in case. These types are awfully suspicious."

He meant the crime families, not the authorities. "Because maybe in their pasts, some of them have faked their deaths?" *Oh, let that not be the reason. Let it not.*

"Exactly." Lester glanced over. "Just get to Paul. He'll handle the rest." Lester looked out the window. "It'll be daylight in about an hour." He cleared his throat. "You got no time to waste."

Reaching over, I clasped Lester's bony hand. "If I do this, who's going to post your bond and get you out of jail?"

"I'll remember my pants, Daisy." His eyes watered. "It was handy, being ditzy. And a good way to get to know you and keep an eye out. Ain't safe for a kid your age nor right neither, having nobody."

I stilled. "It was a test. To see if I was getting close to you for a reason or just because."

He grinned. "That, too." He took in a deep shuddery breath and gave my hand a little squeeze. "Getting me a post card from Lily Nichols now and then would be nice. So I know you're all right."

I nodded, my throat thickening.

"There's somebody coming to that charter. Captain Dave's. See him?"

I did. "Thank you, Lester." I grabbed the door handle and looked back at him. "I'm going to miss you."

"I'll be fine, Daisy girl. Emily's here, and you'll drop me a note now and again. That's more than I've had most of my adult life." He motioned, his voice gruff. "Get going now — and rig the boat's radio so it takes the captain a spell to get in touch with anybody. He'll call for help as soon as you hit the water."

I looked back at Lester. "You never asked me if I could swim."

45

"You learned when you were nine and Jackson slipped off the bank of the creek. Figure if you swam good enough to save his hide, you can swim good enough to save your own."

A flood of emotion swamped me. "Lester," I swallowed hard, "I love you."

"I love you, too, Daisy girl."

I tried but couldn't make myself part with my cash. I bought a few things at a twenty-four hour boutique, stashed some clothes a mile down the beach then rushed back to the harbor.

The sky hadn't yet started brightening, but it wouldn't be long. Spotting a man working on the pier near a boat, I walked over. The slatted boards creaked under my feet, and the sounds of water slapped at the posts supporting them. "You have time for a short trip this morning?"

"Two hours long enough?" Stooped down and checking the ropes mooring his boat to the dock, he straightened up and looked over at me. "Rest of the day's already booked."

I smiled at him and double-checked the sign above his slip. "You're Captain Dave, right?"

He nodded. "Yes, ma'am."

"I'm not sure two hours will do the trick, but I'll take what I can get. I've had the night from hell, Captain." I dragged my fingertips over the raspberry scrape on my face. He'd remember the scrape. "A short trip can't hurt and it could help."

He spotted the scrape and then my bruised and swollen ankle. "No offense," he said, looking beyond my shoulder. "But I don't need no trouble." He glanced at my left hand, clearly checking for a wedding ring.

"Trouble is the last thing I need or want." I lifted my hand and wiggled my bare fingers. "There's no crazy husband or boyfriend. I fell in the parking lot at work. I'm local. A hostess at the Summer House." I offered him twice the fee his sign said he charged. "Sound okay?"

"It's too much." He grabbed the wad of cash. "But I'm short on rent money, so since you offered, I'm accepting."

I boarded the boat wearing a muddy-looking swimsuit as close to the color of the water as I could find. In my purse, I had stowed a floppy hat in the same dull shade of gray-green. Whether it'd really help me be harder to spot in the water or if that was just wishful thinking on my part, it was worth a shot. Of course, everything looked muted and gray at dawn. In the bright sunlight, the water could vary from blue to deep green. I should be back on shore by then. "Where should I sit?" I asked Captain Dave.

I hadn't even noticed the name of the boat. Odd for me. Normally I'd have looked for some kind of symbol in its name — *Survivor* or something to reassure me this was *the* boat I should take.

"Seat at the bow's probably best for you with that ankle."

Grateful it was closest, I sat down and looked back at the captain. He was about my age, tanned and leathery skin, black close-cut hair and a hint of a beer belly.

He coiled the last of the mooring rope onto the deck, then boarded. "So what's your name?"

I hesitated, considered lying to him, but then remembered I wanted him to think I'd drowned and everyone to conclude I was dead. "Daisy Grant."

He cranked the engine, eased away from the dock and out of the harbor. The light breeze felt good on my face. The smell of diesel didn't blend well with the gulf's salty tang and as the boat slipped away from the harbor and through the pass into open water, my stomach lurched. *Please don't let me throw up on his boat. Please.*

Captain Dave radioed the harbormaster, then made small talk with me and he kept talking until finally I told him what he wanted to know. Well, sort of. I told him what I wanted him to know, which was enough to tell the police who I was and to halt his questions so I had time to think. "I didn't just fall in the parking lot," I said. "Well, I did, but I fell because I saw a man on the street get shot. I've never seen anybody get shot before. Frankly, it's knocked me for a loop. I was on the way home, already dreading the nightmares, when I saw you at your boat. I thought maybe a quiet boat ride would help me relax. The water's soothing, you know?"

Surprise flickered over the captain's face. "Is he all right — the guy who got shot?"

"Only if he loved Jesus." I looked at the captain. "He's deader than dirt." I let my head loll back a long moment, then stood up and circled the deck. "I still can't believe it. I mean, who expects to leave work on a normal day and see something like that in the parking lot?"

"World's crazy these days. But that's really nuts." He grunted. "Sounds to me like you need a stiff drink. I would." Captain Dave's expression turned solemn. "Afraid all I've

49

got on board is beer."

"A beer would be great." I hate beer. Don't just not like it, I hate it. But I needed a second of privacy to disable the radio. "I'll take the wheel."

"You know how to drive a boat?"

"Sure. My dad had one." I didn't like lying, but maybe I wasn't. He could have a boat. Course, I'd never know it since I have no idea who he is or what he has. And I had no idea how to drive a boat. But it couldn't be much different from driving a car. Besides, what could I hit? There wasn't a thing in sight moving but water. The boat passed another channel marker. I looked back to shore and pegged the lighthouse. If I aimed for it, I'd stay on target, swimming back.

The captain took the ladder down and disappeared below deck. I reached for the radio's wire but hesitated. Like me, he worked hard and worried about paying the rent. I couldn't destroy the wiring and cost him money. Compromising, I disconnected the cable and wedged it in place so he'd think it just had worked itself loose. Wave action could do that, couldn't it? Who knew? But any evidence of actual tampering would only arouse suspicion, and suspicion was the last thing I needed. Everyone —

absolutely everyone — had to believe I was dead. For my sake and for Jackson's.

Dave returned with two beers.

I turned the wheel over to him, popped the top on the beer can, heard the little hiss, then sat down in the back of the boat. It was closer to the water than the seats at the bow, and more importantly, I sat at Dave's back. "I'm not much of a drinker, but after last night . . ." I took a swig. *Nasty!* I forced myself to swallow.

"Anywhere special you want to go?"

"No, just ride along the coast. Not too far out." I'm a lousy swimmer. With my bum ankle, I really wasn't sure how strong I'd be in the water or for how long, and I wasn't at all eager to make my fake death a real one.

He turned the boat and upended his beer can near a buoy.

There'd never be a better time.

I dropped off the back of the boat, released my beer can, jammed the muddy hat on my head and made for the buoy.

The boat kept going . . . and going . . . Hanging onto the buoy, using it as cover, Captain Dave got smaller and smaller. He wouldn't not notice my absence for much longer, and it wouldn't take forever for him to reconnect the radio. Soon he'd double back with reinforcements and the area would be swarming with people looking for me. I slung my purse strap over my shoulder, and swam hard for the shore.

My whole perspective shifted. In the water, the shore looked distant, and I couldn't see the lighthouse, but at least I could see land. If I could see it, I could eventually get to it.

Stay calm, Daisy. I stroked, smooth and easy. *The hardest part's over. You're dead.*

I did either the smartest or dumbest thing I've ever done. I hung out on a sandbar near the shore until after dark. The lighthouse was nowhere in sight, but the area was populated. I know, of course, sharks feed at dusk, but shark or bullet, I choose shark.

Once the sun set, the cool water felt cold. My arms and legs cramped every few minutes; they needed rest, and frankly, I didn't think my ankle would make it the last couple hundred yards without it. The distance might be two or three times more than it appeared. Being low to the water messed up my distance judgment.

I stood on the sand bar, my teeth chattering, rubbing the chill from my arms. The gulf temperature had come down from its summer high, but the weather had been warm so far, keeping the water warm, too. Still, the night breeze on wet skin felt cold and had a bitter bite, and when my goose bumps had goose bumps, all I could think about was getting to shore, getting dry and getting warm.

The burning desire stayed with me, and about a half hour after dark it occurred to me to float.

I rolled onto my back, my mouth so dry I was tempted to drink salt water, which even I knew would really kill me, and used my good leg to kick hard and the other to stay stable. I floated in the last of the way, and was never so happy in my life to scrape my backside on sand.

The beach might typically have been deserted, but a big group having a party littered it. I came out of the water downwind of them, blended in, weaving through the group, and skirted the volleyball game and bright lights, then ambled toward the parking lot. So far I didn't recognize anything or anyone, which was a good thing, considering.

"You okay?" A tall guy with a winsome smile asked. His waxed chest looked smoother than mine. "You're limping."

I didn't want to talk to him. I didn't want to be remembered. "Fine, thanks," I said, ducking so the brim of my hat hid my face. I kept walking.

Figured. First decent guy to notice me since my breakup with Andy six months ago — not that I was attracted or could ever get past the smooth chest thing — but even if I was and could, I couldn't do squat to encourage him because I'm dead. In my new life, my luck was holding steady at lousy. Odd, but it seemed kind of comforting to be able to count on *something.*

The neon lights of a casino came into view. I headed toward them. It wasn't one in Biloxi. I drove by those all the time. Must have drifted west in the water. Gulfport maybe — I recognized a bank — yes, Gulfport. I really had drifted. Should have thought of the drift, but I hadn't. It was too far to walk to retrieve the clothes I'd stashed, but at least I'd kept my money with me.

There was something about stashing my purse and money that the woman in me just couldn't do. So I'd bought a waterproof bag, dumped my old purse in a trash drum and kept my cash with me. Now, I was grateful for the little female idiosyncrasy. I wasn't without clothes *and* flat broke.

Tour buses lined up in the casino's parking lot. I could catch a ride — no records.

But where did I go?

I hung out at the edge of the beach until I stopped dripping water, shoved every strand of hair under my hat, then entered the casino to get some clothes. The stores were open around the clock. Approaching the first person I saw, I asked about the shops. She had no idea where they were located. Neither did the second person, or the couple that followed her.

A woman in uniform walked toward me. Not wanting to be seen or remembered, I tried skirting her, but she proved persistent. Running would have aroused more suspicion so I slumped and paused near a bank of slot machines.

Petite and in her forties, she intercepted me. "Why are you bothering our guests?"

"I'm not. I asked for directions," I said. "I didn't see you in your uniform or I'd have asked you." *Could she hear my heart thundering?* "Where are the shops?" Frowning, I lifted a hand. "Some jerk stole my clothes off the beach."

"He took your clothes and left your purse?" Her eyebrows shot up on her forehead.

"It was with me. Good thing, as it turns out."

She nodded. "Hotel won't cover items left

unattended on the beach." Frowning her thoughts on their policy, she motioned. "All the stores are down the east corridor. You'll find everything you need. Guests get a discount, but only if you ask for it, so be sure you do."

"I will. Thanks." Letting her continue with the assumption I was staying at the hotel, I wound between banks of slot machines to the corridor and then stepped into the first clothing shop.

Within minutes, I walked out wearing a pair of jeans and a Crimson Tide t-shirt, sneakers and a red baseball cap. My next mission? Find a drug store.

A block down the street, I found a Walgreens. There, I bought a box of red hair dye and applied it in the restroom. The smell probably didn't make the employees happy, but I left the place tidy so they'd have no complaint other than the fumes.

As I left the store and stepped into the night, my stomach growled, demanding food. Considering hunger a good sign — for a while, I thought I'd never be able to eat again — I walked back to the casino and grabbed a burger and soft drink then exited out at the garage near the long row of tour buses.

Lester's warning to avoid rental cars and

public transportation seemed like sound advice, but while his heart had been in the right place on sending me to his friend, Paul Perini, in Dixie, Florida, I couldn't actually go there. If something went wrong with my drowning death and push came to shove, Lester would know where I was hiding. I didn't want to burden him with the secret or to give anyone a reason to beat the information out of him. Dead is dead, until it isn't, you know? So, just in case, I didn't want to take any chances he or his friend, Paul Perini, would be hurt. And that meant I had to find somewhere to go. Somewhere away from Jackson and Dallas.

I ate the tangy burger while walking between the long rows of buses, gazing up their windshields to their destination head-signs. *Jacksonville . . . Dothan . . . Montgomery . . . New Orleans.*

I stopped, sipped at my soda. For a while, Jackson's friend in Dallas, Craig Parker, had worked with Mark Jensen in New Orleans. Mark had been in chef's school with Jackson and Craig. Unlike either of them, Mark had family money behind him. Going into chef's school, he already owned a restaurant in the French Quarter, Jameson Court. I could go there. Nothing connected Daisy Grant to Mark Jensen or Craig Parker, but

Lester's Lily Nichols knowing Craig could help me get a job with Mark. Hey, maybe eventually I could somehow get a covert message to Jackson. Not right away, of course, but one day . . . The possibility brightened my mood.

The bus driver came up, dampening it. "Ready to leave already?" He checked his watch. "You've got another hour."

"Tapped out my gambling budget." Feigning a yawn, I asked, "Do you mind if I wait on the bus?" Standing exposed out in the open gave me the willies. "I'd love to grab a nap."

"You do look tired." He motioned to the open door. "Go ahead."

I got inside and walked to the very back. Hunching down, I begged my ankle to stop screaming its agony, closed my eyes, and took my first half-easy breath since witnessing Edward Marcello's murder.

CHAPTER 4

In the French Quarter, the tour bus rolled past St. Louis Cemetery No. 1 then stopped on Basin Street. About half the passengers exited the bus. Why they went to Mississippi to gamble when there was a casino right on the riverfront in New Orleans, I had no idea, but I left with them and walked into one of a dozen specialty shops lining the sidewalk. Grabbing a map and a soda from the cooler, I made my way to the cash register near the front door.

A young man in his early twenties rang up the purchase. "$7.47."

I passed him a ten. "Do you know where Jameson Court is? It's a restaurant —"

"I know it." He dropped his voice. "A little pricey for someone on my salary, but I hear people rave about the food all the time." He motioned toward the river. "Two blocks down the street. Second building on the right."

Glad it had a good reputation, I smiled. Had to be a good sign, right? "Thanks."

He gave me a slow look. "No offense, but I wouldn't go in Jameson Court dressed like that. Not if you're expecting to be seated."

I stilled. "Formal?"

"This time of year, definitely." He nodded, his dark hair swinging toward his face. "Local bigwigs hotspot."

"Great. More money I don't need to spend." I shrugged. "I've already had everything but my swimsuit stolen on this trip."

"Shame they missed the gaudy purse." He pressed his hand over his mouth. "Did I really just say that?" Surprise lit up his eyes. "I can't believe I said that." He winced, then lowered his voice, glanced at the bag and wrinkled his nose. "Sorry, sugar, but truth is truth."

"No problem." His reddened face warned me he often spoke his mind and then wished he hadn't. "The purse is gaudy." No sense lying about it. "In a pinch, you take what you can get." Waterproof, not style, had been my top priority.

He pursed his lips. "There's a consignment shop three blocks over, Basin Boutique. Ask for Ruth. Tell her Jason sent you." He passed me the change from my ten. "Give me your name and I'll call her. She'll cut you a good deal."

My name. "Lily. Lily Nichols." I cocked my head. "You really think I need different clothes?" I frowned. "I'm not going for dinner. I'm looking for a job."

"Then, you'd definitely better upgrade. Formal isn't necessary, but if you're not well-dressed, you won't make it past the door to even ask to leave your resume. Not at Jameson Court."

"To Ruth's boutique it is, then." I smiled again and extended my hand. "Thanks, Jason."

"No problem, sugar." His eyes turned kindly. "Been in your sneakers myself. Good luck — and don't worry. I didn't see you."

I stopped, went statue-still. "What?"

He winked. "I don't see anyone or anything. No one does. Works best for all in the Crescent City."

Buying a map, asking for directions; he realized I was new here. That's all. "Appreciate the help, and the tip, Jason." I hurried out.

Living in the Vieux Carré, where no one saw or knew anything, could be a huge perk for a dead woman.

Things were looking up.

An hour later, thanks to Jason and Ruth, I

stood dressed for success in a black suit, white shirt, and black pumps — and I paid less for everything than for the new shoes wrecked at Edward Marcello's murder. Cruising down the sidewalk toward Jameson Court at a snail's pace — pumps and a bum ankle do not mix — I still felt my spirits lift. Maybe my luck was changing.

Ruth thought the restaurant stopped serving at ten, so my timing should be about right. Job first, then somewhere to spend the night. I set my priorities then checked my cash. Hotel rates had to be outrageous in the Quarter, but if I secured a job with Mark, I could handle it until I found a place, provided I was careful. My stomach fluttered. I grabbed my Grant half-dollar and rubbed it hard. If nothing else good had come from being on my own for so long, I knew how to be careful.

Something hard collided with the back of my head.

My knees collapsed, and my world went black.

"Hey, lady. Lady, you okay?" I knew that voice. I cranked open my eyes. Jason. And Ruth stood beside him. They hunched over me. "Why am I on the ground?"

"Some jerk knocked you senseless and

stole your purse," Ruth said, her voice shrill. Her gelled spikes of hair rammed toward my face like lethal weapons. "I yelled at him, and he took off. You okay?"

"Jason, why are you here?"

"Ruth called me. We've been trying to get you to come around for ten minutes, sugar." He blew out a long breath. "I was scared to call the cops. Scared to even call you . . . anything. We didn't know what to do."

"No cops." I struggled to sit up. "I'll be okay." I still held my Grant half-dollar. At least the jerk hadn't gotten it. "Who hit me?"

"I've never seen him around here before. He was big. Huge. No way could I tangle with him and win." Ruth looked apologetic. "Sorry. I lost my gun in Katrina when they confiscated them."

"No." I rubbed my head, felt the goose egg. "You'd just have been hurt." Ruth was petite. Maybe a hundred pounds, soaking wet — less without hair gel. "Thanks for coming to help me."

"What is your name?" Jason asked loudly enough to be heard by others.

This wasn't a memory check but a cover. He had no idea what I'd told anyone else aside from Ruth. "Lily. Lily Nichols." I reached for his hand and felt dizzy. "Can

63

you help me get to my feet?"

He grabbed one arm, Ruth the other and they lifted me then held on to make sure I stood steady. Dizzy, I hung on until my head finally cleared. "Thanks. I'm good now."

"He took everything." Ruth cringed. "What are you going to do?"

Good question. "Walk over to Jameson Court and try to get a job."

"You know anyone in town?" Ruth brushed the street grit from my sleeve and skirt.

"No. No, I don't."

"Then you can stay with me until you get a place."

Temptation to accept burned strong. But if discovered by the Marcellos or Adrianos or Boudin, or by Detective Keller or the flat-nosed FBI guy, Johnson, I couldn't be responsible for dragging their wrath down on Ruth's head. She too could wake up dead. "I can't impose, but thank you for your offer."

Ruth kept dusting me off. "What you can't do is go into Jameson Court with dirt clinging to your clothes, and you can't stay on the street. You've just seen that it's not safe, Lily. Where are you going to go?"

"I'll work it out." I smiled at them. "I . . ." Words failed me. "Thank you."

Ruth frowned and called after me. "If you change your mind, just come to the boutique."

Standing under the street lamp, I nodded and then resumed walking toward Jameson Court.

So much for my luck changing. Apparently, I'd come into my new life carrying a lot of baggage from my old one.

Stepping into Jameson Court had butterflies in my stomach. It was elegant, decorated in crisp white and deep green with understated splashes of gold and fine art dotting the walls and lush greenery filling quiet coves to give diners privacy. I loved the place on sight. The old woods and antique pieces that were both massive and scaled to appropriately fit the places they occupied set the perfect tone of tranquil elegance. My feet floated on ancient rugs I would never have expected to see in a restaurant or in any high-traffic area. Yet anything else would have seemed out of place for Jameson Court.

I glanced around, feasting my eyes. The dining room was full, the restaurant busy yet quiet. Peaceful. Serene. For a woman who had known too little of either peace or serenity, both called to me as much as the charming, understated elegance. Probably more.

A blonde woman, also elegant, in her mid-thirties and dressed in a black sheath and heels, approached me. "May I help you?" she asked, her southern drawl natural, not affected. Definitely, a native.

I stood a little straighter. "I apologize for showing up during the dinner rush. I intended to wait until tomorrow, but shortly after arriving, I was mugged —"

"Mugged?" Her eyebrows lifted. "Where were you mugged?"

Too much information. "Across from St. Louis Cemetery," I said quickly, avoiding its number, and then shifted subjects. "I need to speak to Mark Jensen. I'm looking for a job."

The mention of his name had the tension in the woman's face changing to concern. "Were you hurt in the mugging?"

"I was knocked out, but I'm fine now." She'd been staring at the freshly scraped raspberry on my face and would assume I'd gotten it during the mugging. I let her.

"Why don't you come with me? I'm Rachel." She motioned for me to follow her. "We'll get you a cup of tea and you can talk to Mark."

"Thank you." She led me through a hallway paralleling the dining room. We passed several waiters on their way to tables with artfully arranged food that smelled delicious. It reminded me I hadn't had a bite to eat since the burger on the bus at the casino, and now I had no money to buy food. Somehow I couldn't picture a soup kitchen close to Jameson Court.

We walked into a sleek and modern kitchen at total odds with the old-world charm of the dining room. It shouldn't have surprised me, but it did. Well-equipped, sleek, clean and functional. On the far end stood a glass-walled office. In it, behind a long oak desk, sat a man who had to be Mark Jensen. He fit Jackson and Craig Parker's descriptions.

By both accounts, Mark had been the lady killer of chef school and much envied but also much admired because he wasn't full of himself. Dark brown hair, bright brown eyes, and a quick smile. His face was all angles and his skin tinted but not from sun, by heritage. French heritage, if I had to guess. Definitely some Cajun in his gene pool.

"Mark." Rachel escorted me into the office. "Do you have a minute?"

Staring at a computer screen, he looked up. "Sure. What's . . . up?" He spotted me and faltered in a way that made it clear Rachel didn't often bring strangers into his private sanctum.

"Me." I smiled. "I'm looking for a job."

He studied me. Not in a sexual way, but definitely assessing. "What do you do?"

Rachel interrupted. "Your ankle's a wreck. Go ahead and sit down." Rachel motioned to a brown leather chair opposite Mark's desk. "I'll get you that cup of tea."

"Thank you." I took the seat and turned to Mark. "I was a hostess most recently, out of state. I just arrived here and I'm afraid Rachel was right. My ankle is wrecked, and I've already been mugged." Of all times, my stupid stomach growled.

"Before you had supper."

"Sorry." I felt my face heat. "He took everything I had."

"Not everything." Mark lifted his chin. "What's in your hand?"

I'd forgotten I held my coin. Apparently, Mark had noticed me rubbing it. I rubbed when stressed and always had. "A Grant half-dollar. It's my good luck charm." Now considering my circumstances, *luck* sounded like a whacky stretch even to me.

"They're rare coins."

Surprise rippled through me. "You're familiar with the Grant?"

"A little." He nodded and rocked back in his seat. Its springs squeaked. "An old friend of mine had one." Mark touched his cheek and sobered. "Mugged, huh? I guess the luck in yours was on hiatus today."

Had that old friend of his been Jackson? Aside from his coin and her own, she'd never seen or heard of another Grant half-dollar. "I survived it. That's some luck." Actually, I guess I hadn't been as unlucky as I'd felt. I'd died, started over, gotten here, and survived a mugging. That wasn't half-bad. "I apologize for barging in on you without an appointment."

"Not a problem. Did the police catch the mugger?"

"No. I was knocked out and he got away."

"Sorry to hear that." Mark rubbed at his neck. "Your ankle got messed up and your face is scraped. Are you okay, or do you need a doctor?"

"Oh, no. I'm fine. But thank you."

"She's fine for a woman with an ankle the size of her thigh." Rachel returned, interjecting her opinion.

Mark waited for her to set the tea cup down in front of me on the edge of his desk, then told her, "We're going to have dinner. Can you set up the private dining room and let me know when it's ready?"

Rachel smiled. "Absolutely."

Cute. Compassionate. And comfortable in his skin. I liked all those things about him, and more. "Very kind of you, Mr. Jensen."

"I can't have you think we're all barbarians."

"I appreciate it." Okay, he'd surprised me, too, in a most attractive way. I admit it. I guess I'm used to being mugged and having my apartment trashed and my TV stolen, but when it comes to being hungry and someone caring enough to feed me, well, I don't have a whole lot of experience on that front. I know how to watch out for unspoken needs in others. Jackson. Lester. But someone else looking out for me? Honestly, I didn't know how to act. Grateful, of course, but help without groveling? Totally new to me.

"So you've been a hostess. At a restaurant comparable to Jameson Court?"

"Is there a comparable restaurant? I can't peg what it is, but there's something special about Jameson Court." My face heated. "My restaurant was a four-star, but the atmosphere was more relaxed and less . . . whatever that special something is here." I sent him a level look. "The food did smell almost as good."

"It's love — the something special. That's

70

what my mother used to say, anyway." He smiled, bittersweet. "So tell me about yourself."

I sipped from the fine china cup to buy time. I should have thought more about creating a new life history, but I'd been so intent on getting out of Biloxi with my life, I hadn't thought beyond the immediate. "What would you like to know?"

A lovely twinkle lit in his deep brown eyes. "Your name would be nice."

That whack in the head must have been worse than I thought. "I didn't tell you my name?"

"Not yet."

"I'm sorry. Honestly, I'm not quite myself today." I flushed again, deeper, and thought of all that had happened and of Lester. "Lily," I said. "Lily Nichols."

"That's a start."

He was going to ask where I was from. I just knew it. So I beat him to it. "I used to live in New Orleans — before Katrina."

"You were here before the storm?" His face turned dark.

"Before and during." I nodded, still haunted by the memories. "My brother and I were evacuated to Houston. About a year ago, Craig Parker gave him a job and I went east." I swallowed a knot of fear. Had I lost

71

my sense? Telling him about Jackson? *Stupid. Stupid. Stupid.* Now he'd ask about my brother. *Stupid.* I shifted the focus, and hoped Mark veered with me. "Craig used to talk about you all the time."

"So you know Craig?" Mark asked. "That's why you came here?"

"Yes." I let him see my trouble in my eyes. "I really had nowhere else to go."

Rachel appeared at the door. "Dinner is served."

"Thanks, Rachel." Mark stood up. He towered over me, at least a head taller and broader. I'm no shrimp, but I felt like one standing beside a mountain. "Ready?" he asked.

I nodded and followed him down the hallway, around a bend, and then up a narrow flight of stairs to the second floor.

The private dining room felt cozy. A fireplace filled with twinkling lights that burned amber winked from behind a stained glass screen, and a white cloth-draped round table stood before it with two stuffed chairs trimmed in intricately hand-carved wood. "Beautiful."

He smiled. "The chairs are about the only things left from my pre-Katrina home. I'm glad you like them." He motioned for me to sit.

I eased onto a chair. "We were totally wiped out, too."

"So many were." He sat down across from me then paused. "It's not the stuff I mind losing so much. It's the people."

"You lost family?"

He nodded. "Both parents and my brother and sister." He unfolded his napkin. "It's just me now."

My heart squeezed and my eyes burned. "Mark, I am so sorry."

"Did you lose family, too?"

"I didn't have any to lose, except for a brother." I glanced down, avoiding Mark's eyes. "I never knew my father and my mother deserted us when I was six. We grew up in foster care." Sticking as close as possible to the truth made remembering what you said easier. I needed easier right now.

"Foster care." His eyes clouded. "Were they good to you?"

"Some were, some weren't. I learned a lot about a lot of different things. I can change a flat, cook a meal, or grow pot in an attic — not that I ever would." Pausing to restrain myself, I took a refreshing sip of water. "I checked out of foster care when I was sixteen."

"Sixteen?" That surprised him. "Did you finish school?"

"Yes, I did. School during the day, work at night, on weekends and holidays. I've made it to an associate's degree. I would have gotten my BA by now, but I had to back-burner my education to help my little brother." *Too much information. Way too much.* What about this man made me talk so freely? My old boss knew none of this.

Something flashed in Mark's eyes. Something that made me fear my instincts were right and he had all he needed to make the connection between Jackson and me. I shouldn't have revealed all the personal stuff, but in addition to the something about him that addled my brain, I'm new to this hiding out business and having secrets, and all those things entail. Reminding myself everything was different now and I had to watch it or my next bit of jewelry would be a toe tag, I smoothed the napkin in my lap. What if he asked to see my degree? I couldn't produce it. Daisy Grant was dead and Lily Nichols had nothing but a Grant half-dollar.

"You'll be safe here, Lily," he said, as if picking up on my unease. "We refugees stick together."

I swallowed hard. "So you have a job for me, then?"

"Of course." He smiled, then sobered.

"Provided you like the food."

I looked at the plate set before me. "Spinach salad." I sniffed. "Warm apple bacon vinaigrette dressing with pecans —"

"Spiced pecans."

"Spiced pecans and feta — what's not to like?"

"The salad is just a warm up. We'll see how you react to the main course."

"What is it?" I took a bite of salad. "Sweet."

"It's the shaved onions." He took a bite. "Gulf Shrimp Remoulade."

"One of my favorites."

We chatted about the city trying to come back after the storm. About the special challenges created in a life-altering event that just can't be understood unless you've experienced it firsthand. Mark was quiet, confident, unassuming and totally charming. I could see the man behind all Craig Parker and Jackson's stories about him, and it appeared neither of them had been exaggerating. Admittedly, I'd thought he and Jackson were making Mark Jensen seem like Mr. Perfect to get under my skin for refusing so many blind dates with him, but now I wondered.

Knock it off, Lily. Attracted to your new boss? Crazy. Good way to end up fired before you're truly hired. Daisy had her chances with him and blew them off. Too late now.

A waiter brought in the main course.

My senses exploded. I took a bite, seriously amused at Mark's expression. He definitely sat anticipating my reaction, and as adorable as he was, he felt uncertain of what the reaction would be. And *that,* I pegged it, was his magnetism. Exposing his soft underbelly. Strong but vulnerable. Confident but not cocky. I loved that, knowing I shouldn't.

"Well?" he finally prodded me.

I took a second bite, chewed slowly — and then groaned. I wouldn't have, but couldn't help myself. "I think I've just glimpsed heaven."

His wariness faded and he smiled. The tender skin at the corners of his eyes crinkled. "I guess you've got a job, then."

"Seriously?"

"Seriously." He stilled. "I can't start you out as a hostess, but I can use some help in the kitchen and . . . what I really need is help with the business side of things." Hope lit in his eyes. "Do you happen to know anything about computers?"

"Actually, I do." I'd taken a lot of related courses. "I'll do my best at whatever you have in mind."

We talked through the rest of the meal. By the time we'd finished, my world seemed less traumatic and the nasty business with Edward Marcello's murder and the organized crime families and Detective Keller and the FBI seemed like a bad, distant memory. I dared to hope they'd all stay distant and, my belly full, I placed my napkin on the table. "Thank you, Mark. Craig spoke highly of you. I see now why he admired you so much."

"He's a good man, and the admiration is mutual." Mark shrugged. "Just so you don't get the wrong idea, I really can use the help, Lily. I'm lousy with computers — mainly because I hate them."

Jameson Court seemed to be running like a well-oiled machine. He didn't need the help. But I needed the lie as much as he apparently needed to give it. "You fed me, too."

"I wanted to know what you thought of my cooking."

"Ah, I see. Fishing for compliments." I grunted. "Men like you don't need the approval of someone like me."

"Need it from anyone? No." He looked me right in the eye. "Want it from you specifically? Definitely."

"Why?" I hadn't meant to ask. Truly. The

question just kind of slipped out of my mouth.

"Because I think you'll be honest with me. That's important."

"It's easy to be honest. The food is fantastic."

He smiled, then sobered and let truth shine in his eyes. "I'll count on you, then. But I want you to know you can count on me, too. You're alone here and when you get down to it, so am I. Every refugee needs someone to rely on — an ally. We can be allies for each other." He darted his gaze to the fireplace, as if he'd said more than he intended or wanted to say. "You can start work tomorrow at nine."

He missed his family. I missed Jackson, too, and just knowing I couldn't call him had me reaching for my Grant half dollar and rubbing it hard. "A job and an ally. Fantastic." Things were looking up. I slid back in my chair.

"You're leaving?"

"I thought we were done." I stilled. "I'm sure you have a zillion things to do."

"Wait. You were mugged. You'll need an advance."

"It would be helpful, but I don't want to impose further —"

His eyes kind, he dabbed the corner of his

mouth with his napkin. "It's not an imposition, Lily. What kind of ally wouldn't — am I coming on too strong too fast? Sorry." He pursed his lips then tried again. "Craig would do the same for a friend of mine. Is that better?" Mark didn't wait for an answer, but lifted a staying finger. "Wait here. I'll be right back."

I watched him leave the room and disappear down the hall. He too was attracted and feared he was overstepping so fell back to Craig and the friend bit. And that presented problems for me. Craig might do the same to help out Mark's friend, but likely the person would really be Mark's friend whereas Craig was Jackson's friend. Oh, we were friendly, Craig and me, but the friendship bond was between the two of them.

Guilt snaked through me for usurping it. I gritted my teeth, resigned to bearing it. I didn't have the luxury of not bearing it.

CHAPTER 5

I guess my luck, while looking up, hadn't yet changed.

Mark had given me a check to tide me over until my first paycheck, and while generous, paper did me no good at ten o'clock at night. Knowing it futile, I tried one bank and then another I'd passed on the walk over to the restaurant, but both were, of course, closed. Out of choices, I walked down to the riverfront and into the casino hoping I wasn't slitting my own throat. Who knew how far the Marcellos or Adrianos' reach extended? The sixty-odd miles between Biloxi and New Orleans never had seemed a shorter distance.

The banking services desk sat dead center in the first floor. Risking a glimmer of hope, I kept my head down and stepped up to the U-shaped desk. "I need to cash a check, please."

A birdlike woman wearing glasses on the

tip of her nose smiled. "Yes, ma'am."

I slid the check over the marble counter. She picked it up and looked it over. "I'll need a photo I.D."

The glimmer of hope snuffed out. "I don't have one." She stared and me, and I added, "I was mugged earlier tonight, and the guy took everything. If you'll just call Mark Jensen at Jameson Court, he'll vouch for me." I said it and knew it was true. A little ribbon of gratitude I had *someone* to call rippled through me.

"How awful. I'm so sorry. New Orleans really is a friendly city," the woman said with conviction. "But I can't do a thing without your I.D."

I didn't fight her. It wouldn't do any good. "Thanks anyway." I took the check from her outstretched hand and left.

Back on the sidewalk, I had no clue what to do next. Panic threatened to edge in at the corner of my mind, but that's the last thing I needed. The bottom line was Mark's check couldn't do me any good tonight and I couldn't stay on the street. I'd have to impose on Ruth and pray hard she remained safe.

I walked back to the Basin Boutique. Maybe Ruth could cash the check. It wouldn't put her at risk the way me staying with her would. Feeling calmer now that I had a plan, I picked up my pace, wishing my ankle would miraculously heal. The constant throbbing worked from the ankle all the way up through my knee and truly grated at my nerves.

The boutique was dark inside. No lights, and no one in sight. When I got close enough to actually read the sign on the door, it confirmed what I already knew. Ruth had closed shop for the night, and surely Jason had closed his store, too.

Now what?

Jazz floated on the cool night air. The music wasn't from one of the many bars in the Quarter. A midnight funeral's procession made its way down the street. I walked toward it, down Chartres Street toward Jackson Square. The spires of the St. Louis Cathedral stretched up into the darkened sky.

Its real name was Cathedral-Basilica of St. Louis King of France, or something like that, but the only time I'd seen or heard it called anything other than the St. Louis Cathedral was on a sign in a convent's gift shop when I'd taken Jackson on a field trip one weekend a very long time ago.

A church would be about the safest place to pause and regroup — *if* it was open. It should be. When I'd taken Jackson to see it — the ceiling paintings alone were worth the tour — we'd been told it was the oldest cathedral in continual use in the entire nation. Hopefully, Hurricane Katrina hadn't changed that but I wasn't betting on it. For so many people and places, the storm had changed everything.

Mark flitted through my mind. Guilt followed. Not for usurping Craig's friendship; at least, not this time. Because I'd griped myself breathless about losing our home and stuff in Katrina. Mark had lost his family. The guilt in me sank deeper. How petty I'd been. How ungrateful. Jackson and I survived. We had the chance to start over. Mark's family . . . they'd paid the ultimate price, and he'd go on paying it all the days of his life.

Feeling small and shallow, I hobbled past the statue of Andrew Jackson on his horse and made it through the black wrought-iron gate, then kept moving toward the cathedral's door, daring to hope I'd find it open.

It was locked up tighter than a drum.

Deflated, the pain in my ankle shooting all the way up through my thigh and hip now, I spotted a bench near the main entrance and sat down. At a total loss, I rubbed my Grant half-dollar and closed my eyes. *God, if you can forgive me for faking my death, lying, and everything else wrong I've done . . . well, forever, and You'd cut me a little slack here, I'd appreciate it. I'm out of ideas, my ankle's killing me, I'm worn to a frazzle, my nerves are shot, and I'm just too tired to move another inch.*

Silence settled over me in the stillness, and the tension knotting me up inside began to ease. A gentle gust of wind blew across my face, almost caressing and somehow comforting, and I permitted myself to enjoy it. It'd been a long time since I'd felt comforted, and I couldn't make myself give it up just yet. Drifting in it, I flirted with sleep, and knowing I should shake myself awake, I didn't. Since I'd walked out of work and seen Edward Marcello get shot, I had been riding an emotional roller coaster. *Scared. Panicked. Stunned. Terrified. Relieved. More terrified.* This dying business was hard work, but trying to live after it? *Alone, mugged, losing everything . . .*

Mark popped into my mind. Well, almost alone and almost losing everything. Still, I needed a respite. "Just for a second," I told myself. Surely I wouldn't be arrested for loitering if I rested just a second. "Relax so you can think . . ."

■ ■ ■ ■

"Lily, finally!" Mark plopped down on the bench beside me, startling me awake. "I've been looking all over the Quarter for you."

"Mark?" What was he doing here? It was still night. I couldn't be late for work. I gave myself a second to clear the lingering cobwebs of sleep and then asked, "Why were you looking for me?" Had he changed his mind about the job?

"It occurred to me the banks were closed and you wouldn't be able to cash the check. But you were gone, and I had no idea where to look for you." He sent her a look laced with apology. "I'm sorry. I wasn't thinking, Lily."

"I tried the casino. But no cash without a photo I.D." Her mouth went dry.

"I really am sorry. I've been all over the Quarter, looking for you." He stood up and offered her a hand. "Come on. You're obviously dead on your feet."

"Truer words have never been spoken." I looked over at him. He wasn't smiling. Neither was I.

"I have an apartment over the restaurant. You can stay there until you find a place."

"Very kind of you, but it wouldn't be

right . . ." Her new coworkers would get the wrong idea.

"I won't be there." He dragged a hand through his clipped hair. "I started out in the apartment, but I don't live there now. Once in a while I stay over, usually on Mardi Gras. People get crazy in the Quarter on Mardi Gras. You never know what to expect."

"If memory serves me, they party hard every chance they get."

"True." He grinned. "Can you walk back to the restaurant?"

I sent him a questioning look.

"You're limping," he explained. "Did that happen during the mugging?"

"Before," I said, determined not to lie to him any more than I absolutely had to. Lying at all rankled, but sometimes a woman just had no choice. "The heel of my shoe got stuck in a crack in the sidewalk and I twisted it." I stood up and paused a second to get my bearings. "Thank you for coming to look for me."

He looked down and dipped his chin. "You should be cursing me. I should have thought of the problems converting money with no identification before you left. I'm sorry, Lily."

"No." I couldn't let him beat himself up.

"For pity's sake. I'm not your responsibility. If anything, you've been my hero."

"You deserve a refund." He shoved a hand in his pocket. "A hero would have thought about the check-cashing issue *before* you left Jameson Court."

I smiled and ticked items off on my finger. "Food. Job. Ally. Advance. Now a place to stay." I shrugged. "Hero. Down to the bone."

He tugged at the collar tips on his white shirt. "Well, at least I'm useful."

Mark Jensen genuinely wasn't comfortable accepting gratitude. Why? "Hero," I stubbornly insisted. "Now, unless you want to carry me back to Jameson Court, we'd better move. I don't think I've ever been this tired in my life. Not even after pulling double shifts for three weeks straight without a day off."

He offered his arm. "What kind of monster did you work for — three weeks of doubles without a break?"

"He was great." I shrugged. "Christmas was coming. I needed the money."

"That, I understand."

"I thought you had always been wealthy." The words popped out of my mouth before I quality-control checked them through my brain. My face burned hot. "Stop. Ignore me. I had no business saying anything personal."

"It's okay." He patted my arm, reassuring me. "I am wealthy now. But I wasn't born with a silver spoon in my mouth."

"I didn't mean to imply —"

"No, you didn't." He led me through the gate and down the sidewalk. "I'm a little defensive about it, I guess. I worked hard for everything, and I took some healthy risks. I got lucky, too." He glanced over at me. "People just remember the luck."

And apparently they never let him forget it. "Unfortunate. And unfair." My gaze drifted to the curb where a man got into a sleek black car then drove off. His red-dotted tail lights looked like a grimace. "My luck isn't awful, but it's not been exactly great, either. I've been relying heavily on the hard work side of things." I smiled. I have no idea why. "Honestly, work's not produced exactly stellar results, but I've made it, day to day. That's not all bad."

"Lean on me," he said, looping our arms. "Give your ankle a little rest."

"Thanks." I leaned into him, grateful for the reprieve, and we crossed the narrow road then headed toward Chartres Street.

"Well, starting now, your luck's going to be good here. It's New Orleans. Great things can happen to people here, and you're overdue a break."

I felt my burdens lifting, the heavy weight sliding right off my shoulders. "I think it already has changed." I smiled up at him. "It changed when I met you."

His eyes twinkled. "I'm glad, and I'll try a little harder on the hero front. Refugees stick together."

Sweet and kind, but . . . "I don't expect you to take on my burdens. I wouldn't want that, and trust me, you don't want them, either." I chuckled because no one in their right mind would willingly change places with me at the moment. "But having an ally is a blessing." The smell of roses filled my nose. A courtyard trellis. Late for roses. "I'll try to be a blessing for you, too," I said. "Thank you for taking an awful day and making it better."

He nodded a greeting to a couple passing us on the sidewalk. We walked in comfortable silence back to Jameson Court and then Mark led me around the building into an alley on the river side. At the foot of an outside staircase, he stopped. "Can you make it up the stairs?"

I nodded.

It took a little longer than I expected, and I was less graceful than I wished I could be especially with him watching, but between the two of us, leaning on him, I made it.

"Okay?"

"Yeah." If I had to do it again, I'd have slept on the bottom step.

On the top landing, he unlocked the door, reached inside and flipped on the light. "Here you go." He stepped aside to let me in. "It's not grand, but it beats the socks off a wrought-iron bench."

It was far nicer than my apartment in Biloxi. A quaint kitchen, living room with a brown leather sofa and plush tan pillows. A TV, too. And a bedroom decorated in oversize, heavy wood and masculine colors. "All this and a bath, too?" It had a shower and a tub. *Bliss!*

He laughed. "I keep the fridge stocked. Help yourself to whatever you want." He walked to the other end of the kitchen, to a door. "You can get down to the restaurant through here to get anything you can't find and might need."

"I'm fine." And uneasy. And overwhelmed. In all my life, no one had ever opened up themselves or their home to me like this. I felt a great deal — more than I wanted to feel — but I had no idea what to do with all those emotions. Could I trust them? What I really wanted to know was if I could trust him.

Leaning against a doorjamb, I looked over at Mark. He stood just inside the outside door. "Why are you being so good to me?"

"We're allies. That's what allies do."

I shot him a deadpan look. It had always cracked Jackson and made him tell me the truth.

Mark worried at his lower lip with his teeth then shocked me with a toothy grin full of mischief. "Because I can."

It was all I could do not to laugh. "Cute, but I'm serious."

"So am I." The deep timbre in his tone backed up his words. Another stern look laced with reprimand, and he sighed. "Okay, cute isn't enough. I get it, Lily. You can nix the glare."

I waited.

It took him a second to figure out how he wanted to say what he had to say. When he had, he continued. "The truth is, everyone in my life wants something from me. Money. Cars. Tickets to the Saints games — *something*. You wanted to work." He shrugged. "I respect that."

Truth, but not all of it. "And?" There was more. I could see there was more in his eyes and oddly, though he'd told me enough, I wanted to know the rest.

"And you looked dead on your feet, like you'd been dragged through the mill — which you had — and you needed a break, so . . ." Suddenly seeming shy, he let his words trail.

"So you gave me a break because you could."

"Respect is a big thing with me." He nodded. "So is genuine affection."

"Affection?" He'd lost me on that one.

"Yeah. It was in your voice when you mentioned school and back-burnering your education to help your brother. I heard it again when you mentioned Craig Parker. I like Craig. He was a good friend to me after the storm."

He'd talked Mark through a lot of dark nights. That much I'd gotten from Jackson during the move to Dallas. I leaned against the kitchen counter. "You know Craig's an orphan, too, of course."

"Yes, he's told me." Mark let her see his sadness. "I'm still having trouble being orphaned. You'd think by now, especially at my age, I'd be used to it, or mature enough to accept it, but . . . I'm not."

I patted his shoulder. "Hate to break it to you, my friend, but you don't get used to it. You just get better at coping with not being used to it."

He looked down into my upturned face. "Which is harder, do you think?" he asked. "Having and losing parents, or never having them?"

"Hmm." I slid onto a barstool at the breakfast bar and looked at a white-rope ceramic bowl. Made to hold fresh fruit, it stood empty. He really didn't stay here. "I've experienced both. In one you know what you're missing, and in the other you dream of what could have been, or what you hope would have been, and you also wonder if you're the reason it never was. With my dad, I've always half-blamed myself for him not being a part of my life. Over and over, I've asked myself if I did something wrong. Course, he never knew me so I couldn't have done anything right or wrong, but that's logical, and there is absolutely nothing logical about emotions."

"You said your mom left you. Do you know why?"

"Not a clue," I confessed. "It gave me fits for years, I have to tell you." It had. Every time Jackson had asked, it ripped up my heart and the shell around it got it a little bit harder. A mother's love was supposed to be unconditional. If it wasn't, then the fault had to be mine. And if my own mother couldn't love me, then no one ever could. It was a simple, logical deduction I'd made early on and years of foster care had re-inforced until it stuck. Nothing in my life since then had even tempted me to recon-sider.

I looked at the stove and then back to Mark. "It's a mystery," I confessed. "One day, she seemed fine — for her, that is — and the next day she went to park the car and never came back." I paused, then said without apology, "All of which rolled to-gether means, I can't answer your question. Whether you know them or not, when you lose your parents, even if you never had them, it sucks." I paused and then added, "But I think if you had parents and your family was close and then you lost them, that would have to be harder."

"Why?" He slid onto a barstool across the breakfast bar from me.

I grabbed two sodas from the fridge and passed him one. "Because you've relied on them your whole life. There isn't a wound or a triumph you've had that they've missed. They've been right there, helping you over the hard spots, celebrating the good things, holding onto you through all the worries . . . Losing all the support would have to be hardest."

"You never had any of that kind of support, have you?" He popped the top. The soda in the can fizzed. "Even when your mom was there, she wasn't there, right?"

Pride made me want to soften the truth, but I couldn't do it. "No, she wasn't. We — my brother and me — were always . . . inconvenient," I said, finding an appropriate word. "Knowing it was hard on him. I tried to be there for him, but a sister, even one trying hard, isn't a mom, you know?"

"You were there. He wasn't facing the world alone. That's what mattered most to him, I'm sure."

I returned to my seat and sat down. "I'm sorry about your folks, and your sister and brother. It's hard to lose people you love one at the time, but everyone at once . . ." My eyes stung and I blinked hard. "I can't imagine."

His gaze drifted. "I felt guilty for the longest time. Sometimes, I still do."

"Because you lived and they didn't?"

He nodded. "Survivor's guilt. They say it's normal. I don't know if it is or isn't. I do know it also sucks."

"Forgiving yourself is always hardest."

"What?"

I sipped from the can. The bubbles burst on my tongue and the cool drink eased my throat. "It's easy to forgive people you love. It's not so easy to forgive yourself."

"No, it's not." For some reason, his intense expression lightened. "You know, I like you, Lily. You talk straight. I don't get a whole lot of straight talk."

"I've never had the luxury of indulging in fantasies. Not complaining, just stating facts. Reality tends to make you blunt." I lifted a shoulder. "And I like you, too."

"Blunt is good. Bitter isn't. But you don't strike me as bitter. I'm curious about that. Actually, it fascinates me. I'd think you would have every reason to be bitter."

"I considered it. Many times, if I'm being honest. But I couldn't afford that luxury, either." When his brow shot up questioning, I added, "Too busy looking forward, trying to make a life for my brother and me. I had to choose." I lifted my hands and weighed the options. "Bitterness." Lowering one, I raised the other. "Looking forward. I chose to look forward." I lowered both hands and ran a fingertip around the rim of the soda can. "I used to tell myself as soon as he was grown and on his own, I was going to have myself one serious ticked-off, pity party."

"Did you?"

"No. Couldn't afford that luxury, either." I smiled. "Too busy trying to make a life for myself without him."

"Probably for the best."

"Definitely. I haven't made time for pity or blame or even resentment. All of those things take too much energy. I just don't have it to spare."

"Wise." Mark pulled out his wallet. "After the storm, I wasn't so wise. I had plenty of *all* of those things — bitterness, resentment, blame and anger." He grunted. "Man, I was so angry it was like a poison inside me."

"You'd lost your family and home. In your situation, I'd expect all that and more."

"Oh, I had plenty of more. You name it, and I wallowed in it." He shook himself. Clearly, his memories of that time were not good ones. "I was seriously self-destructive."

I swallowed a sip of my drink. "Ah, you took a trip to the abyss."

"The what?"

"It's what I call that place. The abyss."

"The abyss." He sounded bewildered, still not tracking my meaning.

"Yeah. Dark, depressing, destructive. So far down you can't see up much less get there from where you are. It's an awful place." I propped an arm on the counter-top. "I hate the abyss, and do my best to avoid it." I brushed back my hair. "How'd you drag yourself out of it?"

He smiled. "The hard way."

"Of course." It hadn't been an easy lesson. I'd bet on that. "How hard?"

"I got drunk and drove my car into the Mardi Gras fountain out on Lake Ponchartrain." Shame tinged his voice. "Craig wired Rachel the money to bail me out of jail."

The graceful hostess at Jameson Court. "Is Rachel your wife?" I shouldn't ask, but he was so charming and open and I had no idea if he was married. I needed to know. Okay, I didn't need to know, but I wanted to know. He touched me in ways I hadn't been touched ever. I liked it, and him.

"No, I've never married. Rachel's married. She's worked with me since I opened Jameson Court."

"You in love with her anyway?" I had no right to ask that, either. What was I thinking?

"No. I've known her forever. She just married Chris a couple years ago."

I studied Mark, and my honed bull-detector swore he was telling the truth. "I guess after losing everybody, the idea of committing would stick in your craw."

"Honestly?"

I nodded. "Always."

"It scares me right out of my skin. Not the committing. I commit to business deals and people around me every day. But —"

"Loving someone is what rattles you."

"Yes." He stiffened. "I don't ever want to hurt like that again."

"I understand."

"You do?" He tilted his head. "I'd think you'd find me cowardly. In fact, I'm betting I've just blown a hole the size of the state through my hero image."

"Not by me." I grunted. "Loving and being abandoned — willingly or not — hurts forever. I totally get it." I dropped my chin into my cupped hand. The downside, of course, is you never feel connected or loved again, and that sucks about as much as losing people you love."

"Which is why we refugees have to stick together," he said, effectively closing the subject, then opened another.

We talked about everything, about nothing. About business and funny antidotes of restaurant events. We talked about life and death and about growing up. About people we'd dated or not dated, and why. "We sound like two sides of the same mirror," I told him. "Not on the family stuff, but on our past loves."

"I fell really hard only once," he said with a wry grin. "Jenny Singleton."

"How old were you?"

"Six." He chuckled.

"I thought so." I laughed with him. "Had to be serious puppy love to warrant a look that wistful."

"You mean it doesn't happen to adults?" He lifted a hand. "No, don't tell me. I need to heal enough to want to feel that way again. Knowing I might keeps me going."

That shocked me. "He who fears loving wants to be swept up in the chaos of puppy love?"

He stilled. "No, not swept up in the risks, just in the chaos." He rubbed at his neck. "Which makes me totally loony, doesn't it?"

"Actually, it makes you totally charming — and a little loony. But only a little."

We laughed and then talked some more. And we kept talking until I couldn't mask a yawn.

"I'm sorry. I knew you were dead on your feet, but I — I don't get the chance to talk like this much. I was selfish, Lily."

I rested a hand on his forearm. "Not at all. Talking openly is as rare for me as it is for you. I enjoyed it." I smiled, wondering where it all came from. Feelings I just didn't discuss with other people. "I don't think I've told anyone so much about myself and what I think in my whole life."

His eyes warmed with a delicious twinkle.

"Then I'm a lucky man."

"Thank you." Her smile widened. "I'm feeling pretty lucky myself."

"There's something about you . . . I'm not sure what it is, but you make me want to . . . never mind. It sounds crazy."

My smile faded. I knew what he meant. "It's not crazy."

He lifted his gaze to mine. "It's not?"

"No."

"You feel it, too?"

I nodded. "I don't know what it is, but, yeah, I feel it, too."

"I'm glad, Lily." He stood, drained his soda can, and then passed me a business card. "Here's my number. If you need anything, call me at home or on my cell any time. Seriously."

"What should I wear for work? I have to buy clothes in the morning."

"Tomorrow, whatever you can find. After then, black slacks and white shirts. You'll wear a white coat in the kitchen."

"Heels?"

He looked down at her feet, his focus lingering on her bruises. "Sneakers."

"I really do like you."

"With a bum ankle, I knew you'd appreciate that. I'm trying to reclaim some hero points." He flashed her a grin and opened the door then stepped outside. "Lock up now. I'll see you in the morning."

"Night." I closed and locked the door behind him, my goofy heart fluttering like a teen's. What was this connection between us?

Lester's voice cut through my emotional high. "Daisy girl, now ain't the time to lose your head. Get yourself some rest while you can."

Good advice. Already, I was craving a hot bath and the sheer joy of crawling into a soft bed. Memories of the hard bench and the bus seat where I'd napped flashed too fresh in my mind.

Half an hour later, I turned on the TV and checked all the local channels. News of Edward Marcello's death was on every channel, but I didn't spot so much as a mention on the disappearance of Daisy Grant. I guess Detective Keller was keeping the name of his murder witness under wraps for the moment and he hadn't yet caught wind of my drowning. Whatever had come to light in Biloxi apparently had little effect. Simply put, a Biloxi hostess falling off a fishing boat into the gulf didn't warrant airtime on TV in New Orleans.

Relieved and saddened, I turned the TV off and went to bed. Settling in, I scrunched a fluffy pillow and inhaled the scent of fresh, clean sheets. *Thank you, Mark.* I sighed and let myself totally relax.

The image of Edward Marcello being shot fired through my mind.

I forced my thoughts from it. To Mark. To the look on his face when he awakened me on the bench. His regret at letting me leave Jameson Court with a check I couldn't cash. The pain losing his family caused him, and his willingness to let me see it. Mark Jensen wasn't a simple man and his hadn't been a simple life. Not at all. Weighing it all out, the truth seemed as clear as a stubborn chin. I'd misjudged him based on Craig and Jackson's constant attempts to hook us up. I thought something serious had to be wrong or some woman would have snatched up such a paragon. But now I knew for myself. He was a good and decent man. Too often used by others for their own gains, but still good and gentle. I loved that about him, and how he'd come looking for me.

I'd had foster parents who had waited a day or two before reporting me missing. Some had been terrific, and I was grateful for them. But some shouldn't have been allowed anywhere near kids much less been paid to care for them. And Mark, a virtual stranger with only a thin thread of a mutual friend binding us, had come to find me right away.

He'd given me a job, food, an advance and a place to stay. And most amazing, he'd opened his heart. He hadn't said it, but I'd felt it. Surely he didn't do this all the time. No, he'd said he didn't. God had to be nudging him for him to be so generous with me. He sure was nudging me. Never in my life had I reacted like this to any man.

A tender hitch formed in my chest. I'd surely kept the whole of heaven hopping today, but things had worked out every time. I wanted to pray my thanks, but I'd never really been taught to pray, so I don't know how to do it properly, and in fifth grade, another orphan, Marta Boudreaux, had told me if you pray wrong, God gets mad, so I'd better not risk it.

I carried that warning with me for the longest time, but the fact is life's just too hard to face alone without faith. So I decided to risk praying. If I kept it short, I thought, there'd be less for me to mess up, but He'd still know me and that I believe in Him. Finally, I worked up the courage, knelt down in a cold sweat and got my voice to work. "Thank you," I said.

That was my prayer. It's all I dared to speak direct for years, though I thought nearly everything deliberately, aware that He might just be listening.

Years later, sitting on lawn chairs in the front yard one hot night, Lester and I got on the subject and I confessed my fear of insulting God. He snorted, gave me a Bible and said nowhere in the Good Book would I find God mad at His creation for opening her heart to Him. I read and learned and read some more, but that fear of upsetting Him never left me — until now.

With everything going on, seeing Him working in my life and putting what I need in my path, I felt a powerful urge to risk saying more. Oh, I didn't need to tell Him I'm scared to death. He knows that. But I did want to tell him I'm not hopeless. Who wouldn't be grateful for not being hopeless? And I couldn't be sure, but I wondered. Had He brought me to Mark for a reason beyond me needing him and his help?

The possibility set my mind to racing. Mark's so hurt inside and I totally understand hurt. I need his help, but maybe he needs my help, too. If that's the case and what our connection's all about, I want to let God know I'm willing — without making him mad, just in case Marta was right.

My insides shook. Fear put an odd taste in my mouth and it dried out. But ready to take my leap on faith, I pushed on anyway and whispered inside my mind. *Thank you, God, for everything. I'm willing for . . . whatever. I'm just willing.* I swallowed hard and dared say what I'd yearned to say for a long, long time. *Bless Jackson and Lester and keep them safe. Oh, and Emily, too. Help her with her eyes because she sure doesn't need to be behind the wheel of her clunker without good vision. Amen.*

My heart pounded hard and fast. I braced for whatever came, but felt only the nighttime quiet. Maybe I hadn't offended too much, or prayed too much the wrong way.

Long, tense moments passed and finally my heart rate slowed down and I accepted that the world wasn't going to come crashing down around my ears. Still, I had blown it. The certainty I had filled me. With everything going on, I thank God for not being hopeless? I winced.

Clearly, I've got a lot of learning to do and a long way to go, but surely if He thought about it, He'd see my gratitude isn't really *that* off-the-wall. Maybe to most it sounds dopey, but not to anyone who's walked in my shoes. If I live to be a hundred I'll never forget standing outside the *Piggly Wiggly* waiting for my mother to park the car and come join Jackson and me. Deep inside, I knew when she handed me the two Grant half-dollars that she wasn't coming back, but I'd hoped and hoped, clinging onto it down to the tips of my nails. For hours, I stood there, holding Jackson's hand. And then it started getting dark, and I had to accept it. My mom was gone forever.

That moment, the one when hope died, was the most horrible moment I've ever had in my entire life. Not even knowing everyone wanted to kill me made me feel so empty and worthless. All the space inside me filled up with despair and when my entire body couldn't hold it all, still more despair oozed out my pores . . .

Remembering what I didn't want to remember, I squeezed my eyes shut. If He knew my heart, He knew all that. Right or wrong, I prayed the best I knew how and that should be enough. It shouldn't make Him mad enough to walk out on me, too. I flipped over onto my other side. *I will not go there. Not today, and certainly not now.*

It had taken so long for hope of any kind to come back. If it hadn't been for Jackson, it might never have returned. Well, until today.

After today, with the way people like Jason and Ruth just seemed to cross my path and help me, and then Mark . . . well, how could I not have hope? And having stood in front of Piggly Wiggly how could I not be grateful to not be without hope?

Closing my eyes, I considered myself not abandoned *and* blessed.

But when I drifted off to sleep, it wasn't hope or Jason or Ruth or even Mark Jensen that filled my mind or my dreams. It was Edward Marcello, his angry father, Victor. It was Lou Boudin, and the Adrianos. Those perfectly creased slacks on Detective Keller, and him arguing with Special Agent Ted Johnson, pulling me back-and-forth in a tug-of-war. Those men all warred inside me and turned my dreams into nightmares.

I ran and hid but they found me again and again. And they shot me and shot me and shot me.

I awakened drenched in a cold sweat three times.

The fourth time, I ran through a dark alley in the Quarter. Lou Boudin, the Adriano hit man, chased me, and for a big man, he moved fast! Hard on my heels. Clashes boomed like thunder. Loud. Louder. Persistent. They startled me awake, and I realized the noise wasn't thunder at all.

Someone stood banging on the door.

CHAPTER 6

I peeked out the window beside the door. A uniformed officer stood on the landing at the top of the stairs. *What now? Was he a real cop? A fake? A mole?*

He knocked again, harder.

"Who is it?" I asked. My heart pounded so hard, I doubted I'd hear his response.

"NOPD. Open up," he ordered. "I want to talk to Mark Jensen."

I rolled my gaze heavenward. Ninety beats a second slowed to sixty with the mention of Mark's name. "It's four in the morning. I'm *not* opening this door."

"Where's Mark?"

I spotted his business card. "You have a phone?"

"Yeah."

"Call him."

"Why? I'm standing right outside his door." The cop's irritation multiplied. "Does he know you're here?"

For some reason, that question made me feel better. If the man wanted to bust in, he'd have done so by now, wouldn't he? "Of course, he knows I'm here. Would you just call him? He'll vouch for me."

"Who are you?"

"A friend of his. Lily," I said, deliberately avoiding giving him my last name. "Just call him."

I peeked through the hole. He was pulling out his phone. "Don't you try running, you hear me? If I have to chase you down, you'll regret it."

Even if I wanted to run, I had nowhere to go. "I have no reason to run. I work for Mark." I let the man hear my exasperation. "Just call him, okay?" They must be friends. What cop who wasn't a friend took this kind of personal interest?

I heard mumbling on the other side of the door and held my breath.

The cop spoke louder. "Okay, then. I saw you drive off a couple hours ago and then the lights went on and off. I figured I'd better check."

The cop was authentic. Had to be.

"Hold on, Mark," the cop said. "I'll ask her."

I braced.

He shouted through the door. "You okay,

Miss Nichols?"

Relief washed through me and I locked my knees to keep from crumpling to the floor. "I'm fine." *Fine? Not hardly.*

He mumbled something else to Mark and then spoke to me again. "Sorry to disturb you. Like I said, I saw Mark leave and then saw the lights come on and go off again."

"I had to go to the restroom."

"Sorry to disturb you," the cop repeated. "Mark says you'll be here a couple weeks. I told him I'd keep an eye out. If you need anything, let me know."

"Thank you — what did you say your name was, Officer?"

"Just call me Tank. Everybody does."

"Thank you, Tank." He was probably built like one. Big, bulky, solid.

"Good night, then."

"Good night." I stepped away from the door, looked at the bed, then the clock. With all the adrenalin gushing through me, there's no way I'd get back to sleep. In the kitchen, I found coffee and put on a pot, then sat down and checked the news on TV.

This time, there was a mention.

The Lucky Lady, a charter boat owned by Captain Dave, proved to be anything but lucky for Biloxi hostess, Daisy Grant. My driver's license photo appeared on the screen. *Miss*

111

Grant seems to have been suffering a streak of bad luck. Biloxi P.D. sources have unofficially confirmed that she witnessed the execution-style shooting of local business-man, Edward Marcello. At police headquarters, she photo-identified Lou Boudin and Tony Adriano as Marcello's shooters. Warrants have been issued for their arrests but neither has been apprehended. Grant disappeared from the police station. It had been feared that she was kidnapped by this unidentified man. A grainy image of Lester in his ski-mask appeared on the screen. *Reports are he forced her to withdraw maximum sums of cash at multiple ATM machines along the Gulf Coast, which is consistent with a kidnapping. But in an exclusive interview with WDSU, Captain Dave, owner of the Lucky Lady, insists she chartered his boat after the ATM withdrawals and that she was alone. She mentioned the Marcello shooting but said nothing about any kidnapping. As you know, early reports in such cases are often riddled with inaccuracies. We'll sort through them and report our findings as soon as possible. Anyone with information on the unidentified man, Lou Boudin or Tony Adriano should contact Biloxi PD or 1-800-crimewatch. All three men are considered armed and dangerous.*

"Lester wasn't armed." I sipped from my cup.

Captain Dave, owner of the Lucky Lady, reported that during the charter, Miss Grant fell overboard.

Captain Dave's face appeared on the screen. *I radioed for help as soon as I could. Had a bad wire.*

He stood next to his boat, careful not to block the view of the sign advertising his charter business. *We searched until dark. All the fisherman, the Coast Guard, everyone with a boat, but we didn't find any sign of her. We'll start again at sunup.*

A fissure of guilt opened inside me. They needed to be working, earning to care for their families, and instead, they'd be searching for me.

A second reporter, shouldered in front of the first and stuck a microphone in Captain Dave's face. "You're sure it was the same woman?"

"Oh, yeah. She even told me she needed the boat ride to calm her nerves. Seeing a guy shot down like that really rattled her."

The in-studio anchor's image returned to the screen. *Miss Grant remains missing. The search will resume at dawn, and hopefully she'll be found. Authorities say this is still a search and rescue mission. At this time, Miss*

Grant's case hasn't yet been reclassified to a recovery operation.

I looked at the last flash of my driver's license photo. It wasn't half bad. I missed my blonde hair and — *Jackson!*

I sucked in a sharp breath. If this much was on the news in New Orleans, it could be on in Dallas, too. According to Keller, the Marcellos and Adrianos were famous in the way organized criminals are, not that their fame mattered. If the Biloxi police information officer had told the media all of this, then Detective Keller had to have contacted Jackson, her next of kin.

My poor brother, mourning me . . . and feeling orphaned.

I cried between sips of hot coffee.

And prayed Mark Jensen wasn't up watching the news.

Would he recognize me? Would Rachel or Jason or Ruth? What about the tour-bus driver, or even the mugger?

I didn't have a clue.

Until Mark arrived at Jameson Court looking well rested and glad to see me, I had knots in my stomach that had knots. If he'd discovered Lily Nichols and Daisy Grant were one and the same, he'd have been mortified. Finally, the fear and dread I'd been hauling around since seeing myself on the news began to ease up.

Wearing black jeans, and a white shirt, he crossed the kitchen, creating a trail of fresh smelling soap, snagged a cup of coffee, then offered one to me. "Do you know anything about creating websites?"

"A little." I took the steaming mug. I'd had way too much coffee already and half-expected my stomach to slosh. "I'm not a techy, but I can handle the basics. Why?"

"We need a website."

"For Jameson Court?"

He nodded, set his cup down on a long stainless counter. "That's got priority over kitchen help, if you can do it."

"Sure. I can come up with something. Whether or not it'll be what you want, I don't know."

"Anything's better than the mess we've got right now, and I hate computers. See what you can do."

Rachel came into the kitchen and hung her purse on the rack by the backdoor. "The nuts are already filling the square this morning. Why it acts like a magnet for them, I have no idea." She smoothed her slacks and reached for a cup, then poured herself coffee. "Mark, did you see the news?" she asked without looking back at him.

"No, I haven't had it on."

Rachel turned and frowned. "Edward Marcello was killed."

"Seriously?" Mark stilled. "What happened to him?"

"I didn't catch it all, but from what I heard, it sounded like the families are squabbling again." Rachel blew into her cup. Steam lifted toward her face. "He was shot on the street in Biloxi — or was it Gulfport? Could have been Gulfport. I'm not sure."

"It was Biloxi," I said before thinking. *How did they know Edward Marcello? They weren't supposed to know him.* When Mark and Rachel swerved their gazes to look at me, I willed my heart rate to slow down and added, "Tank woke me up at the crack of dawn. I turned on the news."

"Sorry about that," Mark said. "He's been a good friend for a long time and keeps watch on the place." Mark swiveled his gaze to Rachel. "Wow, an Adriano shot him." He grunted. "I guess they'll both be moving their operations bases again after this. I sure hope it isn't back here."

"Do you know these people?" I asked Mark. I couldn't imagine why he would, but he sounded familiar. So did Rachel.

"We went to school with Edward in

Gretna, just across the river. Then, the Adrianos ran their business on the east bank, and the Marcellos were across the river, on the west bank. They had a squabble —"

Rachel harrumphed. "A turf war's more like it."

"Whatever." Mark went on. "They all ended up leaving here."

"And both families landed in Biloxi?" I encouraged that line of discussion, hoping Rachel wouldn't report more on the disappearing witness and Daisy Grant's disappearance.

"Apparently. You'd think with fifty states they could get away from each other, but they didn't. More's the pity." Rachel sighed. "Edward was nice in high school. He sat behind me in science in our sophomore year. I was sorry to hear he got killed like that."

"How did he get killed?" Mark asked.

"Shot dead on the street."

"I warned him, senior year, to get away from them all. He said there was no getting away from his family or its rivals. Poor guy was kind of hopeless." Mark headed to the stove and pulled out a bin of flour.

He looked so sad. I glanced at Rachel. "He's okay. They weren't close friends," she whispered. "It's another person he knew dying. Loss gets to Mark like nothing else."

"Does he always cook when he's troubled?"

"Of course." Rachel smiled. "He's a chef."

I nodded. That made sense. When something bothered me I did what made me comfortable — clean. Otherwise, I'm not exactly a domestic goddess. "I'll get busy on the computer and see what I can do about a website," I said in a normal voice so Mark could hear.

"Use the computer in my office. It's up and running and you'll have a reasonably quiet workspace." He paused pouring milk into a large bowl of flour. "Have I mentioned I hate computers, Lily?"

About a dozen times. "I believe you mentioned something in passing."

He nodded, clearly oblivious he'd shared that tidbit of information on any occasion. "If you could keep that thing out of my life, I'd love you forever."

"Careful, Mark." Rachel giggled. "Lily isn't one for frivolous words. She'll hold you to them."

He looked from Rachel to Lily. "I know exactly what kind of woman she is."

That he might terrified me. "If that's the mission, then I'm on it." I turned for the office and didn't dare acknowledge anything to do with the loving forever comment. It was just an expression of gratitude. He didn't mean anything by it. Actually, I was more than a little surprised Rachel called him on using it. Innocuous enough, and there were no PC police in Jameson Court. Still, it must be an odd thing for him to say to snag Rachel's attention. I didn't know what to make of that.

"I'll call you when breakfast is ready."

I stopped and looked back at him. "You're cooking breakfast for me?" No one had cooked breakfast for me since I was twelve. Even in my foster homes from twelve to sixteen, if breakfast required cooking, I'd cooked it. Well, aside from Jackson's pastries. But I was his taste-tester, so that was different.

Rachel's gaze darted between them. "He cooks every morning, Lily."

"Oh. Great." Oddly disappointed, I walked into the office and sat down at the computer with two goals: Create a website. And then work at making it unnecessary for Mark Jensen to go near his computer.

I'd love you forever.

Just words. He didn't mean them, of course. But for a woman who has heard too little of love and forever, and too much of earning my own way, I seriously debated putting him to the test. It'd be an interesting experiment — and a way to pay him back for being good to me. Daisy Gra— Lily Nichols always paid her debts.

Breakfast came and went and I returned to Mark's office and the website project. Then more mornings and afternoons like it passed the same way, and not every evening but most evenings, Mark came up to the apartment after work to talk. He ended up cooking dinner for the two of us and we'd go for a walk and talk or if it rained, just sit and talk until midnight. Day after day, we'd do it all again.

By the end of the second week, news of Edward's murder faded. The search was abandoned on Daisy Grant much sooner, and I finally began breathing easier. Working days at the computer in Mark's quiet and serene office, chatting with Rachel and Mark off and on during the days and then Mark and I adopting our evening semi-routine . . . it formed a predictable and peaceful life. While still nervous — more at times than others — I found myself settling in, and I liked it. Honestly, Mark had a lot to do with that.

Well, being totally honest, Mark had *everything* to do with that. He was all Craig and Jackson had said and more. I kicked myself for refusing those blind dates at least a half dozen times a day. Mark tugged at things I'd buried so deep inside me I didn't know they even existed anymore. The biggest shock came on one of our walks. We had just passed Jackson Square and I went to step off the curb. He called out, "Stop!" I did. Immediately. He grabbed my arm and a car veering too close to us jerked back into its lane. I didn't pause to ask questions, to check things out myself, I just stopped. That was new to me. And I realized why I had stopped. I trusted him. Completely trusted him.

Trust happened to be something I'd not experienced since Mom had dumped us at the Piggly Wiggly. I liked many people, I shared things with many people, but trust them? No, none of them. I couldn't do it. Even Jackson got edited versions of me from me. But Mark . . . I didn't withhold from Mark and keep secrets to protect myself. What I withheld from him, I withheld to protect him. That was a first for me. Frankly, I wasn't sure I liked it.

But like it or not, I trusted him and our pattern had been set. It felt normal and good. Comfortable, and oddly exciting. I, who rarely had a minute to spare and definitely didn't share those I did with anyone else, had a routine with Mark that wasn't at all routine. I think because I actually let my emotions show with him, and that was not usual or routine for me in any sense of the word with anyone. As odd as it feels and weird as it is to admit, I am enjoying my life. Imagine that? Enjoying it.

Who ever would have thought?

At breakfast one morning, I half-listened to him chatter about football season starting and half-pondered why he had this all-encompassing effect on me. Unsure, I prayed I wasn't imagining that I seemed to have a similar impact on him. We finished breakfast and I headed to the office, where I worked on the website the rest of the morning and a big chunk of the afternoon.

The other staff began gearing up, prepping for dinner, but I remained lost in my own world in his office. It was liberating, a new experience, to be able to hide away and just be creative. Mark's instructions on the site had been simple: hours of operation, address, map, and a photo of the building from the street. That first day, he'd passed me his cell phone to snap a photo.

I'd taken it, knowing I could do a lot better website than that, and I had. As well as what he'd asked for, I'd added the lunch and dinner menus, an online reservations form, and other unsolicited treats he and his diners might enjoy. The site was gorgeous — and almost done. I studied it intensely, and bubbles of joy and surprise floated up in me. Even I hadn't known I could create something so utterly charming on the web. What can I say? The man inspired me.

That afternoon, I got the surprise of my life when my drifting thoughts coalesced and I realized Mark could also break my heart. I steadfastly believed he wouldn't do it, but that he could . . . I scarcely believed it. I never let anyone get that close. Ever.

The shock took a while to work through and a good while longer to stop terrifying me. Then, I broke for a cup of soothing peppermint tea and wrestled with all it meant.

Two cups of tea later, the truth slotted in my mind, pulled into focus, and wouldn't be shunned or denied. Knowing he could and wouldn't hurt me was the most precious gift I'd ever been given in my life.

Unfortunately, my conscience got wind of it and nagged me half to death.

Mark had been everything good and kind and decent to me, and I'd been dishonest with him.

No matter why I'd kept secrets — even if I did it for his own protection — I wasn't being honest. I'd lied and lied and lied to him. In doing so, I'd broken the refugee's golden rule. I knew the worth of my ally. But, boy, he'd gotten the short end of the stick with his.

The sparkle in my day dimmed, and guilt held a banquet inside my head.

"Lily, it's after four. You've been staring at that screen again all day today."

Startled, I jumped, then looked toward the doorway and saw a dashing pirate standing there holding a white, diaphanous dress and clear shoes. "Mark?" The voice was his, but with the garb and patched eye, I couldn't be sure.

"Take it easy. If you'd come up for air now and then, you'd know it's Halloween."

I rolled back a bit from the computer. "You're going trick-or-treating?"

"You really have been buried in here." He laughed. "We wear costumes every year and tonight after closing, we have a Halloween Ball. It's a Jameson Court tradition." He lifted the dress toward her. "When I got mine, I took the liberty of picking up one for you."

Why would I need a costume? I'd never worn a Halloween costume. "You got me a Halloween costume to wear in the kitchen?"

"No, for the ball after the kitchen closes."

He'd mentioned there was a ball tonight, and that explained all the extra activity in the kitchen itself. "I'm invited to the ball?"

"I told you on our walk a few nights ago." He frowned. "You weren't listening to me. I called you on it, too, but you assured me you had heard every word."

He had. The memory of that came back to me. "Yes, you did. Sorry. I forgot for a second. Actually, I guess I didn't realize it was Halloween today." A ball meant a ton of extra work for the staff. I stood up and stretched. My muscles were cramped from being bent to the computer screen all day. "Do we need to convert the dining room, or what?"

"No. There's a ballroom on the third floor. Everything's done."

"Wow. Terrific." From the outside steps to the apartment, I knew there was a third floor but I had no idea what was up there. That was one of the few things they hadn't talked about. "You make a great pirate."

"It's my trademark. I'm always a pirate."

"Jean Lafitte fan?" The Civil War pirate was well known in the city. I walked over and touched the long white dress he held on a hanger. Soft. "Pretty. Thoughtful of you to get this for me."

"I guessed on the size for it and the shoes. Hope I got close."

So did I. My ankle finally felt better and I didn't want do to anything to set it to throbbing again. "We'll soon know."

He smiled. "So how's the website coming. Can I look?"

I blocked his path. "I've told you a hundred times. You can't see it until it's done."

"Did I ask for too much?" He lost his smile. "If it's too hard, I can hire —"

"You asked for very little, and it'll be done soon. I just have a few finishing touches to put on it." Another ten minutes and I'd have been done.

"Finish it tomorrow or the day after," he said, dropping his voice. "Rachel told me you didn't even break for lunch today."

"I had tea this afternoon."

"Tea is not lunch." He dipped his chin, his tone chastising. "Don't do that again. Eating is very important to your health, Lily."

"I was enjoying myself," I said honestly and, well, amazed. Now he worried about my health, too. Neither Craig nor Jackson had exaggerated about Mark at all, and I liked him too much — even more than Craig and Jackson swore I would, which was a lot. Those two always had been trying to hook Mark and me up, which is exactly why I'd made sure I never met him. I regretted that now but, liking him as much as I do, scared me right out of my sneakers. "After all the excitement of the last few weeks, I needed the calm and quiet."

"That's what Rachel said," Mark admitted. "Try the shoes."

My gut-alarm sounded. Had she recognized me from the news? "Oh?"

"Moving, getting mugged and all."

I let myself breathe and set the shoes on the floor then toed off a sneaker and stepped into the slipper. It actually fit. I drew in a breath.

"Too tight?" He let out a frustrated sigh. "I consulted with Rachel and we really thought a seven would fit." He wiggled his fingers. "I'll run back to the shop and exchange them. What size do you need?"

So eager to please me. I smiled. "They fit perfectly."

"Really?" His lips spread into a smile.

I nodded. "Like they were made for me."

"Good." That pleased him immensely.

"Well, I'll run upstairs and put this dress on, then you tell me what you want me to do down here — and don't you dare peek at that website, Mark Jensen."

He frowned. "Why not? You know I'm

eager to see it."

"Yes, but tomorrow will be soon enough. I want it completely done before you start picking it apart."

"Why would I pick it apart?"

"You'll notice every flaw, and tonight I want to be happy at having created it before I have to start changing it to suit you." He was the boss. I should do what he wants. "Is that asking for too much?"

"No, but you're fretting for nothing. I'm not that hard to please, I promise you."

I grunted. "You're very hard to please," I said with a deliberate sniff. "If you weren't, this wouldn't be the best restaurant in New Orleans and you'd have disgruntled employees. Half the reason your staff is so loyal is they enjoy the prestige of working for you at Jameson Court."

"Seriously?" He looked genuinely surprised. "I thought it was because I pay them well and treat them decently."

"That comes in lower on the totem pole. They leave here, they can handpick their next job anywhere. Do you really not know this?"

He paused. "I think I'll take the fifth."

"So you do know it." I took the dress and then stared at him, waiting.

With a sigh, he answered, reluctant as all

get out. "Think hero points."

"What?" He'd lost me.

"If I say I did know, I'm a conceited jerk. If I say I didn't know, I'm a dumb jerk. When either way I'm a jerk, how can I answer, Lily?"

Darling. "Honestly, you can't and get away with it." I shrugged. "I can spot a liar at twenty paces."

"I won't lie to you. Ever. About anything. Refugees don't do that."

Guilt rammed through me. "I appreciate the reassurance, but don't be so set on that line of thinking, okay? Sometimes things happen and people lie — omit, really — to protect not to deceive." Oh, I hoped my face wasn't telling him more than my words. They gave away too much already.

"Have you lied to me?" he asked, proving my hunch was dead-center and on target.

A knot rose in my throat. There it was. A straight out question I couldn't avoid. But just the thought of answering it struck terror in my heart.

"Mark?" Rachel stuck her head in the door. "There you are. Back in the office again, eh? I'm not used to finding him in the office," she said to me. "He's always avoided it at every possible opportunity." She smiled at me, then looked back to Mark

129

and her smile faded. Worry filled her eyes. "You need to get out front."

"What's going on?" The change in his tone signaled he picked up on her worry.

"Victor Marcello's just come in. He's having a memorial service for Edward — friends and family — here, because they have deep roots in the city, and he wants you to cater the dinner afterward."

Mark sobered. "When is it?"

"Monday, and we're booked, but you can't tell him no. Edward apparently talked about you to him. He knows you knew each other in high school and he'll be really offended if you don't do this — for Edward."

My luck had fizzled. Of all people and places, Victor had to remember Mark and Jameson Court and Mark's connection to his dead son. *Why do things always work this way? Finally, something good and now this. Just figures.*

"Book it," Mark told Rachel. "Then phone Maxie at the Courtyard. She'll send over extra staff. I've done it for her."

"You don't want to see him?" Rachel's jaw dropped loose.

"No," Mark said honestly, "but I will." He glanced at me. "Victor Marcello isn't a good man to tick off."

"Never make an enemy on purpose," I

said, repeating one of Lester's favorite sayings. Where it came from, I hadn't a clue. But this wasn't about making an enemy. People in business were tied up all the time. Mark didn't want to see Victor Marcello's grief. It would bring back his own and make it fresh again. That's what this reluctance was all about. My heart hurt for him.

"Are you okay, Lily?" Mark studied her. "You're as pale as a ghost."

"I'm fine." For a woman scared to death, I was fine. If Victor Marcello recognized me, he'd kill me for sure, for running and not testifying. In his eyes, it'd be solely my fault that his only son's murderer was free. But him showing up here didn't mean I'd messed up my death and he'd found me at Jameson Court. Marcello hadn't come for me. He'd come for Mark about cooking for the gathering after Edward's second memorial service. Totally different connection. *Thank heaven.*

Marcello already had held a funeral in Biloxi. I'd seen clips of it on the news. It was quite a star-studded event. Tons of celebrities and powerful politicians.

You're safe. He has no idea Daisy isn't dead and you're here.

I wasn't rationalizing. He couldn't know, or he'd be marching into the office with or

131

without approval, grabbing me and then dragging me to the authorities, insisting I'd testify or else every step of the way. "You go ahead."

Mark glanced at Rachel. "Lock that computer and don't let her get back on it today. She needs a break — whether or not she wants one."

"You've got it, boss." Rachel smiled.

Mark went through the kitchen and disappeared. My nerves jangled.

Rachel shut down the computer then powered it off. "Well, Lily. I don't know what you've done to him, but I think our Mark is finally back."

"Back? He's been gone?"

"Oh, yeah. If we knew where, maybe we could have gotten him back sooner, but it didn't work that way." Seeing my perplexed look, Rachel clarified. "Mark's been MIA since Katrina. We've all tried to reach him, and we thought after the incident at the Mardi Gras fountain, we had. He has stopped being self-destructive, but he still distances himself from everybody else." That worried her; it showed in everything about her. "He can't let himself care about anyone or anything — al least, he couldn't. You somehow changed that." She hugged me, then pulled back. Tears brimmed in her eyes. "Thank you, Lily."

I didn't know what to say.

Rachel sniffed, grabbed a tissue from the desk and dabbed at her nose. "Are you afraid Mark's hooked in with the Marcello family?"

"Is he?" I hadn't even thought of it, but maybe I was wrong about why Victor had showed up here. Maybe it wasn't Mark's knowing Edward. Maybe . . .

"No!" Rachel's reaction proved beyond her words the idea was absurd.

"Good." Breathing again, I lowered the hand I'd unconsciously pressed against my stomach.

"Okay, girlfriend." Rachel closed the office door. "Sit down. It's time for you and me to talk turkey."

My pulse raced. She had a look that filled me with dread and terror. "About what?"

Rachel tensed all over and her eyes glittered. "Daisy Grant."

CHAPTER 7

My knees gave out and I slid onto the computer chair as if I had no bones.

"The red hair threw me off," Rachel said, leaning against the door. "But the second time I saw your license photo on the news, I knew you were Daisy Grant."

"You're mistaken. I'm Lily–"

"I'm not mistaken, and you're a lousy liar, so don't bother." Rachel frowned. "You haven't checked the news this afternoon, have you?"

"No." I hadn't left the computer — and I'd totally enjoyed getting lost in the creativity of crafting the website and, frankly, of forgetting my problems.

"Well, it seems the clothes you had on when you went missing from the police station were found stashed about a mile down the beach from the harbor where you rented the *Lucky Lady.* And your handbag was found in a trash drum near a store where you bought a swimsuit, a hat and a waterproof purse."

"But it's been two weeks." Surely they empty the trash drums more often than every two weeks. I should have been home free on that. "How can this be happening now?"

"How?" Rachel shook her head, lifted her hands. "Who cares? What's important is that you know what's happening."

Fear beat through me, hard and fast. Rachel had put the pieces together which meant the police, FBI and both crime families had, too. "Oh, God, Rachel. I messed up my death!" How could I mess up my death? I'd tried so hard to do everything right.

"Yeah, you did," Rachel said. "Which, I fear, is why Victor Marcello is really here."

I jumped to my feet. "Mark!"

"Is fine, and we'd like him to stay that way, so stay put." She grabbed my arm and held me into place. "He doesn't know a thing about Daisy Grant. Victor will know that as soon as they speak."

"How did he track me here?" I asked, seeing no sense in pretense now.

"Marcello has an army of goons and a lot of friendlies in New Orleans. It was his stomping ground for decades. Apparently, a tour-bus guide got them to New Orleans — he was interviewed by some police detective, and that's as effective as a bullhorn."

"Gray hair, rumpled looking?" When Rachel nodded, I said, "That's Detective Keller from Biloxi."

She frowned again. "I'm not sure who got them from the Quarter to Jameson Court. But the point is, they know you're here."

"And now I've brought all this down on Mark's head." Tears burned my eyes. I blinked hard and fast. "I never dreamed they'd find out I wasn't dead, or that they'd find me here or I wouldn't have come. I tried to be so careful . . ." I swiped at an errant tear. "What am I going to do?"

Rachel pulled up a chair and sat down beside me. "I'm no expert at this stuff, okay? But your actions make it obvious you don't think the authorities can protect you."

"Their witnesses are all dead."

"I figured." Rachel sighed. "You've got to run again. Fast. Before Victor or Adriano gets the idea in their heads that Mark's protecting you. Otherwise, they'll go after him, too, for helping you. I take it you haven't contacted Jackson."

She even knew about Jackson. "Has he been on the news, too?"

Rachel nodded. "Afraid so. He looks really

good all grown up — even grieving."

Mixed emotions slammed through me. Jackson wasn't mourning anymore and that was good, but he had to be terrified about the mob and the authorities being after me. Now, in making a mess of my death, I'd put Jackson *and* Mark in jeopardy, and knowing Jackson, he'd be beating a path to New Orleans. I stood up, sniffed. "He'll come here. He's probably already on the way." I swiped at my eyes. "I have to leave now. Lead them away from Jackson and Mark. It's the best I can do to keep them safe."

"You can't just leave now. You'll be dead before you cross the street." Rachel's voice went shrill. "Victor will have people watching to see if you run while he's here or after he leaves Jameson Court. If you want to get out of New Orleans alive, then we have to be more subtle and sly." She rubbed at her temple. "It's Halloween. We'll use that. A costume will help."

"Mark got me one." I hiked my chin to where it hung on a hook near the door.

Rachel glanced over at the white diaphanous dress and transparent heels. "Okay, Cinderella. You put on the dress and glass slippers. I'll work up a mask. That with the red hair should be enough. You'll hide out here, stay for the ball, and then when the bulk of the guests leave, you'll leave with them. There's usually a hundred or more people at this thing, so it should be easy for you to blend in and fade away."

"Rachel, this all sounds clear-cut and simple. But I have no way to just leave." Lester's warning about public transportation replayed in my mind. "Buses, planes, trains — they'll all be watched."

"Leave transportation to me." She clasped Lily's hand. "I hate it that this happened to you. You seem like a special woman and Mark's totally crazy about you. Any other time . . . well. He'd have fallen in love with you. I just know it."

The truth sounded crazy so I kept it to myself. I think maybe we both already had fallen in love. At least, we'd fallen into something. I can't explain it. What I know about love would fit in a thimble with lots of room left. But there was an instant connection between us. I'd sure never felt anything like it before, and gauging by his comments, I don't believe Mark has either. Maybe it was our shared refugee status. Or the fact that we're both alone. Or all the stories of him I'd heard from Jackson and Craig, though of course, Mark knew none of them. Honestly, the connection wasn't that simple. It was more like spontaneous combustion without the external explosion. Somehow I recognized him, knew him. I can't explain it even to myself, but it wasn't as simple as love at first sight or a mere attraction. This was something beyond chemistry that happened at soul level I'd never before experienced — and I wanted it. More of it. All of it. But now . . . I had to walk away from it.

That made me want to cry. "I can't think about what might have been. It's not going to happen." The words tasted bitter. "I could get him hurt, which means I have no choice. I have to go."

Rachel slid me a knowing look. "That's the reaction I thought I'd be getting. You're already crazy about him, too."

"I am," I admitted. "I'm not sure how it happened. Seriously, this sort of thing has never happened to me. Naturally, it would finally happen at the worst possible time. My bum luck." Some things never change. "Oh never mind that. The bottom line is I am crazy about him and that's why I'm leaving him and never looking back. I'll get as far away from him and Jackson as I can." My hands shook, my heart felt squeezed. "But what do I tell him? He'll feel abandoned again." Her chest went tighter still, and memories of her holding Jackson's hand outside the Piggly Wiggly swamped her.

"You'll come up with something — other than the truth. It'd just put him in danger and we both know he'd move heaven and earth to keep you from leaving."

The idea of lying to him about this made me sick, but he was protective and Rachel was right. He would jeopardize himself to protect me. I couldn't let him do it.

Rachel walked to the door. "Change into Cinderella, and don't you dare leave this office until I come back with the mask."

"I won't." My throat constricted. "Rachel, thank you for not telling anyone."

She sobered. "You're a victim, Lily. I won't make you one again, and I don't want your blood on my hands."

"Neither do I — want anyone's blood on my hands, I mean."

"I know. You're easy to read."

"What?"

"Your character," she explained, gripping the door's edge. "It shines through in everything about you — which is why I'm helping you."

She was helping me for Mark. "You're protecting him."

"He's been good to me and to my husband, Chris. Of course, I'm protecting him. But I'm protecting you, too. Because you

140

matter to him in a way I've never before seen a woman matter to him."

"Really?" My hungry ears loved hearing that, and it filled my hungry heart.

She nodded. "True. I promise."

"Thank you for helping me."

"You're welcome." Rachel turned and walked out.

I stepped into the office's bath with the dress and heels and put them on, wishing they were like Dorothy's and I could click my heels three times and be home. Problem was what it always had been: I have no home.

It is what it is. You can let it define you, or you can define you. Which is it going to be?

Squaring my shoulders, I answered my conscience. *I choose what I've always chosen — to define myself.* Rushing to the computer, I hacked through the simple lockdown and then put the finishing touches on Mark's website. It didn't have all the bells and whistles I wanted for it, but it was lovely. Elegant and warm and charming, just like Jameson Court. I left the home page up on the screen, wrote a note and then put it on the keyboard. Just as I put down the pen, Rachel returned.

"I locked you out of the computer." She frowned. "How'd you get back in?"

"One of my foster parents had a knack for hacking," I said with a shrug. "I watched and learned. I didn't hurt anything, I just wanted to finish the website."

She scooted in and looked at it. "Lily, it's gorgeous!"

I smiled. "Thanks."

Rachel turned to look at me. "No, I mean it. It's really gorgeous." She glanced back to the computer, studied the photos of the staff. "How did you get all these?"

"I observed you all doing what you do. It was simple, really."

"Not so simple. It's not just the photos. You got the personalities of the people. Mark is going to be knocked out by this!"

Music to my ears. An absolute symphony. "I hope he likes it."

"He won't like it," Rachel said. "He'll love it." She went silent, then softened her voice. "Oh, Lily, I get it. This is your something for him to remember you by, isn't it?"

I nodded, feeling the burning swell of tears start at the back of my nose and work up to my eyes. "And to repay his kindnesses."

She clasped my hand and gently squeezed. "I was right about you. You're a good woman." Gazing down, she focused on the bejeweled mask in her hand.

I didn't have to be a mind reader to know

she regretted that Mark and I wouldn't be together. It showed in her face and seemed about as bleak as I felt inside.

"Here you go." She passed the mask over.

Its rhinestones winked in the light. I lifted it to my face. It covered the top half. "Well?" I asked, peering at her through the eye slits. "Will it get the job done?"

"No one will have a clue." She kept assessing me. "Seriously, I know and can't tell who you are."

"Great." Relief washed through me. If Rachel had doubts, she'd express them. The last thing I needed was to cause a blood bath at Mark's ball. Jameson Court's reputation would be destroyed and, through no fault of his own, Mark had lost way too much already. I just couldn't — *please, God* — cost him more. How had this all gotten so complicated?

Rachel softened her voice. "Do you need anything from the apartment?"

"No. The mugger got everything but my Grant half-dollar. I've got it on me. The rest I'd be scared to take. Someone might recognize it from when I was here. There are some personal items to get rid of though. Would you bring them to Ruth at Basin Boutique? Maybe someone will come in who needs them."

"Sure. I can do that." Rachel stood up. "Stay here," she told me again. "I'll come and get you when you're to come up to the ballroom. Then just watch me. I'll signal when it's time for you to leave. There'll be a black limo at the curb out front. Chris will be driving it. He'll take you to a car, and you can take it from there."

Chris. Her husband. Good. She'd kept the circle of who knew about this tight. "Wait. He'll take me to a car? Whose car?"

"Don't ask. It's not stolen, and no one will connect it to you or to anyone else from here. That's all you need to know. Now, what about money?"

"I have most of the advance Mark gave me. I'm good." I'd tucked it and the Grant in a little pouch and attached it to my bra. "I'll send it back as soon as I can. No card or anything, just the money. You'll tell him it's from me, right?"

"I will, though with the website, you've earned whatever he gave you." More regret rippled across her face. "I'm so sorry this has happened to you, Lily."

"So am I." Understated, but factual. "But it did happen. All I can do now is deal with it."

Rachel started for the door, then stopped, her hand on the knob. "I admire that about you. All my life, I've been told that what happens prepares us to cope with what's coming. But I really didn't believe it until now. In your situation, I wouldn't have the first clue about what to do to stay alive. I'd probably find a corner, collapse and curl up in a tight ball and stay that way for the duration. But you're a fighter, and even though you're in deep trouble, you don't use other people without a care about their safety." The look in her eyes softened and admiration lit them from the bottoms. "Had you been able to stay, I think we would have been great friends."

I liked her. Admired her even, but I had to be honest and not leave her with false illusions. "I'm not that good. Seriously, Rachel. I have no idea what I'm doing. None. I'm just trying to stay alive and to not get anyone else killed. That's all. But I think I would have loved being your friend."

Rachel smiled and left Mark's office.

A friend. A real friend. And Mark. I sat down and squeezed my eyes shut. The things I've always wanted most, next to taking good care of Jackson and us having a real home, and here they are. Finally. But all I get is a glimpse of them.

I shook myself. At least I got a glimpse. At least I know those things aren't pipe-dream fantasies, they exist. That's more than a lot of people got in their whole lives.

It was.

But still, I wanted more. I wanted these people and my dreams in my life.

Lester's voice rang inside my mind. *Forget it, Daisy girl. What ain't meant to be, ain't meant to be.*

I sighed. Long and deep. Lester had survived most of his life alone. If he could do it, then I could, too. No sense whining about it. It changed nothing.

I'd made do most of my life. And I hadn't minded it really, except during the hungry times. I hated being hungry. I'd seen to it Jackson had been spared that, at least. But for the first time, I resented having to accept less than what I wanted most.

I really, *really* resented it.

CHAPTER 8

The third-floor ball room was packed.

Mark Anthony and Cleopatra stood talking with the Statue of Liberty and Benjamin Franklin. A wide staircase leading down to the street was littered with more costumed people; mostly couples, but a fair number of singles stood in clusters on the rungs, leaning on the ornate handrails. Dinosaurs. A man in a diaper carrying a five-foot baby bottle that I mistook as a prop until it laughed. His wife, Sunny, he told a Dorothy and Tin Man standing nearby.

A five-piece band with a female singer performed on a stage constructed at one end of the room. Soft music rippled through the crowd and flowed out multiple sets of open French doors. I kept an eye on Rachel. She seemed at ease and familiar with most of the guests. So long as she didn't appear panicked, I supposed everything was okay.

Mark made the rounds, greeting everyone from the mayor and council members to vendors I'd seen delivering fresh vegetables in the kitchen. That he treated all of them with the same respect impressed me. It was too natural to him to be done for show, and too deliberate to be disingenuous. My heart sank a little deeper. I'd never before met a man like him, and instinctively I knew I never would again.

The lead singer in the band introduced Mark. He joined them on stage, grabbed a mike, then formally greeted the guests, welcoming them all to Jameson Court. "It's become tradition that I kick-off the festivities with the first dance, but I seem to have lost my partner. Cinderella? Where are you?"

The spotlight roved through the crowd, seeking me. I darted a frantic look at Rachel and saw her expression stiffen with the worry I felt. *Oh, no.* How was I supposed to fade away now? I evaded the searching light, ducking behind a couple dressed as New Orleans Saints football players.

"Cinderella?" A woman shouted from the crowd. "I'm right here, gorgeous."

The light landed on an elderly woman and the crowd parted to let her advance toward Mark. Bright-eyed and spry, the silver-haired senior lifted the hem of her ball gown and moved toward the stage. "Well, get down here, boy, and let's heat up this dance floor."

Peeking around heavily padded shoulders, even I grinned.

Mark laughed, met the capricious woman on the dance floor, then signaled the band to start playing.

The woman stepped into Mark's arms. She looked an awful lot like Emily. *Emily!* It was, which meant . . . *Lester?* Scared to death he was here, I anxiously scanned the crowd.

A man whispered near my ear. "You ain't gonna find me out there, Daisy girl."

I spun to face him — Abraham Lincoln, that is, complete with stovepipe hat. "What are you doing here?" I couldn't hide my upset.

He hushed his voice. "I might be asking you the same thing." He elevated his whisper. "This ain't Dixie."

"I know." Swallowing hard, I confessed. "I didn't go there because I didn't want someone to figure out you knew where I'd gone. They'd beat it out of you, for pity's sake."

"And knock my friend, Paul, around, too. I'm sure as spit you thought of that." Lester shook his head. His hat wobbled, and he

149

reached up to seat it on his head. "You shoulda known better, but there ain't no help for it now." His expression sobered and resignation had the lines running nose to chin alongside his mouth deepening to shadowy creases. "You gotta fly, girl. They know you're here."

That much I knew. "How did you find me?"

"Wasn't hard, I'm sorry to say. Put the pieces together same as they did. Just had to get myself arrested and then keep my ears open. If you want my advice, girl, you best be doing better at staying dead next time than last time or you're really gonna be toes up, pushing up daisies."

"Don't you think if I could do better I would? My neck's on the line here. Worse, Jackson's neck is on the line." What could happen to him petrified me. "What did I do wrong?" I had no idea what had messed up my death, which meant I could repeat my mistakes and mess up again. Even a cat only had nine lives. I couldn't afford any more missteps.

"Your stash on the beach. Why didn't you go back and get it?"

"I drifted too far, swimming to shore. Somehow — I don't know how it happened — I ended up in Gulfport."

"Well, Detective Keller found your stash. From there it wasn't a puny frog's jump to finding you. I expect he and that FBI agent, Johnson, will be here directly."

I didn't mention Edward Marcello's dad, Victor, had already been to Jameson Court. It'd just make Lester worry more and he looked plenty worried already. "Great." My rotten luck. The mob *and* the authorities after me again. Couldn't I catch at least one break from them? Just one?

"We got us a disaster in the making here. Even Emily with no eyes sees it clear as day. We figured we'd best come haul you out of here or else we'd be burying you."

I waited for two jailbirds to pass us, then whispered, "No, you can't get involved. It's too dangerous." No way could I run with him and Emily in tow. I honestly wasn't sure I could do it alone.

Clearly bent on blistering my ears, Lester sucked in a heavy breath. I touched his upper arm to spare us both. "It's arranged. I'm leaving in a little bit. If you two could just help me not get waylaid before then, everything will be under control." I spotted Rachel and smiled, letting her know all was well.

"You're set on protecting me again." He stepped closer and lowered his voice. "Ordinarily, I wouldn't stand for it, but Emily and me probably would slow you down, and right now you need wings." Pausing a long moment, he added, "Well, all right, then. So be it. But you get your backside to Dixie this time, Daisy girl. I done lost everybody else in my life, and I ain't hankering to lose you, too. I won't stand for it, I'm telling you true. You're a good soul, but you got the street smarts of a gnat. You need Paul to stay in your skin, and that's all there is to it."

I did. And it was exceedingly apparent I was incapable of pulling off anything like this on my own. I would go to Dixie to Paul Perini, but I would not admit it to Lester. He couldn't be forced to tell what he didn't know. I lifted a hand and cupped his weathered face. "Thank you for coming to rescue me."

"You've pulled my fat out of the fire plenty of times." His eyes shimmered. "Go dance with your young man before Emily stomps his toes right off his feet. Woman's a wonder, but she can't see a thing or dance a lick."

"I love you, Lester." He'd done more for me than anyone else in my whole life.

"Course." He nodded. "I'll be expecting me a post card from Rose Green now and then — so I know you're okay."

Rose Green. I committed it to memory. "All right."

"Do your best to stay dead this time, you hear me? I don't know many more flower names that suit you."

He tried to look disappointed but all I sensed was fear. Bone deep, chilling fear. "I will," I promised, forcing a cheery look on my face. It took a fair bit of effort because I felt more fearful than he looked, and that's saying something.

Spotting Rachel laughing with two people dressed as pretzels, I stepped away and walked over to Mark and Emily, then lightly tapped Emily's shoulder. "May I cut in?"

"I suppose, since we're sister Cinderellas." Emily showed no signs of recognizing me. "Thanks for the dance, Mark. *Cinderella and the Pirate.* We could start a new trend. Maybe Disney could make us a movie." Emily smiled. "Oh, and I'm sorry about your toes, boy. They should be good as new in a day or two." She released Mark and stepped away.

Still smiling, Mark turned to me. "I've been looking for you."

"Sorry." I smiled, seeing Emily hook up with Lester then dissolve into the crowd. "But I'm here now."

"Dance with me?" Mark lifted his hand.

I smiled. "Can your toes stand it?"

"To hold you in my arms? Absolutely."

I stepped into Mark's waiting arms and my troubles melted away. We circled the floor and when the music changed to a waltz, he whispered, "You're a good dancer, Lily."

His breath warmed my face. "Mr. Granger taught me. He loved to dance and Mrs. Granger hated it, so we danced a lot. He said I had a knack for it."

"I'd agree."

"You'd be wrong," I confessed. "I struggled to remember every step. I didn't like it, which made it harder, though at the moment, I'm seeing its merits."

"Why didn't you tell Mr. Granger you didn't care to dance?"

"I wanted them to like me so they wouldn't send me back."

"Ah, I see. The Grangers were more of your foster parents."

I nodded. "Good ones. I was happy there almost seven months. It was a new record for me being in one place."

"You didn't want it to end."

Every night for a week, after the others had gone to bed, she'd locked herself in the bathroom, stuffed a towel to her face and cried her heart out. "No, I didn't want it to end. But, like most things, it ended anyway."

"What happened?"

I swallowed a lump that had risen in my throat. "Mr. Granger and I planted a garden. One day, we were weeding it and he was telling me stories about growing up in Illinois. He had a house on a lake there and they'd fish in the summer and in the winter, when the lake would freeze over, all the neighborhood kids would gather and play ice-hockey." Vivid flashes of memories burned in my mind. "He started laughing — he liked sharing his stories and Mrs. Granger had heard them all a million times — then he had a heart attack, dropped dead on the green onions, and that was that." I paused to let my emotions settle. The horror of that day, losing him so suddenly like that, and then the trauma that came afterward. When I could, I added, "After the funeral, Mrs. Granger moved to Birmingham to be close to her sister. All they had left was each other." *Oh, how those words had cut me to the quick.*

"All she had?" Mark looked confused. "But she had you."

Bittersweet, I smiled. "How like you to think of that." Touched, tender, I leaned in and kissed him. "Thank you, Mark."

"I take it Mrs. Granger didn't think of that."

"No. No, she didn't."

"I'm sorry, Lily."

"Me, too." The music shifted to a lovely ballad. "But it was a very good seven months. I got to see my brother nearly every weekend, and they treated me well. It wasn't a real home, but it was the best I'd ever had, and I was grateful for it."

He pulled me closer, and looked down into my upturned face, then whispered close to my ear. "If I could, I'd take all of the hurt and every bad memory away."

Sunny fields of daisies and rainbows only happen in the movies, the pot-growing-in-his-attic, Mr. Venier, had told me. I had to agree that it seemed that way so far, but that Mark wanted a happy life with sweet memories for me touched me deeply. I nuzzled his neck. "One of many reasons you're so special to me. You're a good ally, Mark."

He kissed me again. This time, longer, deeper, and with more tenderness than I believed a woman could be kissed. It emptied and filled my senses all at once.

We danced three more dances, then Rachel motioned to me. My stomach clenched. This wonderful man finally had come into my life, and now the time had come for me to walk away and leave him. I had no choice, yet knowing what leaving him would do to Mark . . . everything inside me rebelled. It took every atom of strength in me to not grab hold of him and hang on for dear life.

You could get him killed. You want him dead?

I didn't. Above all, I wanted him safe and happy. I pulled back. "I have a surprise for you."

He smiled.

"Your website is ready," I said softly. "I wanted to add a few more bells and whistles, but . . . well, I hope you'll like it. It's up on the screen in your office, if you want to sneak away for a look." Before he could say anything, I passed him my Grant half-dollar. "And I hate to ask, Mark, but this ally needs another favor." I put a lilt in my voice to tone down how important this favor was to me. Jackson needed to know I was okay. He'd have his stomach acting up again and pouring acid. He didn't need another ulcer. "Would you give this to Craig Parker for me?"

"Your Grant?" Mark's expression turned solemn. "Of course, I will. But why?"

I shook my head, signaling I didn't want

to answer. "It's important. Craig will understand what it means."

Something akin to jealousy lit in Mark's
eyes. "I'd like to understand, if you'll give
me the chance."

Rachel lifted a staying finger at me. Now
wasn't the time to depart, after all. The relief
of a reprieve and a few more minutes slid
through me, eager for whatever time with
Mark I could get.

"Lily?" Ruth from the boutique joined us,
sparing me from having to answer Mark —
or from having to refuse to answer Mark.
"Excuse us for a moment, will you?" Ruth
asked him. "I've got to consult Lily on a
website problem."

"Okay. He seemed torn, and I expect he
was torn and wanting me to explain why I
couldn't give Craig the Grant myself. "I'll
grab us something to drink," he said, then
warned me, "We *are* going to finish this
conversation."

"Of course." I nodded, knowing we
wouldn't. Ruth led me through the French
doors onto a veranda at the east end of the
ball room. "I've been looking for you in here
for an hour."

Not good. That kind of hunt had to signal
more trouble. "What for?"

"The guy that mugged you. I saw him on

TV." Ruth leaned in close. "His name's Lou Boudin."

One of Edward's shooters. "That explains a lot."

"He's a goon for the Adriano family, Lily. This is serious. They pegged you being here and sent him after you. Jason says Victor Marcello followed them. You're in a heap of trouble, woman."

Tell me something I don't know. "You know about me, too?"

"Jason and I watch the news. How could we not know?"

Great. I messed up my old life, my death, my new life, and I dragged a lot of others into the mess with me. *Batting a thousand.*

"You realize that jerk didn't mean to mug you, he meant to kill you, right? It scares me half to death to think of what could have happened if I hadn't interrupted. Calling attention to him saved your neck. That's why he took off."

"Thank you for that," I said. "I'm sure you're right."

"I don't need to be right. I need to know you understand what all this means."

"What?" I couldn't track the path of her mind. It was a whacky, gel-spiked maze.

"It means Adriano isn't happy that Boudin didn't kill you in the mugging. Tony's still on the hook for Edward's murder. That leaves Boudin in a situation. He'll have to try again. The fact is, either he takes you out or the Adrianos take him out — unless Victor finds him first." Her pink-tipped black Mohawk warbled. "Then, Lou's pretty much dead."

Ruth clearly had street smarts. "So you came here to tell me this?"

"Well, yeah." She shrugged. "You needed to know he'll be back. You gotta run, Lily. Now, before Boudin finds you again. It won't take him long — not with both families coming down on him, locked and loaded."

It wouldn't. Actually, I was surprised I hadn't run into him already. I squeezed Ruth's hand. "Thank you. You've been a good friend to me."

"Hey, we look out for each other down here." She darted her gaze. "I've got to get back to work. You leave now, Lily, and don't come back to the city. These people you're messing with are all business, and they're mean."

That much I knew. Especially when protecting their sons. There was nothing Victor wouldn't do for revenge for Edward's murder, and nothing Adriano wouldn't do to keep his Tony out of jail for murdering the man. Frustrated and scared out of my wits, I made myself a promise. *From now on, I know nothing and see nothing and report nothing — ever again.*

Wouldn't help me much this time, but I'd learned a lesson I'd never forget. "Rachel's going to bring you some clothes and stuff. Maybe someone can get some good out of them."

"That's thoughtful, thanks. There's always someone who needs a few things."

I'd been one of them. "Thanks, Ruth."

"Take care of you." She nodded, then disappeared into the crowd.

Mark had lingered to speak to a few more guests. Now he returned to me holding two wine glasses. "It's water," he said. "We both need clear heads for the conversation we're going to have."

"What conversation?" I tried playing stupid. It could work.

It didn't. "The one where you explain to me why you're sending Craig the Grant half-dollar."

"It's a signal that I'm okay."

"Is Craig your brother?"

"No, he's not." He was a terrific guy, a good friend to Jackson, an excellent chef and the African American son of two now-deceased African American parents, which of course Mark knew since he'd been at their funerals. A pang of regret that I hadn't been able to scrape together the airfare to get both Jackson and me there when Craig needed us settled heavy in my heart. "You know he isn't my brother."

"I do." He frowned, shoved a hand in his pants' pocket. "Are you two in some way involved?"

"No, Mark — not like you're apparently thinking."

Relief washed over his face, flooded me with guilt. He didn't push, just looked at me and waited. Finally, I said, "He'll know what to do with the coin. It's important."

"You're my refugee buddy. I'm your ally. I should do the things important to you."

Possessive. Any other time and my knees would be weak for a couple days over that remark. I might even gush. But right now, being attached in any way to me could be bad for him. "I'm grateful to you for that. More than I can put into words. But Craig has to do this thing." I sipped from my glass. My hand wasn't steady.

Mark noticed. "You're leaving, aren't you?"

My voice didn't want to work. I took a long sip of water and tried again. "I have a bit of an emergency."

"So you'll be back." Less worried, he cocked his head. I paused, and he added, "Oh. Oh, I see that you won't." He read the truth in my eyes. "Lily, you're welcome to take whatever time you need but I want you to come back. You're . . . special to me."

"I know, and I feel the same way. It's beautiful and rare, this thing between us. I've never felt anything like it." I wanted to cave. Wanted it so badly I wasn't sure I had the will not to cave. An image of Edward getting shot ripped through my mind, and for once, the vivid reminder happened at just the right time. I stiffened my shoulders and did the right thing. "The problem is, this isn't something time can fix. I wish it were. You have no idea how much I wish it were."

Hurt warred with confusion in his expression, in his eyes. "I don't understand."

"I know you don't, and I am sorry about that." I stopped talking until a couple brushed past us, then added, "But I'm not free to explain."

"You can't explain, or you won't?"

I shrugged. "What's the difference, Mark? I'm not going to do it."

He studied my face a long, tense moment. "This is what you were talking about when you said, 'Lying not to be dishonest but to protect.' "

Could he read my mind? I recoiled and started to back away.

He clasped my hand and held me in place. "Don't protect me, Lily. I've waited a long time to find you and I can't let you just walk out of my life because you're afraid I'll get hurt. Let me answer that question for you. If you leave, I *will* be hurt."

I wanted to cry, to scream. "You're the most amazing man I've ever known, but this . . . us . . . it's just the wrong time." I *don't want you to die with me. I don't want them chasing you and for you to give up your life and Jameson Court and all you've built — not for me.* I thought it all, but had the luxury of saying none of it. "You're going to have to trust me, that I know best. I know how hard trust is, but I'm asking you for it."

"I see." The hurt inside him shone in his eyes, pounded off him in waves. "So when do you leave?"

"Soon."

"Tonight?" He looked a shade shy of panic.

"No, not tonight," I lied, knowing if I didn't, he'd stick to me like glue, try to stop me, and that could get us both killed. "Tomorrow evening at the earliest. Flight is

164

being arranged." He'd assume I meant air travel and, God forgive me, I let him.

"By whom?"

My face burned like fire. *Oh, but I made a lousy liar.* Still, I had to do it. This was for him. To spare him and keep him safe and out of danger. "My brother." I pecked a kiss to Mark's cheek. "We'll talk more about it tomorrow. Right now, Rachel needs something. She's signaling me to come to her. I'd better see what it is."

"Mark. Great to see you." A rowdy man clasped Mark's shoulder and claimed his attention.

I cut through the crowd, paused to give Rachel's hand a last squeeze. "Take care of him. One day when it's safe, tell him the truth, and tell him I didn't want to leave him." He would feel abandoned. Again. I knew and hated it. But what else could I do? Plunk him down right in the middle of all this? Have his neck on the line, too? I couldn't do it. I just couldn't.

"I'll tell him. When it's safe," Rachel promised.

My eyes stung and I bit my lower lip to divert my attention. Tears never had solved anything. "Tell him, I'd have given everything to not leave him, but I couldn't risk getting him killed." His family and now her.

165

Even if given no choice, they'd all left him and he did feel abandoned. That hurt so deep I couldn't tell where the pain even started, only that I felt it skin to bones. Memories of Jackson and me waiting for our mother to come back flashed through my mind, making the pain worse. The despair. The desolation. Abandoned and deemed worthless. *Alone.*

"I'll tell him." Rachel interrupted the assault. "Be safe, and hurry." Her gaze wasn't on me. It was on the door.

Lou Boudin had arrived — and not ten feet behind him, Victor Marcello and his entourage of body-guard goons walked in. My heart skipped a full beat and my legs turned to jelly.

"Go!" Rachel whispered a shout, motioning away from the men.

I couldn't move. It seemed like I'd frozen in place. *Why couldn't I move?*

Lester and Emily moved in and planted themselves between Boudin, Marcello and me.

Emily shrieked, then yelled. "Don't move!" She spread her arms wide and spun in a circle. "I've lost a contact. Help me find it. I can't see a thing."

That caused a stir that had everyone around her halting in place, bending their necks to look at the floor.

Rachel provided cover for me, and my legs decided to work. I slipped out the door, seeking one last look at Mark before heading down the steps.

He'd apparently been watching me and now pushed through the crowd toward the door. I turned and flew down the steps, determined to get to the car before he could catch me. Honestly, I just wanted him safe, and I wasn't convinced I had the strength to walk away from him twice.

At the curb, I spotted a man standing outside a black limo dressed as a carriage footman. He motioned to me.

Had to be Rachel's husband, Chris. I headed toward him.

He opened the door. "Hurry, Daisy. Mark is —"

I dove into the back of the car. The door slammed shut, Chris ran around, got in, and pulled out into traffic, leaving half his tires on the pavement.

"Uh-oh."

"What?" I righted myself in the back seat, unwrapping the gnarled gown from my legs.

"Lou Boudin just tackled Mark."

I spun in the seat to look through the rearview. "Why?"

167

"It's obvious. They think he knew about you."

"Slow down."

"No way." Chris hit the gas and did a one-eighty in the street, then stomped the pedal and headed back to Jameson Court, whipped into a slot across the street. "They'll kill him, Daisy. He can't stay here any more than you can. Not now."

My heart ripped open. The heavy tint on the windows protected me from being recognized, but I cracked my window so I could better hear. The street was well-lighted so everything outside the limo was clearly visible, and chaotic. "Oh, God. I didn't want this. I've ruined his life."

Boudin and Mark fought in the street. Marcello walked out with his goons and one did something at the corner of the building. They hustled into a waiting limo and sped away.

"They've done something bad over there." I sensed it down to the tips of my toes.

"I saw it." Chris apparently agreed. He whipped out his phone and hit someone on speed dial. "Rachel, get out of there. Get everyone out — now!" A pause, then, "Are you leaving yet?"

Lester and Emily came down the stairs to the street, Lester yelling for everyone to run.

He and Emily kept moving. What had alerted him to the danger to others?

People flooded down the stairs and kept going, running down the street. Rachel ran among them, snagged a megaphone from uniformed police officer and, holding it to her mouth, she ordered everyone to vacate the premises.

A second police officer, one the size of a mountain, yelled, "Mark!"

"Tank. What's going on?" Mark and Boudin paused swinging at each other long enough for Mark to answer, and Boudin used the distraction to back into the crowd. He disappeared beyond the light, swallowed by the shadows.

Tank bellowed over the hysterical din of terrified voices. "Bomb threat!"

My heart stopped. Just stopped. "What should I do?"

"Stay put," Chris said. "Marcello obviously tipped off the cops. He's giving them time to clear the building."

"There's a bomb in Jameson Court?" Mark looked dumbfounded.

"Another minute and it'll be empty. Get out of here."

"Not while anyone is still inside."

"We've got it, Mark. Go." Tank shook Mark's arms. "They want you dead, man.

You hear me? They want you dead."

"Me?" He looked baffled. "Who? Why?"

"Lily Nichols," Tank said. "She's really Daisy Grant."

Mark lifted his hands. "Who is Daisy Grant?"

That was the one. The last nail in my coffin. I couldn't stand anymore. If anyone got hurt, I'd never forgive myself. Ever!

"Let her explain. You've got to get out of here," Tank said. "Marcello thinks you lied to him to protect her. He's going to kill you for it and so long as you're here, all these people are at risk. Go, Mark. Go!"

Mark looked devastated, destroyed and as lost as I felt. I should never have come here. If I'd had any idea Mark had known Edward or that the Marcello family had operated here before moving to Biloxi, I wouldn't have come to New Orleans or to Mark. But that was history and it was too late. I had come, and now I'd cost Mark everything. His home and business and perhaps his life. Tears flooded my face.

Chris groaned, opened his car door and then jumped out and waved. "Mark! Over here!"

Rachel joined Chris. "I'm going to get a few blocks away but I need to be close since Mark can't be here. I'm the only other one

170

who can do things at the Court."

"Get in," Chris told his wife. "I'll take you to the casino on the riverfront. You can wait there until Tank calls and gives you an all clear."

Rachel nodded, then slid into the front passenger seat.

"I'll call as soon as I can," Tank said to Rachel and then looked at Mark, his eyes deadpan serious. "Disappear. Don't come back. There's a contract out on you, buddy. A big one. I can't protect you." He urged Mark into the limo in the seat beside me.

Too choked up to utter a sound, I relied on silent tears to let him know my regret.

Tank took a call on his radio. "Building's empty," he relayed to Mark. "Go — and don't look back. Never come back."

Chris got in, slapped the gearshift into Drive, and then took off down the street.

Mark didn't say a word. He wouldn't even look at me. Rachel turned in the front seat, looking back at Jameson Court. "Police are pulling back," she said. "Everyone's definitely out." She blew out a deep sigh. "Thank goodness."

That was good. Very good.

Mark stared straight ahead as if stunned. "Who is Daisy Grant? What's she got to do with me?"

I opened my mouth to confess, but Chris checked the rearview and blurted out, "Isn't that —"

Rachel gasped. "It's Anthony Adriano."

Edward's shooter. I craned my neck but still couldn't see well. "What is he —"

An explosion down the street rocked the car.

I hunched down, covered my head with my arms, then sprung up and looked back toward the sound at the same time Mark spun to look.

Windows shattered. Doors blasted off. Flames licked at every opening and all of Jameson Court belched thick, black plumes of billowing smoke. My quiet tears turned to unabashed sobs.

Mark stared at his burning restaurant, his face as impenetrable as carved stone.

Rachel dialed her phone. "Tank, Tony Adriano did it. I saw him."

"Are you crazy?" Her husband crashed the steering wheel with the heel of his hand. "You want to be on their hit list, too?"

"Unofficially, Tank," Rachel said. "Just so you know." She paused, listened, then told Chris, "Drop me off at the casino, then get them out of here fast. Tank says the car is still safe but not to mess around."

So Tank had helped protect the waiting

car. He was in on my flight, too. Would Mark do as they suggested and leave with me? I expected that as soon as I admitted I was Daisy Grant, he would want to get as far away from me as possible.

He could take the car Rachel had intended for me and put me out of the limo and onto the street. I wouldn't blame him, any of them, for that. In fact, I should be brave enough to insist on it myself. I needed to get far, far away from all of them before someone found me and hurt them.

I cleared my throat, hoping my voice worked. "When we get to the car, Mark, you take it. I'll find another way."

He looked a little stunned and immensely angry but said nothing, and he didn't ask again about Daisy Grant. Either he'd figured out Daisy and Lily were one and the same, or that no longer mattered to him. Considering he'd just lost the last traces of his family — the antiques at Jameson Court — his silence could be due to either or both.

At this point, it didn't really matter. Nothing he could say would make me feel any more guilty than I already felt. I cared about him, and I had ruined his life.

The full weight of that pressed down on me in the way only messing up really bad on something critically important that can't be undone or fixed can bear down on a woman.

How in the world was I supposed to live with this? He'd worked so hard to build his future and I'd cost him everything he had. I didn't even have the right to apologize for it and ask his forgiveness.

Once he learned the truth — that I am the reason he'd lost everything — he'd hate me forever.

I couldn't blame him. I hated myself.

Chris's gaze snagged on the rearview and then he turned to look. "Oh, no."

"What's wrong now?" Mark asked.

"Someone is following us."

Mark and I both turned to look back, but it was too dark to make out more than headlights. Chris hooked a last-minute turn that removed all doubt.

We definitely had picked up a tail. The words tumbled out of my mouth. "I'm sorry. I'm so . . . sorry."

CHAPTER 9

Three turns later, Chris out-maneuvered the car tailing us and it lost track. Once certain it wouldn't pick us up again, he made a beeline for an old warehouse near the river. It wasn't the sort of place you'd drive in the light of day much less deep in the night. Lights peppered the street, though more than two-thirds had been busted out, and groups of rough-looking men loitered on every corner. No women were in sight, and considering the odds ranked high that I'd be walking out of here alone, that fact elevated my anxiety level which already flirted with straddling the stratosphere.

Between two tall brown buildings, Chris braked to a halt. The shadows dragged so deep I couldn't see a thing beyond the tinted glass. "Why are you stopping here?"

"Two buildings down, in the back alley, you'll find a black Honda Civic. He passed back the keys with a little grunt and a ruffle of fabric; his sleeve brushing against the back of his seat. "There's a spare key in the glove-box."

I didn't reach for the keys. I didn't have the right.

Frowning in my general direction, Mark took them.

"Will you two be together?" Chris looked back at us. "Rachel's going to want to know . . ."

Before Mark could answer, I did. "No. I'll be going on alone."

"She won't," Mark contradicted me. "Tell Rachel, yes, we'll be together." Pausing to glare at me, he went on. "I'm not losing everything else and you, Daisy. Wherever we go, we will go together."

Daisy. He'd worked through it and put the pieces together, and still, he wasn't kicking me to the curb to face my enemies on my own. I swallowed hard, so moved and relieved I didn't dare try to speak.

"Where are you going?"

I started to answer Chris, but then thought better of it. The less he knew, the better. Safer for him and for Rachel.

"I have no idea. Someplace . . . else," Mark said, then focused on me. "Did you hear what I said?" He pushed for an acknowledgement I didn't want to give him.

The less Chris knew the safer we'd all be, including Mark. "I heard you."

"And you planned to go . . . where?"

I looked Chris right in the eye and said nothing.

Mark frowned, short on patience and not bothering to hide it. After what had happened to him tonight, who could blame him? "I don't think she has a clue. But even if she did, with the Marcello and Adriano families up to their necks in all this *with* the FBI and locals, you don't want to know. They'll just add you to their hit list."

"I can't tell Rachel that," Chris objected. "She'll stay wired for sound, worrying about you. We're trying to get pregnant, remember? No stress."

Something in Chris's body language had my internal radar alerting. I had no idea why. The man had been nothing but good and kind and had put himself at considerable risk for me, but something warned me that stress and Rachel conceiving came secondary to something else. I couldn't see him crossing Mark. And he and Rachel had put their necks on the proverbial chopping block, helping me. Still, something wasn't quite right there, and because it wasn't, I kept my intentions to myself. "She won't stress," I said. "Rachel is practical and she

177

would agree. The less said the better."

"But she'll —"

The thread of Mark's patience broke. "Listen, you can't know, okay? They'll hurt you or Rachel — or both of you — to make you tell them. You can't tell what you don't know. It's that simple. Now let it go, Chris. The subject is closed."

"I get it," he said, his mouth flattening to a thin seam. "I'm just thinking of my wife. She loves you, Mark. She's going to be terrified. Give me something."

"I already did," Mark said, his tone thick with frost. "I told you we'd be together and we will." He motioned, frustrated. "Do either of you even hear a word I say? We are going together, Daisy. That's it. Let it go."

"I hear you." I placed a hand on Mark's, resting on his knee. "And I am sorry, Mark. If I'd realized —"

"So you've said. Drop it. I need to process all this, okay? Give me time." He let out a stuttered sigh. "Let's move. Sitting here isn't a good idea."

Chris turned in his seat, looked at Mark. "To get word to Rachel, text my cell. Ditch yours now and get another. Text me or leave a draft email in my gmail account. Don't send it. Just start a draft to David and save it. I'll check it a couple times a day. We'll send money, whatever you need."

Mark's expression soured. The weight of all this was coming home and bearing down on him. It showed in his posture and grim expression. "It's a good thing I gave Rachel full power of attorney."

"I'm sorry we need it." Chris avoided looking at me. "Draft emails are a way for us to converse without anyone being the wiser. Since they're not sent . . ."

"That doesn't work anymore," I corrected Chris. "NSA sees even the drafts."

"So be cryptic — unless you have a better idea."

"Cryptic works," Mark said.

Something about this whole exchange with Chris bothered me. I couldn't pinpoint why. It just felt . . . off.

"Better get going," Chris said, vigilant, watchful. "Daisy, be well and stay safe."

"Thank you." I faked a smile and kept my misgivings to myself. "Thank Rachel for me, too."

Chris nodded.

Mark and I left the limo and half-walked, half-ran across the uneven, cracked concrete to the Honda. By the time we got there, my ankle was throbbing up to my knee. Dancing with Mark had it tender. Running had pushed it back over the edge.

In the weeks since I'd gotten to Jameson Court, Mark had tried multiple times to get me to go to the doc, but I didn't want to expose myself any more than I already had. Too many had seen me already. Maybe Detective Keller had been right and I had broken a bone in the original fall.

"You okay?" Mark asked, holding the door and motioning me to get inside.

"Fine." I scooted onto the seat and buckled up.

He went around, got in, then shut his own door.

I dreaded mentioning the internal alarms Chris had triggered, but I couldn't not mention them to Mark. I worked at a logical reason to not say a word. I just couldn't find one, and so I gave in. "Mark, something wasn't right with Chris. I don't know exactly what, and I started not to mention it . . . I know you trust Rachel implicitly, but —"

"I picked up on it, too. He pushed way too hard, wanting to know where we were going. Rachel, I trust. Chris? Not so much. He's a little secretive. But we'll talk about that later." Mark ditched the pirate patch and wig, tossed them into the backseat, then finger-combed his hair while cranking the engine. "First, you've got some explaining to do, and you'd better get started. Just so you know, I'm trying hard not to explode here, but frankly, I'm having to work at it. The only thing that's keeping you in this car right now is that I know Rachel. She helped you, setting up this escape and she wouldn't have, and she sure wouldn't have involved Chris, without good reasons. So tell me, Daisy Grant," Mark paused and nailed me with an expression more flat than any I'd ever seen on his face. "What reasons do you have for your actions that's worth everything I've worked for and ever had in my life?"

Oh, he was hostile all right. Beyond angry and upset. More like, livid on steroids, and it was justified. I cleared my voice. "I don't have a reason worth any of it."

From his dropped jaw, that answer he didn't expect. "You cost me everything for nothing? Is that what you're telling me?"

"No. I didn't intend to cost you anything." Tears threatened but I fought them hard. There was a time to mourn, but this definitely wasn't it. This was a time for truth — and for watching someone who had been only kind and good and caring come to hate you and resent ever having met you. The kicker was I'd earned every bit of his bitterness and resentment and more.

"Daisy, I'm not amused."

"I wasn't trying to amuse you. I really didn't intend any of this. You're the best thing that's ever happened to me and you think I'd really dump all this on your head deliberately?"

"No, I don't. But I'm afraid I don't really know you. I thought I knew you well. But do I? How much of all you told me was true?"

"All of it," I said. "I just didn't tell you my brother was Jackson and that you knew him. I didn't tell you what I was running from for the same reason I didn't tell Chris where we were going. He'd be at risk."

"I don't think so." Mark slanted me a telling look. "You had a feeling, you said."

"That's beside the point. If I had a bellyful of bad feelings about him, I still wouldn't want him or Rachel hurt."

When Mark passed the same property for the third time, he growled. "I can't think. Where are we going?" He crossed the intersection and pulled out from between two shabby buildings. "You do have a plan, of course, though I told Chris you didn't. You'd always have a plan . . . wouldn't you?"

"Generally, yes, I would always have a plan. Surprises have never been fun experiences in my life. They generally end with me in pain so I try my best to avoid them."

Something softened in him, but he called back the shield he'd thrown up to protect himself from me. "Fine. No surprises. Am I allowed to know where we're going so I can stop driving in circles?"

"Florida," I said. "Dixie, Florida."

"Dixie? Where is that?" He frowned. "I've never heard of it."

"Up in the panhandle, near the Alabama state line."

"Fine." He took the I-10 ramp and headed toward Mississippi. "And we're going to Dixie because . . . ?"

If he didn't like my other explanations, he'd definitely hate this one. I tried and failed to find a way to make it easier to stomach. "There's a man there who will help us die."

Mark stomped the brake and swerved to a stop on the shoulder. "What?"

I spoke slowly and distinctly. "There's a man there who will help us die."

"Are you kidding me?" He let out a heavy, thick sigh. "We can die, staying right here."

I frowned at him. "Not really die. Just get-a-fresh-start die."

"We're going to fake our deaths?" He looked torn between disgust and disbelief.

Pulling on something Lester had said

183

once, I repeated it to Mark. "Sometimes to live, you gotta die."

It took Mark a long second to absorb that. "Great. Terrific."

"I'm sorry —"

"Stop saying that. Would you just stop saying that?"

The thread taut, he veered closer to snapping it again. I gentled my voice, hoping he'd reduce his from an earsplitting roar. "We can't go back, Mark. They will kill us."

"I kind of figured that out when they blew up Jameson Court." He pressed on the gas and merged into traffic.

"They're not going to let us go forward. There's no statute of limitations on murder. As long as I'm alive, I'm a threat to Tony Adriano and his father and Edward's dad knows it. The authorities want them all, and they'll use me to get them, Mark."

"I get it. The only hope for a life is to leave this one in the dust." He glanced over at me. "Now they want me dead, too."

"Yes." Hard to accept, but true. "I'm so sor—" Recalling his objection, I paused and tried again. "I sincerely regret involving you in any of this. I didn't know about your connection to Edward or that either family formerly operated in New Orleans. I thought it would be perfectly safe or I'd

184

never have come to Jameson Court."

"I was a link to Craig that wouldn't be tracked to Jackson. You'd have someone without marking them for a target."

I swallowed hard. "Yes. I didn't want to be totally alone."

That confession took a little wind out of his sails. "I believe you and I understand, but I'm not going to lie. I'm not happy with what's going on. My life's been high-jacked, Daisy." He dragged in a deep breath and slowly exhaled. "But, I have to say, as angry as I am, I'm still not sorry you came."

The tears I'd blinked back and kept at bay brimmed and spewed forth like a gusher. I let them, not daring to wipe them away because that Mark would definitely notice. Instead, I relied on the darkness to conceal them from him.

He checked his mirrors and pressed harder on the gas to pick up speed. "Okay, I've doubled around enough to feel confident we're not being followed anymore."

"Were we being followed?"

He nodded. "An old clunker of a car. But I lost it."

"When? I didn't see it."

"You've been crying so hard you wouldn't have seen much of anything, Daisy." He flicked on his blinker and passed a green truck. "We'll go to Dixie. On the way, I'll hear you out. Then we'll decide what to do." He paused and looked me in the eye. "I'll drive, you talk. And, I'm warning you, you better not utter so much as a single word that isn't the absolute truth or so help me I'll dump you out in the middle of nowhere on the side of the road."

He'd never do that, and we both knew it. But he wanted to mean it, and I couldn't blame him. All things considered, he was taking these developments pretty well.

"That includes lies by omission and for protection. Those days are over. Talk. Now — and I wouldn't mind a little reassurance that you'll tell me the *whole* truth so I don't have to listen to all this and wonder."

Okay, he was taking these developments reasonably well. My ears would ring for a week, but in the grand scheme of things, that wasn't bad. In his position, I don't think I'd handle any of this nearly as graciously much less all of it. I'd be chomping at the bit to rip him apart for costing me everything. "I promise to tell you the whole truth." I lifted and then lowered my right arm. "I guess it all started when I screwed up my death — my first death."

"Your first . . . *what*?"

Lost already, bless his heart. "My fault.

Let me back up a bit to where it really all started. I was trying to skip that part — not to conceal it or anything. Thinking about it . . . unnerves me."

"Skip nothing. I'm a little unnerved myself. We'll both just have to deal with it."

"Okay." I took in a steadying breath and dumped my Cinderella mask into the backseat with his pirate patch. "I got off work late that night, and I was so tired. I'd pulled a double and we were slammed both shifts. The whole time it was *run as fast as you can to keep up.*" I caught a breath, then continued. "It didn't help that I had on new shoes that pinched and gave me blisters. By the time I clocked out, I was hobbling." He said he wanted it all, so I did my best to spare no details. "Anyway, I'm walking to my car and I hear tires squeal. I spun to look, my heel got stuck in the crack in the sidewalk and I fell."

Now he looked lost. "Your fall has Victor Marcello and Lou Boudin after you?"

Mark knew Lou, too. Now how would he know Lou? Through the restaurant most likely. Lou was too old to have been in school with Mark and Edward and Rachel. "Sort of. Well, actually, no, not the fall."

"Daisy?" His warning grumble scraped at my ears.

187

"Be patient. I'm trying to be exact and that's hard, you know?"

"It's not hard. Losing everything in your life in a finger-snap, that's what's hard. Talk."

"I'm trying." A little heat of my own escaped. I warned myself to get back in control; I had no right. "You see, when I fell, I saw a man across the street, standing under the streetlight like he was waiting for someone. The car with the squealing tires barrels down the street, screeches to a stop, and these two men inside it start shooting. They shot the guy standing under the light dead. That's what started all this."

"Edward was the guy standing under the streetlight?" Mark guessed.

I nodded.

"And you called the cops?" His incredulity matched Lester's.

"I did." When Mark groaned, I went on and told him every detail I could recall of everything that had happened between then and now. I held back nothing. Not a single thing.

He listened mostly, but somewhere between being mugged and being told my clothes stash on the beach had been found, he silently passed me the Grant half-dollar I'd asked him to give to Craig Parker.

He knew my predisposition to rubbing it when anxious, and that he gave it to me was a very good sign that I wouldn't be walking to Dixie.

Dixie, Florida looked more like a village than a town.

Surrounded by woods on three sides and a lake on the fourth, it wasn't exactly laid out for high speed or dense traffic. The closest town of any size was thirteen miles away, and it didn't warrant a pinprick on most maps. That's not to say Dixie didn't have its charm. It did, in that small-town Americana way. *Mayberry-ish* with white picket fences and old-oak lined streets and charming bungalows with front porches littered with wooden rockers and hanging baskets of flowering plants that would, no doubt, be heavy with colorful blossoms in spring and all summer.

We went through the sole traffic light and down four or five blocks into an historical-type district of post World War II homes that had been restored. "Pretty neighborhood," I said, eyeing a tire swing tied to a low-slung tree limb. A bicycle lay across the brick sidewalk. Obviously, this wasn't a high-crime area. "When I get a home, I'm going to put up a fence like that."

"Did you develop a picket-fence fondness from one of your foster parents?"

"What?" I glanced from the houses to Mark.

He shrugged. "You seem to have picked up something from all of them. I just wondered if you liked the fence because one of them had a picket fence."

Interesting observation. I had picked up things from each of the foster parents. Some were the kind of skills you talked about, others were the kind you tried to forget. But I hadn't thought about associating things I love with any of them. I needed to think on that, but not for this. My fondness for picket fences belonged to me alone.

They marked a friendly boundary. What stood inside the fence was mine. It belonged to me. I haven't had much that belonged to me, so that carried a lot of weight. "No, I didn't develop a fondness for them from anyone. I just like them." I started to stop there, but I'd promised myself to keep no more secrets from Mark. "Did I ever tell you that I used to keep a notebook full of pictures I'd cut out of magazines?"

"No, you didn't. What kind of pictures?"

"All kinds. It was an eclectic collection of things I loved about houses. Kitchens, lamps, even stepping stones in the gardens."

Revealing that cut closer to the bone than I expected. Had I ever before shared my dream of a home with anyone else? No, not that dream. Not even with Jackson. Wanting a real home was just too personal, and it meant too much. "Now I take photos."

"Of all the things you want in your home?"

Not a *house.* He'd switched it to a *home.* With everything going on, the odds of me ever having a real home looked slimmer all the time. I choked back a sudden lump in my throat and nodded. But how like Mark to not mention that, and to know it wasn't just a house I wanted but a real home.

He switched lanes, passed an SUV in serious need of new shocks, judging by the way it bounced, and then pulled back into the right lane behind a blue truck hauling a refrigerator. That was just downright strange. Who hauled a refrigerator around in the backend of a pickup at three in the morning?

"How many photos have you taken?"

"About nine hundred — give or take twenty or so." I sounded obsessive. And maybe I am, but it didn't seem obsessive or excessive to me. Not in my position. For somebody who's had a home, it would set gut alarms to firing off. But for a woman who'd never had a home? Nope, not strange in the least. Totally normal.

He half-chuckled. "You're very specific on what you love."

"You bet, I am." Wasn't everyone? Shouldn't they be? I wondered and shifted on my seat, tapped the vent to blow its stream of warm air away from my face. "If you care enough to dream it, then dream it right."

"Good point," he said. "I have a question for you, Daisy."

"Okay?" This was going to be bad. Suck-lemon, stink-a-week rotten. I could hear his hesitation and feel the bad vibes radiating off him every bit as much as the air vent's stream. "Go ahead. Ask." I braced.

He looked over. "How long does it take to get used to home not being there anymore?"

My heart squeezed as if captured in a mighty fist. I sensed more than heard his sadness in his voice. *Adrift. Abandoned.* After losing his family, abandonment was the ultimate horror for Mark. "You look a little . . . frazzled. Do you need for me to candy coat it? Or can you take the truth?"

"It's a big adjustment," he defended himself. "But always tell me the truth. You promised, remember?"

"I haven't forgotten." But boy, did I wish the truth on this wasn't so ugly? Absolutely.

"Honestly, you never get used to it. You get better at coping with knowing the truth won't ever change and there'll always be a part of you that feels betrayed and abandoned and a little lost. That makes it bearable."

"I was afraid of that."

"I know." I reached for his hand. He let me cover it with mine.

"It's tough to take as a adult. I can't image what it was like for you as a kid."

"It was hard. It's still hard." I patted his hand in apology for passing along the bad news. "No matter how old you are, eventually you work your way around to the facts and you accept that your life is what it is, and you have a choice. You can make the best of it, or not. It's your call." I adjusted the vent so it stopped drying out my eyes. "I try to make the best of it."

"And you dream of the life you want with your pictures."

I nodded.

"Sounds like good advice."

"I don't know how good it is, but it's the best I have to offer." It was, and I hoped he'd heed it. Otherwise, the hunger for what wasn't — home, family, roots — would eat him alive.

"Did we miss the town?"

193

"I don't know." I looked out, but saw nothing man-made, only clusters of trees and natural brush. "I've never been here."

Mark glanced over. "That's right. The crazy old man . . . Lester sent you here."

"Lester's not really crazy," I said, determined to be totally honest on everything. Mark deserved that, considering, and, feeling lost, I think he needed it even more. "I didn't know he wasn't crazy until all this stuff happened, but — look! There it is."

Ahead stood a roundabout dead-center of an old-fashioned town square. The buildings surrounding it were businesses — all red-brick, all with discreetly lighted, painted signs. A café, post office, shoe store, candle shop. *Charming.* "This has to be it."

"So we're looking for . . . ?"

This admission would earn me a weird look and likely a lot more. "The funeral home." I glanced from one side of the street to the other. "I doubt it'd be on the Town Square, though. That'd strike too many people as morbid, wouldn't it?"

"I wouldn't want to walk past a funeral home every time I came in to town," Mark said. "There's a store on the corner. It's open. We can stop and ask —"

"Let's don't. We don't want to be remembered as the pirate and Cinderella." I pointed to a corner away from the store. "Try a couple side streets. It's a small town. We'll find it."

On the third side-street, Mark wove around a parked SUV and then said, "There it is. Dixie Funeral Home. Paul Perini, Director. There can't be two of them in a town this size."

"I don't know about that, but this is the one we want." Mark rounded a little bend, and parked right out front of the funeral home was Emily's old clunker. "Oh, no." My heart rate tripled. "Don't stop. Make the block!"

Mark kept going. "What's wrong? Why didn't you want to stop?"

"Lester's there." As we rode down the street, my mind flew into overdrive. "Why would Lester be in Dixie?"

"Whatever it is has to be bad for him to risk leading Marcello or Adriano to you."

"Definitely." I speculated reasons aloud, and Mark circled the block.

On the second round, he pulled into the drive.

I panicked. "What are you doing?"

He covered my fisted hand with his. It felt warm and comforting, and he softened his tone to match his touch. "We can drive around and guess all night, but we won't *know* anything until we go in and ask him, Daisy." I opened my mouth to object, but Mark stilled me, lifting his hand to my shoulder. "Listen, if what you told me is fact, Lester would never put you in jeopardy. If he's here, he's either convinced it's safe or so scared he has to warn you of something."

"Maybe." My mouth went dust-dry. "I'm really not a hundred percent sure he isn't a brick short of a full load, Mark."

"He's not crazy. He's sly. Busting you out of jail —"

"In his underwear and a ski-mask."

"Which he didn't wear inside." Mark put the Honda in park and killed the engine. "I'd think he has a compelling reason or he wouldn't have come. Let's go in and ask him what it is, okay?"

"You're right. Of course, you are." Mark was good for me. Calming. Rational. From the moment Jameson Court had blown up, I'd left rational in the dust. It amazed me that he hadn't. How did he do that? "Okay. Let's go." I opened the door and got out of the car before I could change my mind.

We didn't have to wait to get inside to hook up with Lester. The car door shutting echoed in the still night and before the sound settled, he came rushing out of the funeral home's front door.

"Daisy girl." Relief flooded his lined fine. He looked back to the open doorway and raised his voice. "It's them. They made it."

I walked with Mark up the sidewalk and saw a brass sign: *Paul Perini*. Then below his name: *Funeral Home. Justice of the Peace*. Taped to the wood siding underneath the brass sign, someone had taped a note scribbled in black marker. It was bold and I read it easily in the dim porch light. *No live bait this week. Pete Ladner's gone hunting. Charlene at the corner store's got some.*

What kind of hole-in-the-wall was this place? Who bought bait from a funeral home or went there for a justice of the peace? From Mark's wary glance, he felt equally uneasy about this whole Dixie plan.

Lester grabbed me in a bear hug. Thin and wiry, he shook hard. When he finally let go, he nodded at Mark then extended his hand. "You sure you wasn't followed?"

"Actually, we were followed. But we lost whoever it was before we left the city."

"Not to worry, then. That was Emily and me. You're safe for now."

I didn't feel safe. When the people after me stop following, you're anything but safe. Of course, they had just bombed Jameson

Court. They'd want a little distance from that for a short time. But as sure as they'd backed off to avoid authorities on the bombing, they'd be back after me — *us*. They were after Mark *and* me now. "Why were you following us, Lester? And what are you doing here?"

"I wasn't following you exactly, I was trying to rescue you," Lester said, sounding urgent and more than a little grumpy.

The mothball smell of Emily's car — and Lester reeked of it — could do that to a hearty soul, much less to Lester. Poor man probably had a wall-banger of a headache. "Rescue me from what?"

"Not here or now, girl." He motioned toward the door. "I'll tell you inside. Just so you're sure as certain no one else followed you here."

"It'd take a guide with GPS or a satellite, Lester," Mark said. "The roads leading into Dixie are deserted, and I was extremely cautious."

"There's a reason we like our roads empty. We want to know what's coming." A short man, thin and about Lester's age with bright blue eyes and silver hair stepped out on the porch and extended his hand. "Glad you got here in one piece, Mark. I'm Paul Perini."

Mark shook his hand. So did I.

"Daisy." He spared Lester a glance. "Every bit as beautiful as you said, Lester." Pivoting to me, Mr. Perini added, "He always did have an eye for women." A smile curved his full mouth. "Now, I understand from Lester that the two of you want to get married tonight."

Mark choked. "What?"

"Married?" I darted a look at Mark to make sure he hadn't fainted. *Still upright.* Frankly, I was grateful he hadn't tossed me out of the car on my foolish elbow. That was a major score in my book. Nobody had said *anything* about marriage. "Lester, why would you tell Mr. Perini that?" I couldn't make myself repeat the "m" word.

Lester pursed his lips to explain but, before he could get wound up tight, Mr. Perini answered me. "Because he knows you need a reason for coming through Dixie at all, much less this time of night. One that won't raise suspicion. People come here to marry in the wee hours now and then."

While I absorbed that, I primed to ask again why Lester was here.

Mr. Perini snatched the opportunity to divert focus. "Lester says the two of you drove over from Sampson, Alabama to get married." Hiking a slim shoulder, he hand-signaled his brass sign. "Before you say anything, think. You got two possibilities in this situation," he told me and Mark. "Either you're here for a wedding or because you're dead. I don't suppose I need to remind you that corpses don't drive or wed." He scratched at his neck and squinted. "Marriage is common sense, really. Anything but a wedding creates a dilemma."

"Muddles things up good and proper," Lester agreed. "Good and proper."

Justice of the Peace and funeral director. Logical, but problematic. I didn't dare look at Mark to see how he was taking this development. "I see."

"The wedding was my idea," a woman said from behind me.

I recognized her voice. "Emily?" I turned to see her still dressed as Cinderella, as she had been at Mark's party. "What are you doing here?"

"Lester and I had to come for the wedding."

I did glance at Mark then, and he looked reasonably calm. He slid me a questioning look I well understood. Lester and Emily . . . maybe they *were* both crazy. I cringed my uncertainty and asked Lester, "Is that your cover? This wedding?"

"Well, yeah, sort of," Lester confessed,

lumbering a couple steps closer to the door. "But I've been noodling on the matter, Daisy girl, and if you two are going to die together and then run together to start over, you ought to be married or kin." Lester spared Mark a sharp eye. "He sure don't look at you like no brother, and you don't look at him like no sister neither. Ain't no help for it. We need a wedding, and that's all I got to say about that."

I didn't know what to say about any of this, and Mark apparently didn't either. He didn't utter a sound. What was he thinking? Oh, how I wish I knew.

"What's the problem?" Mr. Perini hiked his shoulders. "It's a solid cover."

No one answered.

He went on. "Daisy, Mark. You need to understand. In small towns, there are no secrets. That's not an opinion, it's the way of things. You need a plausible reason to be here for your protection, and we need a plausible reason for you being here for our protection."

Emily piped in, clearly hoping to make the idea more agreeable. "I brought you a wedding dress."

Hopefully it didn't include a ski-mask. "This wouldn't be a real wedding though." I struggled to slot this new wrinkle into

201

Lester-logic and to give Mark and myself a little reassurance. "I mean, Mark and I won't legally be married. It's just a cover, right?"

"Actually, I'd prefer it was real." Mark looked at Lester then at me. "When you were Lily, we were heading toward serious relationship territory anyway, Daisy. Before all . . . this."

Mark *wanted* to *really* marry me? That totally boggled my mind.

Lester, Emily and Mr. Perini all spoke at once. I couldn't untangle their conversation to make sense of it. Frankly, I couldn't grasp a thought or sift through anything.

The uncertainty in Mark and the way his body tensed and he spread his feet, he seemed more like a man girding his loins for battle than a man seriously interested in marrying a woman.

Tired of waiting for a reaction from me, he pulled me off the sidewalk and onto the lawn, then looked me straight in the eye. "Everything between us — I thought it was real. Was it?"

That, at least, I could answer easily. "It was, yes. But I didn't think it put us on a relationship express lane to an altar."

"Put that way, marriage doesn't sound so appealing to me, either."

I'd hurt him. "I'm sorry."

"That's not enough." He stiffened even more and his expression hardened. "Before tonight, I had a home, an apartment, a successful business, money and no significant worries. Speaking bluntly, you're the reason I've lost everything. Even my life is in jeopardy."

"Mark, I didn't mean —"

He lifted a hand, motioning me to stop. "I know, and I'm not judging you. I'm just stating the facts. They are what they are, Daisy."

On the sidewalk, Emily nodded, obviously weary of pretending to be as deaf as a stone. "I have to say, he's right about that, pet."

"Sure is," Lester agreed from beside her. "Though I can't say you're selling the idea of marrying by pointing it out, son."

I shot the two of them a glare that'd stop a clock, then shifted to Paul Perini. "Well, don't you have an opinion?"

"Do I need one?" He sniffed and plucked a leaf from a squatty bush. "Seems to me, Mark has the matter well in hand. Guilt is a powerful motivator, and the fact is, you are guilty, Daisy. No disputing that."

Lester nodded emphatically. "Absolutely, no way to see it otherwise."

"Will you guys please stop helping me?

The woman will run until she lands on a different planet." Mark's admonishment sounded more like a plea. He turned his back to them and faced me on the grass. "If I'm allowed to make my point . . . I don't want to make you feel guilty."

"Well, what's your point, then? Because guilty is exactly —"

"No," he cut in. "Everything I said is reality. Intentional or not, I have lost everything else at your hands, Daisy. Since I have, I think it's fair that you should at least do this for me."

"Marry you?" Who could have expected this? From Mark? I couldn't absorb it.

"It's one little thing."

Marriage? Little? One little thing? At the moment, he sounded as fickle as Lester and Emily. I still couldn't wrap my mind around it. "You want to marry me because I owe you?" I couldn't believe this was coming from him.

"Seems fair," Emily said. "Like the man said, he has nothing else."

"Appears right as rain to me," Lester added. "It's one little thing, Daisy."

Mr. Perini opened his mouth.

I lifted a hand. "Don't." He snapped it shut and I looked at Mark. "Is this because of what Lester said about marriage or kin, because you don't have to —"

Mark went quiet. Everyone did. I held my breath and waited, knowing the next words Mark uttered would forever alter the direction of my life. One way or another, a major change was upon me.

"With all due respect, no. Lester has nothing to do with this. It's about you and me, Daisy. You talked about your dreams and what you want. This is about my dreams and what I want."

His dreams. His wants. Since losing his family in Katrina, Mark had been alone. He didn't want to be alone again. Suddenly his reasons for wanting to marry me made sense, and they touched something deep inside me. Something so deep I couldn't pinpoint where it started or ended but it was there and real and it ignited a yearning in me so strong it nearly buckled my knees. Mark wanted *me* to be his home. His family. Could a person do that? Be that? I had never before considered the possibility.

"Now this," Emily said, "I'm afraid, I don't quite understand."

"No need to." Lester patted her arm. "Look at her, Em. She understands."

Stepping closer, Mark took my hands. "Daisy, think of it this way. What difference does marrying me really make to you? It matters to me, but even if you object, marriage is only 'til death us do part, and we came here to die — at least, legally." His hand trembled on my arm. "I've tried to be good to you and I've never asked you for anything except to spare me from having to ever touch computers. But I am asking you for this. For me. Because I need it. Marry me, Daisy."

The truth slammed into me and stayed put. It wasn't living alone, Mark wanted to avoid. It was dying alone. After losing his family, he couldn't bear to die alone — even if that death was figurative. I mulled a bit. Having lost my family, I understood what this meant to Mark. And after a little thought, I sorted it out in the deepest recesses of my soul.

Emily let out a sigh and leaned into Lester. "Isn't he romantic?"

Lester covered her hand on his arm.

It was romantic, though I didn't say so. But more romantic was a lovely twinkle in Mark's eye. Only he had ever looked at me with that twinkle, and my gut alarm warned me it was beyond rare and special. Only the very blessed saw it, and likely only once. I can't explain it, but I trusted that twinkle.

My heart seconded my opinion, beating hard and deep. Still my head hadn't caught up with what was happening here and, until it did, it wouldn't agree and come along for the ride. "Why do you want to marry me, Mark?"

"I'm sorry to interrupt — especially there," Mr. Perini said. "We'd all like to hear the answer to that one. But we need to move this inside." He jerked his head, motioning across the street to where a woman in a bathrobe had come outside, looking for her dog. "You can finish your debate there — but keep it short — Lester needs to update you on some important information."

The woman neared her sidewalk and shouted. "Everything okay over there, Paul?"

"Just fine, Mrs. Baker. A couple from Alabama, wanting to get married."

"Glad it ain't a funeral," she shouted back. "They sober?"

"Yes, they are."

"Come here, Dutch." She yelled at the tiny, fluff-ball dog. He came running to her, tail wagging and tongue lolling. "Good luck to you, kids."

"Thanks," I called back and, still mired in a mental fog of uncertainty, I edged toward the front door. Mark Jensen wanted to marry me. *Me?* I'd cost him everything and he wanted to marry me. He knew we didn't have to marry to start over together, and that we'd be fake-dying together either way, so his reason for wanting to marry me couldn't be living or dying alone. Those were givens. It couldn't be that we had been moving in that direction anyway, either. We had a bond, to be sure, but it was leap between a bond and matrimony. So what was his reason?

The fact that I'm crazy about the man makes me wish he'd insisted because he had fallen madly in love with me, but I've never seen proof that kind of love exists, so I'm not sure I believe in it. Doubtful I'd know it, if I did see it. I puzzled through it all anyway, but in the end, my money was not on that horse in this race.

Marriage.

The word alone set me to trembling. People I know and marriage hadn't worked out so well. It certainly hadn't been a bundle of bliss for my mother.

Marriage?

Mark had to be giving me a hard time. Didn't he? I wasn't sure. I'd explained everything, and he hadn't come unglued. I'd expected he would and prepared for it despite the fact that him coming unglued didn't fit in with a thing Craig Parker or Jackson had said about Mark. So maybe he wasn't giving me a hard time. Maybe insisting on marriage was just his way of venting. Needling me like Jackson had when he went through that he-man stage. He certainly had just reasons for venting. In his shoes, I'd be a raving maniac.

Venting. That had to be it. I'd cost Mark huge and he wanted me to pay huge. But even then, shackling himself to me hardly seemed the way to do it. Not even in a short-term until-we're-dead-kind-of-marriage shackle. Or maybe it was a control thing. The man had lost everything and all of that had been out of his control. This he could control. Yet that only made the logic cut, if he demanded I marry him. He hadn't demanded, he'd asked. So that couldn't be the reason. I mentally searched for another.

Was he protecting me? Protection would be like him, but it certainly didn't require marriage. Punishing me? That's so not his style. What was left?

I had no idea — and no further time to ponder on it.

Mr. Perini led the pack of us into a large reception area that was tastefully decorated and informal. A large desk sat on the right side of the room, several chairs lined in a straight row on the left. "Barry," Mr. Perini called out, stretching then grabbing a car tag from a stack on a shelf behind the desk filled with books. When Barry joined us, Mr. Perini said, "Replace the plate on that Honda with this one and bring me the old tag."

Barry could have been twenty or fifty. He stood slightly taller than Mr. Perini, but with the long hair and gnarly beard, wearing jeans and a faded t-shirt for some rock band, guessing his age was impossible. He mumbled a greeting to us, then took the plate and eased out a side door.

"This way." Mr. Perini led us through a reception area to a large, comfortable room filled with groupings of cushy sofas and little tables. "Have a seat."

We all sat on the sofas. Mark and me across from Lester and Emily.

Mr. Perini eased down into the lone chair he clearly preferred, gauging by the dents in its seat. "You'd better tell her now, Lester, so she understands exactly where she is before she decides whether or not to accept Matthew's proposal."

"It's Mark."

Paul stared at Mark long and hard. "For now. Soon it'll be Matthew, if you like it. Matthew Green."

Mark thought a second, then nodded. "I'm good with that."

"Tell me what, Lester?" Surely the news this night couldn't get any worse. I mean, what was left? Then it hit me, and I gasped. "Is something wrong with Jackson?"

Mark flinched. Before he could object, I spared him a glance. "I told you Jackson was my brother."

"You did, yes."

"I really did," I insisted. "I'm not keeping secrets."

"I know." He nodded, clasped my hand and gave it a little squeeze. "You told me."

"Well, if the two of you will hush up, I'll tell you this ain't got nothing to do with Jackson," Lester said. "It's about Chris."

"Chris?" I said, momentarily baffled. "Rachel's husband, Chris?"

"That's the one, girl."

"What about him?" Mark pulled himself up, stiffening like a plank of wood. "Was he hurt?"

"Naw, he's fine." Lester looked at Emily. Wary, and hesitant.

"Go on and tell him. He can take it," Emily said, motioning at Mark. "Daisy's told him everything and he hadn't gone ballistic or dumped her. Not that it'd matter if he did. He's got no choice on this bit of business."

"No choice on *what* bit of business?"

Mark asked.

Still, Lester hesitated.

"Good grief, will you just tell 'em? You're making 'em both nervous wrecks, Lester." Emily clicked her tongue to the roof of her mouth and leaned forward. "Before the party, we saw Chris talking to Lou Boudin out by the limo. It was real friendly-like. So we bugged his car."

"You bugged Lou Boudin's car?"

"No, Mark," Lester said. "Chris's limo, though bugging Lou Boudin's car would have been a good idea. We just didn't have two bugs."

"It was you following the limo?" Matthew asked for confirmation neither of us needed.

"Yep. Backed off when he started driving squirrely. Knew we'd been made, so we backed off until you two were in the Honda. Then it seemed to Emily like you spotted us, so we had to trust you two would get out of there on your own. We headed over here," Lester said. "Didn't figure it would take you quite so long."

"After being followed twice — he took the scenic route to be sure we were alone," I explained.

"Figured that." Lester looked at Mark. "Point is, you two weren't outta the limo two minutes when Chris made a phone call.

212

From the conversation, it was clear he was letting somebody know you were in the Honda and headed out. He didn't know where."

"We didn't tell him." Boy, was I glad now we hadn't.

"That's a mercy," Emily said with an emphatic nod. "It surely is."

Mark frowned. "He was probably talking to his wife."

"He wasn't talking to Rachel." Mr. Perini sighed. "Not unless she's related to Victor Marcello."

"Victor Marcello?" My throat turned to dust.

Mr. Perini nodded. "A friend traced the call. The number belongs to Victor Marcello. He doesn't take well to visitors, just relatives."

Mark's expression tightened, then closed. "Why would Chris call Marcello?"

"It seems pretty obvious," Mr. Perini said. "Marcello got to him."

I wanted to sob — and hit something. Betrayed by Chris. Mark trusted him and Rachel. How could Chris do this? Why would he? No matter the reason, that he had would burn Mark deeply, and he'd been burned more than enough already. I mounted a defense I didn't quite believe.

"Duress. He had to be under duress."

Lester harrumphed. "Then he's been under it for nearly a decade."

"A decade?" Incredulity rippled through Mark.

Feeling it, I tensed, wadded my hands into fists in my lap. "What exactly are you saying, Lester?"

"I'm saying, Daisy girl, Chris has been on Victor Marcello's payroll for ten years. That's what I'm saying."

What that meant to Mark hit me hard. Betrayed and wounded didn't begin to describe it. Violated. To the bone.

Mark grimaced at me. "As soon as I use that email he gave me, they all know where we are."

"They would," Mr. Perini said. "But you won't be using it."

"I have to use it," Mark said. "It's my only channel to my assets. Rachel has my full power of attorney."

Mr. Perini spread his feet and leaned forward on his seat, then rested his arms on his thighs. "Let me explain the situation to you, Mark. The first time you use that email, you're signing your death warrant and Daisy's. Without using it, in my estimation, you've got hours not days before they track you here anyway." His expression sobered. "The life you had and everything you had in it — it's all gone, son. The sooner you accept that, the better off you'll be. And, I suspect that's why Chris turned on you. If you're out of the picture, Rachel inherits everything, right?"

Mark nodded, clearly strained but holding together. "I need a lawyer."

"Now?" I asked, not bothering to hide my surprise at that remark. "What are you going to do?"

He looked from Paul to me. "I'm going to revoke the power of attorney and my will. Leave everything to . . ."

"To whom?" He had no one but Rachel.

Mark's expression cleared. "To the brother of my wife, as soon as I have a wife."

"Jackson?" Shock ripped through me. "You're going to leave everything you've got to Jackson?"

"He'll be my family."

Lester cackled. "Well, that'll fix that."

"You're sure about this, Mark?" Mr. Perini asked.

"Positive. Can you get a lawyer over here? A good one that is well versed in Louisiana and Florida law. I want this locked down so tight a gnat couldn't find a crack in it."

"Jackson?" I asked again, dumbstruck.

"Jackson."

My brother had no idea what good fortune had just fallen in his lap — or the danger that came with it. "Is this your way of making me pay for my sins against you?"

"I'm making your brother a rich man because everyone in my life has betrayed me and you ask me that?"

"Jackson." I drew in a breath, wrung my hands. "Will they come after him?"

"Why would they?" Mr. Perini asked. "Neither of you have talked to him. He knows nothing. They've no reason to bother Jackson unless you contact him."

Lester grunted. "They'll be watching for that, all right."

Emily nodded. "No doubt about it. Victor Marcello is nothing, if not thorough."

By Mark's body language, the matter was resolved. He proved my thoughts on that by turning the subject. "Why are you thinking they'll find us in a couple hours, Mr. Perini?"

Barry came rushing into the room. He held something up in both hands.

"Took you long enough," Mr. Perini told him. "You should have found those within the first five minutes. You're slipping, Barry. It's critical you keep your skills sharp."

"Yes, sir."

"What are those things?" I asked, looking

at the little black boxes and the wires attached to them.

"They're why I was certain you had hours." Seeing my confusion, he elaborated. "They're the means by which Marcello and Adriano — or the FBI, depending on who put them in the car — will find you."

Lester groaned. "There it is, Em."

"There's what?" Emily asked, straining to see.

"The stuff in that hand," Lester pointed to Barry's left, "is the bug and tracker we put in the Honda. It's what's in Barry's other hand that worries me."

"Another bug?" My heart slid out of my chest and took up residence in my stomach. "Are you saying someone heard every word Mark and I said to each other in that car?"

"Heard you? No, ma'am," Barry said. "It's just a tracker. It signaled your location, but they couldn't hear you."

"Small mercy." Mark's lips flattened to a slash. "Chris had to do it."

"He did." Lester nodded. "Seen him myself, which is why Em and me were following you."

Fear zipped up my spine. "Then they already know we're here."

"Barry." Mr. Perini moved to the desk and dialed the phone. "Finish getting the car ready and summon the team. I want that VIN number left legible after all this."

"Yes, sir. I'm on it." Barry disappeared into a hallway then from sight.

Paul perched a hand on his hip, spoke into the phone. "Dexter, it's Paul Perini. I need your help, and I need it fast." He went on to explain in some kind of muffled short-hand what he needed and then hung up the phone. "Emily, watch email. The documents will be here within half an hour."

"Was that the lawyer?" Mark asked.

Mr. Perini nodded. "Dexter Devlin. One of the best —"

"In the country," Mark said. "And you've got him on speed dial?"

He shrugged. "We go way back."

"Do you know him, Mark?" I asked.

"Not personally, no."

There was more so I waited.

Mark hiked a shoulder. "Dexter Devlin has one of the sharpest legal minds in recorded history. My dad and I followed his cases. Anytime a high-profile client needs a lawyer or when it seems all is lost, everyone with the resources calls in Dexter Devlin. He rarely loses." Mark frowned at Mr. Perini. "He's also next to impossible to re-tain."

Mr. Perini shrugged. "Like I said, we go

218

way back."

"Then this is good news. Chris won't get away with your assets." I felt compelled to add, "I accept that he's rotten, Mark, but I just don't believe Rachel is. Are you sure this is what you want to do?"

"Yeah." He turned to look at me. "At some time, we can contact Jackson, and he'll be there for us. Chris wouldn't — and Rachel wouldn't because she couldn't be there for us and keep the peace with her husband." Mark turned on the sofa toward Mr. Perini. "You told Barry to summon the team." Paul nodded, and Mark then asked, "What team? Summon them for what?"

"An accident, I think. A fiery one. Lots and lots of heat."

"What are you talking about?" Mark asked.

"You're going to die tonight," Paul said calmly. "Actually, both of you are. I'd hoped for a little more time to train you on surviving off the grid and on evasion tactics, but the families have made the timing choice for us."

"Ain't no help for it. It's out of our hands, all right." Lester shook his head. "Well, it is what it is."

I stared from them to Mark and he seemed as poleaxed as I felt.

"Lester, you best get finished with the paperwork for after." Paul spared Mark and me a glance. "Don't worry. You'll die, then Matthew Green and Rose — that'll be you, Daisy — will get out of here. We'll take care of everything, including seeing to it Jackson has smooth sailing." Mr. Perini stood up and cleared his throat. "All we need to know is one thing."

One thing? At least a thousand things were fighting for attention in my mind.

"What's that?" Mark asked.

"Do you want to die before or after the wedding?"

CHAPTER 10

"Well?" Mr. Perini seated a red newsboy cap on his head, then waited.

The lump in my throat felt huge. "I'll go with whatever Mark decides."

"After," he said. "I want it, and Emily got you a dress and everything."

"You two being hitched will make any legal case stronger on Jackson's inheriting, too," Lester said. "If Chris and Rachel should decide to dispute it."

"Daisy, please." Mark dropped his voice. "Don't let them get away with taking everything I worked for, too."

"All right." I agreed, but I did it knowing this wasn't just about that, it was about Mark having ties to something. To someone. To me.

"Thanks."

"Thank you." I smiled. For the first time, I felt truly special to someone other than Jackson and Lester. That it was a gorgeous man who was good and decent and so much more was the proverbial icing on the cake.

So okay, marrying Mark wasn't exactly crazy but it by no means ranked anywhere near normal or traditional. Still, it made more sense than anything else that had happened in my life since I kissed the concrete in Biloxi and saw Edward get murdered — and I am crazy about Mark and about to die. Jackson would be cared for, too. He'd never lack for a thing. Mark knew, of course, that would seal this for me, but it also showed me how much Mark wanted this marriage. How much it meant to him. And that, I find quite charming and endearing.

Oh, all right. And a little sappy. I'm not blind, and I see it. I haven't had a lot of experience with mushy stuff, but I am human and it does touch me. I can't afford to let it go to my head. I mean, just think a minute. I'm in a bit of an unusual situation here, and I have one shot to marry a man I really care about before I'm lost and gone forever. My life might not seem like much to others, but it's mine. I built it from nothing by myself. It's all I've got, and it's going away. I worked so hard to make Daisy Grant a good person, someone respectable and that I respected, and tonight she will cease to be. Marrying Mark is Daisy's last hurrah. So blame me for taking it. I don't care. I've done without and had less than I needed — forget what I wanted — my whole life. Not just my adult life, my whole life. I'm not complaining, but I'm not kicking this gift in the mouth, either. This is my last chance and my last shot, and I'm taking it. "All right. I'll marry you, Mark."

Emily squealed and ran for the dress.

He squeezed my upper arms and planted a hard fast kiss to my lips. "Go on and get ready. We'll talk more afterward."

I stepped even closer and dropped my voice so only he could hear. "You're really sure you want to do this?"

"Yeah, I am." He tilted his head. "My mom was always on me to find a good wife. I think she would have liked you."

My heart rate sped up. "You're marrying me for your mother?"

"No. I'm marrying you because I'm marrying you," Mark said, his tone steely but level.

This wasn't about me. Not really. Or his mother. It was about everything and more, including abandonment. One can't just walk away from a spouse. I clasped his hand. "All right, then. I'll be back in a few minutes."

"You want a tux for the pictures?" Lester asked. "Paul's got a lot of 'em."

"Let me guess," Mark said. "He does tuxedo rentals on the side."

"During prom season mostly, but he keeps a few around."

"For funerals?" Mark grunted. "Why not?"

"Good attitude, son." Lester smiled. "Daisy will like the pictures. Most women do."

"Daisy will be dead. So will Mark."

"No reason to get all persnickety about it. Jackson will have it. It'll mean a lot to him."

Lester grabbed a tux from a side room, then returned with it to Mark, unaware that standing in the room next door, I could hear every word uttered. Emily was well aware, and she and I both pretended to be deaf as dead stumps while going about our business as quiet as church mice so we didn't miss a thing.

"Here you go." Lester passed the tux to Mark.

"Black." On the other side of the wall, Mark made noises like he was shrugging into the jacket. "I'll keep my own pants. Switching black for black — it's overkill."

A few minutes later, Mark said, "It fits pretty good."

"It does." Lester dusted at Mark's shoulders and smoothed the fabric between his shoulder blades. "You realize that once you're dead, you and Daisy ain't gonna be married no more."

" 'Til death. Yes, I realize it."

"You've had a lot to take in tonight."

"I have."

"I wouldn't be letting you marry her — even with conditions being what they are — if I didn't think you cared about her. For all her little flaws, Daisy's got a head on her shoulders. She's devoted and loyal, and she'll make a good wife to the lucky man she chooses to love."

"She's a good woman, I agree." Mark paused and his voice hinted at him being bewildered. "Does anyone choose to love, Lester? Really? Isn't it something that's just there in you, or it's not?"

On the other side of the wall, I held my breath.

"Sometimes it's that way. You might be dead set against love, but if it's there, it's there. Might as well accept it. Love's got some good in it. Sure as certain."

"Love is a gift," Mark countered. "Unfortunately we don't often realize all the ways it impacts us until we lose it."

"That's the way of things. It's a gift, but it's a nightmare too — when it ain't returned."

225

"Did you love someone and it wasn't returned? Is that what this is about?" Mark's voice lifted. "Or are you afraid I won't love Daisy or be good to her?"

"This ain't about me, though I've had my fair share of troubles with Mr. Cupid. It's about my Daisy." Lester paused, then added, his voice strained. "I know you'll take care of her. But taking care of her and loving her . . . well, that there's two different things." Lester paced a bit then stopped. "The fact is, she's all I got, son. I want her loved. You treat her right because she deserves it, but you love her because you can't not love her. And because . . . she's all I got."

Mark's voice turned tender. "She's all I've got, too, Lester."

"We understand each other, then."

"Yes, we do." Mark coughed. "I hope she's thinking about these things in there like we are out here."

"She's a woman. They don't think like men."

"You know what I mean." Mark straightened his tie.

"Lemme do that." Lester grabbed the tie and began fiddling with it. "Yep, you're wanting to be loved, too. Well, don't you worry. She'll settle in. One thing I know about Daisy Grant. She needs loving. I'm guessing only Jackson ever cared if she lived or died — least 'til I came along."

"You love her?"

"Like a daughter." He pulled at the edge of the bow, straightening it. "She'll never leave you, son, and once you get into her heart, you'll be there to stay. That girl's longed to love somebody her whole life. Make sure you're that lucky man."

Emily and I listened intently, and pretended not to be listening. I don't know about Emily, but Mark and Lester's conversation would have made a lot more sense to me if we weren't going to die soon. Actually, it would have been insanely touching.

Instead it confused me. Oh, it was still touching and insanely sweet, but all things considered, wasn't it also certifiably nuts? I gave up the pretense and looked at Emily, whispering so only she could hear. "Why are they talking about this like it's a normal wedding?"

"Situations can be normal or not, but men are *always* men," Emily whispered back. She caught my blank-expression response and added, "It's the peacock strut, pet."

I looked back at her, standing there holding the dress, and stepped into it. "The what?"

Lifting the diaphanous dress, she motioned for me to slip my arms through the straps. "The peacock strut. Ain't you ever heard of it?"

I seated the strap on the left shoulder, then on the right and smoothed the bodice. The fabric clung then draped, soft and beautiful. Layers of crinkling chiffon and delicate lace in a traditionally cut gown I would have chosen for myself. "Never."

"It happens before every wedding where there's two men in a woman's life." She zipped me up. "The father tells the groom he loves his daughter and the groom better be good to her or else, and the groom says he will be good to her and the dad's got nothing to worry about." She stepped back and lifted both hands, palms up. "The peacock strut."

It fit. The magnificent dress actually fit. "I didn't hear any of that."

"Course not." She fluffed the skirt, waist to hem. The rustle helped cover their whispers. "The men don't warn and reassure each other straight out — it ain't civil on the day of a union — but it's clear as day to both of them if the groom ain't good to the bride, there'll be steep consequences."

"It's like a turf war." I met Emily's eyes but the dress had stolen the lion's share of my attention. Never in my life had I put on a dress that felt like this.

"Exactly." Emily bent deep and straightened the hem, then reached for the veil. "I always looked at it like a transfer of power in a political coup."

I groaned. "Politics bore me to tears, Emily. Too little substance and way too much theater."

She giggled. "Brings out the best and worst in people, and that's what I meant. A lot of truth beyond the surface clutter, too. They talk nice, silver tongues and all, but cross 'em and they'll rip your throat out."

"I guess I see your point." I stood overwhelmed. Me, a woman who thought she had no peacock to strut or transfer power and no man who wanted it, had both, and I didn't even know it until now. My heart hitched in my chest. Lester and Mark cared for me and about how I would be treated. Both would fight for me. Me, an orphan nobody wanted.

That was kind of hard to take in. A rush of raw emotion coursed through me, left me feeling as if my nerves were on the outside of my skin and ragged and raw. I'd never had anyone willing to fight for me before, and truly, I didn't know what to do with all it made me feel. But since I'm now bound to this honesty streak, I have to admit, it feels awesome to know you're special to someone. Alien, but awesome, and humbling. Double that and add breathless for two someones. "The peacock strut."

"Yep." Emily seated the veil on the crown of my head and then straightened it. Our eyes met through the fine netting. "Do you love him, pet?"

I could lie. I probably should lie. But I couldn't make myself do it. Aside from the honesty bit, love is too special a gift. And nobody better than someone whose never had it knows it. "You know, Emily, I don't know a lot about love, but I think I do. I guess that sounds weird. We haven't known each other long, but Mark is all Jackson and Craig said he was, and more." I smiled, bittersweet that Jackson wasn't here for the wedding. Even if it was a sham, it was the only wedding I was going to get, and it would have been nice if he had been here for it.

"Is the smile because you love him, or because you love him and didn't know it until I asked?"

What exactly is love, anyway? I looked at Emily, tempted to ask. But she looked so sweet in her pink tulle suit with her soft silver hair — and so incredibly shrewd! She was a true romantic, and I couldn't pop her bubble by admitting that I didn't know about love. I liked and respected and felt connected to Mark. The twinkle in his eye drew me, dozens of things about him drew me. I wanted to be with him. Missed him when we were apart. I looked ahead and without him with me, the days seemed duller, longer, less bright. But was that love? I couldn't say. I didn't really know. "Probably a little of both," I told her, compromising. "And because, if I'd listened to Jackson and Craig — they tried to hook us up on blind dates dozens of times but I always refused — we probably would have been together a lot sooner." Would we, I wonder, have ended up in this same place?

"Mmm, or been dead a lot sooner." Emily straightened and looked me right in the eye. "Mark lost everyone in the storm. If you'd been there, he well might have lost you, too." She gave my veil one last tug. "Trust God's timing, pet. It's perfect. Ours ain't." She exhaled a content sigh. "You can turn and look in the mirror now."

I pivoted to face the free-standing glass and my gaze collided with the woman reflected in it. She looked like me — well, me with red hair — but she couldn't be. That woman was beautiful and the dress —

oh, the dress. "I look . . . like a real bride."
Breathless.

"You are a real bride."

"You know what I mean, Em."

"And you know what I mean." Emily smiled. "You're stunning, Daisy. Always have been." She cocked her head. "The red hair suits you but your temperament is blond to the bone, hon."

It was. "Thank you for the dress. It's the prettiest one I've ever seen."

"A woman's wedding gown should be special, and so it is."

Emily's eyes. She needed money for cataract surgery. "It is amazing — and from the feel of this fabric, expensive. I have to pay for it."

"No, it's a gift. Don't fret, hon. I didn't buy it." She shrugged. "Lester bought it."

Poor guy wouldn't be eating for months. "You have to tell me how much it was so I can pay him back."

"It wasn't that bad."

"It was," I insisted. "I saw the Vera Wang label, Emily." How many times had I fronted bail money for Lester because he was broke? "His heart is huge, but he can't afford this."

"Can't afford it?" Emily looked at me as if I had lost my mind. "Daisy, Lester could buy half the state, if he was of a mind to do

232

it. Maybe all of it."

"He couldn't. Emily, trust me. Lester's a wonderful man, but he has no money." Had he told her some tall tale?

"Hogwash." She laughed. "Don't look at me like that. I know what I'm talking about. Lester comes from a long, long line of money."

If Lester had money, Emily would have eyes. I had to make her see the truth. "Then why hasn't he helped you get your cataract surgery? He's your friend."

"I won't let him. I ain't ready to see again just yet."

That answer I hadn't expected. "He's offered?"

"Least once a week for years." She sniffed. "I ain't like the others, nuzzling up to him for what he can give me. I actually like him. We have a lot to talk about. Good conversation ain't nothing to sneeze at, pet."

Now I understood, but the shock hadn't yet settled. Lester was wealthy. "But I've paid him out of jail a half dozen times —"

"He wanted to know if you would."

That fit. "Testing me."

She nodded, and I asked, "Okay, so he's got money. Why does he live . . ." How did I say it without insulting Emily and myself?

"Why does he live like us?"

233

I nodded.

"It's real. Lester likes real." She dropped her voice and wiggled a come closer finger at me. "And you might not have noticed, but he does bend a little on the eccentric side, hon."

Understatement of the year, right there. "Just a little."

"Ladies." Mr. Perini tapped on the door. "It's time."

Emily opened the door and we stepped out and then across the hallway to the doorway into the funeral parlor.

"Barry, move that!" Mark's voice carried from within. "She's not marrying me next to a corpse. I don't need fifty years of that kind of grief. We need an altar, man, not a casket."

I tried not to laugh. I really did. Could this situation — this whole situation — get any more bizarre? *Fifty years?* My spirit soared and I checked to make sure I wasn't floating. He really *did* want to marry me — and he wanted to *stay* married to me. He had to love me, then. Didn't he? I dared to hope he did, because he'd been loved his whole life and he knew exactly what it meant.

"I'm sorry, Mark," Barry grumbled. "I forgot it was there, okay? Been a little busy arranging the wreck."

"I know. You've been hustling non-stop. I'm the one who's sorry." Mark grabbed his face with his hands. "I'm a little tense."

That was the one. The remark that made not marrying Mark for real — at least in my heart — impossible. After everything that had happened and all he'd lost, he was *a little tense* and not about marrying me but at marrying me next to a casket rather than at an altar. That and him fearing fifty years of me harping on him just did it for me. Oh yes, I love him. I think I knew it before, but now I *know* I knew it. And every cliché I'd ever heard about love being fickle and unpredictable raced through my mind.

I lifted my chin, not caring one whit.

Mr. Perini shuffled past Emily and me at the doorway and entered the room. He helped Barry and Mark rearrange the furnishings. "The team is ready and Dexter will be here in ten minutes," he told Mark and Barry. "We need to hustle. Where's Lester?"

"He'll be here in a second, he said." Mark set an arrangement of lilies on a curved-legged table next to the altar. "Dexter Devlin is coming here?"

"Has to." Paul pushed a button on the wall. Long royal blue drapes slid across the width of the room, hiding the casket. "I'm not a notary."

Now that shocked me. I mean, Paul Perini seemed to be everything else in Dixie. Why not a notary? I would have asked but I felt more than heard the urgency in his voice.

Apparently, so did Mark. He asked, "What is it, Mr. Perini? What's wrong?"

"They're on the way here."

"Here?" Mark's voice turned tinny. "As in Dixie?"

"As in *here*," Paul said. "We've got four hours and then they'll all be here, standing where you're standing."

"Marcello and Adriano?" Lester entered the parlor asking, looking dapper in a black tux.

"Yes," Paul answered. "And Detective Keller and the FBI."

Even Special Agent Ted Johnson was coming? I groaned. "Perfect."

Emily patted my shoulder. "Don't you worry, pet. We'll have you wed and dead long before then."

What did I say to that? Failing to find anything that sounded even halfway logical, I squeezed my Grant half-dollar hard and settled for the obvious and trite. "Thanks."

A knock sounded at the front door. My heart kicked into overdrive.

"It's all right," Emily whispered. "It's not them."

It had to be. "Who else would be here at four in the morning?"

"The lawyer, Daisy." She rolled her eyes. "Dexter Devlin."

CHAPTER 11

Dexter Devlin stood an imposing six-seven. His face was lean, his shoulders wide, and his neck thicker than my thigh. I knew from Mark he was a successful lawyer, but I have to tell you, I wondered if the reason wasn't his oratory skills but because the sight of him scared people half to death. His hands were the size of hams and his don't-even-think-about-messing-with-me look seemed to be a permanent feature on his face.

Mark sat at the desk next to him, reading and reviewing papers, then scribbled his signature. "The revocation of the power of attorney on Rachel," he said, passing that one over to Dexter, then scanned the next and signed it. "A power of attorney for Jackson." Mark then read and signed the third legal document. "My new will leaving all assets to Daisy Grant Jensen with Jackson Grant as secondary."

Dexter accepted the last of the batch.

"You're certain these are your final wishes?"

"Absolutely."

"Okay, then." Dexter notarized and sealed the documents. "When I leave here, I'll head straight to New Orleans."

"What about Daisy?" Mark frowned up at Dexter. "If she becomes my wife —"

"After the wedding, both of you will sign again. Powers of attorney and wills. They'll read exactly the same so that who died first creates no issue."

"Why is that significant?"

"You can't disinherit family in one of these states. Chris and Rachel could challenge the will on that. This will preclude them from it since it makes the order of death a moot point."

"Okay." Mark stood up, extended his hand. "Thank you, Mr. Devlin. It's a privilege to meet you."

"Dexter. Paul told me about you and your dad following my cases. I hope the real man hasn't disappointed you."

"Not at all. I can't thank you enough for doing all this." Mark frowned. "I just worry that if Chris turned on me, he'll keep giving Jackson fits."

Dexter smiled. "Don't worry. I've got you and Jackson covered."

Looking at him, I believed him. I even bet

myself that Victor Marcello and Adriano didn't mess with Dexter Devlin. Probably the FBI didn't either. If it did, it'd better bring it's A-game. He'd see to it, it needed it.

"I appreciate it." Mark sobered. "Oh, be sure to get Daisy's Grant half-dollar and give it to Jackson."

"Why?"

"He'll understand."

My throat thickened. Jackson would understand that they were okay. Thoughtful of Mark to think of it. It shamed me that I hadn't.

Mr. Perini joined me at the doorway. "Ready, Daisy?"

I nodded and started to walk in.

"Wait!" Emily stopped me with an outstretched hand. "Mark can't see the bride before the wedding, Paul. What are you thinking? Get him out of there."

Mr. Perini escorted Mark out of the reception area, and I walked in. Dexter Devlin sat at the desk and he smiled. Amazing, how it softened his face. "Hi."

"Hello, Daisy." His eyes gentled. "You make a lovely bride."

"Thank you, Mr. Devlin." I smiled back, wondering how I ever thought him intimidating. The man was a teddy bear. "You have some papers for me to sign?"

"Yes, I do. These will transfer everything you own to Jackson." He pulled the documents from a file and spread them out on the desk. "And I'm supposed to get a Grant half-dollar from you for Jackson. Mark said he'd know what it meant."

"He will." I lifted the pen and signed the papers, then took a last look at the Grant. *Thanks for being there for me all these years. You carry my love to Jackson, okay?* I passed the coin to Dexter Devlin.

"You didn't read them."

"Mark signed duplicates, right?"

"He did."

"Then they're fine."

"You trust him."

"With my life," I said, then thought, *And my death.*

"Now," Dexter said. "Let's get you two married so we can do this all over again."

"What?" Do what all over again?

"You're not married now. We're covered," Dexter explained. "You're marrying Mark in minutes. That changes everything. You'll both sign again as married people, and then we'll be totally covered — before and after."

Two minutes later, Lester walked me through the parlor to the altar. I stood before it beside Mark, facing Mr. Perini who

241

held a well-worn Bible in his hands and began speaking the familiar words heard at thousands of weddings, "Dearly beloved . . ."

In a blur, the ceremony progressed, and then Mr. Perini lifted his voice and said, "I now pronounce you man and wife. Mark, you may kiss your bride."

He bent low, his breath warm on my face. "Thank you for marrying me, Daisy," he whispered, then kissed me long and deep, letting me feel his emotional turmoil, sharing my emotional gauntlet. Tender and passionate, both untamed and in control, and by the time his lips left mine, I'd forgotten everything except the feel and taste and scent of him. "Thank you for marrying me, Mark."

He smiled.

I smiled back. Strange but, at that moment, I couldn't imagine any other bride and groom feeling their marriage was more real or more treasured than ours was to us. It was, in every way that most matters, perfect.

A teary-eyed Lester and fluttering Emily enveloped us in hugs, and Mr. Perini and Barry and Dexter added their congratulations and well wishes. Everyone smiling, happy, thrilled — it was a beautiful mo-

ment. One I'd hold dear the rest of my life.
All forty-five minutes of it.

CHAPTER 12

Mark and I signed the marriage license and then the duplicate legal documents.

Dexter Devlin tucked them into his file, and then the file into his briefcase. Its locks clicked closed. "I'm on my way to New Orleans."

"You're absolutely sure you have everything you need?" Mark's fear that Dexter had forgotten something rippled in his voice. "I don't know how we'll pay you, but we will."

"I have everything," Dexter assured him. "On the bill, forget it. It's paid in full."

"Why?" Mark asked the question burning on my lips.

He winked. "Good luck to you," he said, then headed for the door.

"The Grant," Mark lifted a hand.

I clasped it and lowered our hands. "He has everything. The before-and-after papers and the Grant, Mark." I nodded, feeling tender. "Thanks for thinking of it. It'll do so much to ease Jackson's mind."

Mark gently squeezed my hand. "It'll all settle, Daisy. Everything's going to be okay."

Mr. Perini grabbed something from the bookshelf near the stack of license plates and followed him. "Be right back. I'm going to walk Dexter out."

Moments later, an engine rumbled outside and brakes squealed. "What is that?" I looked at Mark. "It can't be them." Adriano. Marcello. Keller and Johnson. "It's too soon."

Mark looked out a window near the door. "It's not them." He looked back at me. "It's a truck — an eighteen wheeler."

"What's an eighteen wheeler doing on this street?" Emily asked Lester.

I wondered the same thing. It didn't belong in a little neighborhood like this unless . . . no, it wouldn't be delivering coffins at this time of night.

"I don't know," Lester said, loosening his tie.

Mark stepped back from the window and faced the three of us. "I don't know either, but Dexter left and Paul's talking to the truck driver."

Emily elbowed Lester. "Best see to it now. No better time."

He nodded and reached to his inside pocket and pulled out a thick envelope then passed it to Daisy. "This is for the two of you. Go ahead and open it."

I broke the seal and nearly hit the floor. It was crammed with hundred dollar bills. "Lester, no." I looked from it to Mark and then to Lester. "There's thousands of dollars in here."

"Yep. Three-hundred fifty thousand, to be exact." He leveled an even look on me. "You and Mark need front money to get started. Paul will explain all that."

"I — we can't take this, Lester." I fought tears. "Where did you get this?"

"It's mine and I didn't steal it, if that's what you're thinking."

"I told you he had money, pet," Emily added. "Don't you remember?"

"I remember." I eyed Lester warily. "But all this time — bail money?"

He couldn't hold my gaze, and let his drop to the skirt of my gown. "I had to know, Daisy girl."

"Know what?"

"If I could trust you." He did look up at me then. "When you used your grocery money to get me out of jail . . . I knew then."

"So you did it over and again?" I'd eaten peanut butter for a solid week every time.

246

"I couldn't believe it." He glanced at Mark. "I'm an old man. She thought I had nothing. I couldn't do a thing for her, and worse, I cost her. But she still stayed put and kept me under her wing. See why I say she'll never leave you, son." He took my hand. "You know I been by myself most of my life, Daisy. I saw what you done with my own eyes, but I just couldn't believe that a woman like you would take me into her heart like we was family. But you did. And then you rescued me again and again, like I was somebody important."

"You are somebody important. You always have been." He tested me. Again and again. "So after you got it through your head I'd keep bailing you out, why didn't you tell me the truth?" A thought ran through my mind that hurt. "Are you telling me after all that, you still didn't trust me?"

"No! I trusted you." He looked away.

"I want an answer, Lester. I deserve one, too."

"Yeah, I guess you do." He shuffled and slumped, then finally looked at me, his wrinkled eyes burning with truth. "Fact of the matter is, I was scared to tell you then. If I told you what I'd done, then you wouldn't trust me. I didn't want to hurt you, girl, but I didn't want you to kick me to the curb, either, and I was scared you might." He looked at Mark. "I was selfish, pure and simple."

He feared losing me. *Me. The orphan.* "You were not selfish." I hugged him. He kept the truth to himself to assure I stayed. "You risked yourself to bust me out of jail and to keep me from walking in on the thugs ransacking my apartment. There's nothing selfish in that."

"You forgive me?" Surprise lit his eyes. "I know you got stuck with a peanut butter diet every time you bailed me out of jail, Daisy, and I'm sorry. I really am. How can you forgive me for that?"

"You're an easy man to forgive." That earned me a blank look, so I made the reason plain. "I love you."

He brightened. "I love you too, Daisy girl."

Mr. Perini came back in and shut the door. "Okay, then. You two better change clothes —"

"Wait." Lester lifted a hand. "What's with the eighteen wheeler, and why'd you take that tracker outside with you. I notice you ain't carrying it now."

"He's astute, no?" Mr. Perini smiled. "That truck will soon be on its way to Minnesota."

"Ah, Minnesota." Lester let out a whoop

that dissolved into a chuckle.

"What?" I asked, then looked at Mark.

"Beats me," he said, every bit as clueless.

"The driver put the tracker on the truck." Paul's eyes lit up. "Divide and conquer, Daisy. Marcello and Adriano will be here, but they'll also have half their people following that tracker. They'll think you're on the move — at least, they will until they find out you two are dead."

"What about the driver?" Their men wouldn't take being duped kindly. The truck driver would feel the brunt of that. "Will he be safe?"

"He'll be fine. He won't know the tracker is on his truck."

Mark disputed that. "You handed him the tracker, Mr. Perini. I saw it. How can he not know?"

"I talked to *this* driver, who happens to own the truck. He doesn't drive loads anymore. I didn't talk to the driver heading to Minnesota. He will have no idea he's carrying a tracker."

Mark grimaced. "Which means Marcello and Adriano's goons will blindside him."

"It doesn't work that way, Mark," Lester said. "Well, not anymore. The families use a little more finesse now. He'll be fine." Lester turned to Mr. Perini. "Clever." Lester rubbed his chin. "Owner's one of ours?"

Mr. Perini nodded.

Ours? Our what? I should ask. I knew it, but I really didn't want to know. I limited my concern to the driver. If Lester said the man would be safe, then he would be safe. Lester wouldn't lie about something like that.

"Okay, the driver's safe." Mark grunted, obviously opting not to explore that *one of ours* either. "But Marcello and Adriano and all their thugs will be back here once they figure out the tracker was planted on the truck and that's a dead-end for them. Which means they'll all be here for the funeral."

"No doubt." Mr. Perini nodded. "But don't worry. I've got it covered."

"Covered how?" Mark pushed. "They're going to demand to see our dead bodies, Mr. Perini."

"Yes. They surely will."

That set Mark back on his heels. "We won't be dead — or will we?" His uncertainty about that triggered my own.

"Technically, yes, but — oh, I see you're concerned." He clapped Mark's shoulder. "No, of course you and Daisy won't be dead, though she'll be Rose, then, and you'll be Matthew Green."

"So how can they see our dead bodies if

we're not dead?"

"I have it covered — and I'll tell you in due time, Mark. It's better that you know only what you must know when you must know it." Paul motioned to Barry. "Get the crew geared up. We'll be there in ten minutes."

"Yes, sir." Barry left without a backward look.

Paul waited until he had gone and the sound of the door thudded closed behind him, then he turned back to Mark. "You're going to have to trust me. I've been through this before and you haven't, eh? Like I said, it's best for you not to know any more than is necessary at a given time."

Trust? On what basis? I have trouble with trust. I've never denied it, not even to myself. And Mr. Perini was, after all, a stranger to me and I was placing my life and Mark's in his hands by trusting him with our deaths. "Why is secrecy important, Mr. Perini?" I asked. "In thirty minutes, we'll be dead."

He looked me right in the eye. "Because you die today. But your final arrangements won't be final for three days. A lot can happen in three days, Daisy."

"Three days?" Mark asked. "Why so long?"

251

"We have to wait for Jackson to get here," Lester told them. "Ain't nobody gonna believe his only sister dies and he don't come to the funeral."

"He's right," I told Mark. Worrying my lip, I thought this through, looking for a way — any credible way — to spare Jackson from getting mixed up in this.

I failed to find one. "Jackson has to be here for this to work. Rachel and Chris, too."

Mark grunted. "Considering the paper-work Dexter is handling later this morning, I doubt Rachel or Chris will come here for my funeral. None of them will. Well, maybe Tank and Craig Parker but not Rachel."

That truth hurt him. I could hear that it did and looped our arms, then said to Mr. Perini, "I've been thinking through all this, and there's one thing I see as a problem. I'm afraid it has the potential to be a big one."

"What's that?" Paul's surprise fell to keen curiosity.

"Okay, so we die and are buried," I said. "What's to stop any of them — Keller, Johnson, Marcello or Adriano — from digging us up and finding our coffins empty?" I glanced at Mark. "We're never going to have a minute of peace. We'll be looking over our shoulders all day, every day, for the rest of our lives."

"Naw, you won't." Lester pulled his loosened tie off and stuffed it into his pocket. The ends dangled at his hip.

"I don't see how we won't." I crossed my arms. "First thing every morning it's going to be, is today the day they dig us up? The day they find us?"

"Daisy's right," Mark said. "Have you considered that, Mr. Perini?"

"Oh, yes."

"Well?" Again, Mark pushed. "What do we do about it?"

The light overhead reflected in his eyes and sparked a mischievous twinkle. "I told you. Trust me."

I looked at Mark and he at me. Simultaneously, we shrugged, accepting that we had no choice.

Who knew what he had in mind? Maybe his mind was as much a maze as Lester's. But things worked out for Lester, who actually was quite clever, and he looked totally relaxed. If I were going to be in jeopardy, Lester would not be relaxed. Knowing that, I relaxed, too. "It's not like we've got other options," I told Mark. "Mr. Perini's handled everything else that's come along. He'll handle this, too."

Mark hesitated. All the reasons against trust ran through his expressions like cars circling a racetrack. But when he spoke, he looked at peace about it. "All right, then. We'll trust you."

"Sensible decision." Paul looked extremely pleased. "Now, you two go change your clothes and let's get you killed."

In the same ante-room where I'd dressed before, I changed clothes and carefully hung the lovely gown back on its hanger. It'd been a perfect wedding. I fingered the delicate fabric and let out a sigh. *If only . . .*

"Daisy, are you ready?" Mark called out from the other side of the door.

Back in my Cinderella garb, I opened the door and faced my patch-less pirate. "Ready."

Together we joined the others in the reception area.

"Ah, good." Mr. Perini stood up. "We're cutting it close. It's nearly dawn. Let's hurry."

"Um, how are we going to wreck?"

"Aided by mother nature, my boy." Mr. Perini shoved on his red newsboy cap then clapped Mark's shoulder. "Barry will tell you exactly what to do . . ."

CHAPTER 13

On the front lawn, Mark got instructions from Barry while Lester and I said our good-byes, and then Mark and I got into the Honda. I buckled up. "So what now?"

"I drive and follow him."

Surprise rippled through me. "That's it? That's our instructions?"

"That's it."

I wrung my hands. I'd always hated it when women did that, but I couldn't seem to help myself. "I don't like the idea of not being prepared. I mean, if we're the ones doing the dying, shouldn't we be prepared?"

Mark gave me a look. "People die unprepared all the time, Daisy."

"Yeah, but they really die. I don't want to really die."

He clasped my hand. I couldn't tell if it was clammy with sweat or freezing. "We're not going to really die."

How could he sound so confident? So

calm? My insides felt like they were stuck in a whirring blender. "What else did he tell you?"

"I told you what he said."

"You didn't tell me all of it." I sniffed in the darkness — loudly, to be sure he didn't miss it. "I know you Mark Jensen. He told you something or you'd at least be tense. You just don't want to tell me."

"I told you what he said," he repeated, sparing me a glance. "Where's your wedding dress? I thought you were going to wear it."

His face even looked good in the green light cast from the dash. How could anyone look good green?

"What am I supposed to make of that?" He gripped the wheel. "I wasn't sure what to make of you wanting to die in it, so I sure don't know what to make of you not wanting to die in it."

"What are you talking about?" Maybe he'd been around Lester and Emily too much. Or I had. Even applying Lester-logic, Mark's comments made no sense.

"Did you want to wear it to signal me that when we die, our marriage dies, too? Or were you telling me that you were taking me with you? Or that you —"

He wasn't as calm as he'd seemed. I'd

have to remember that. Right now, though, he needed reassuring. "I was thinking that I'd be taking you with me through eternity."

"Oh." He smiled. "I like that." A second later, he grunted. "But you didn't wear it. I don't like that you changed your mind. So you are dumping me, aren't you?"

"No, I'm not dumping you." What was wrong with him? Even nervous, the man rarely lacked confidence.

"Harrumph. Interesting."

"Interesting?" I sat here a nervous wreck and he was worried about why I was and wasn't wearing my wedding dress? We were about to *die* — hopefully without really dying, but with Mr. Perini and Lester at the helm . . . who knew?

"Fascinating," Mark said. "I could be wrong, of course, but I think you might not be as opposed to our marriage as I initially thought." He glanced over. "I have to tell you, Daisy, I was a little stung by your reluctance to marry me."

Flabbergasted, I blurted out the truth. "How was I supposed to react? I'm not a mind reader, Mark. They said we should marry. You said nothing. I was stunned by the suggestion. I didn't see it coming, and I had no idea how you were reacting to it. You sure weren't saying. I didn't know how to react anymore than you did. I mean, I don't even know how you feel about me. Isn't that reason enough to hedge?"

"Sputter."

"What?" What was he talking about now?

"You didn't hedge, you sputtered."

I probably had. "I didn't see you jumping in —"

"I did. I said I wanted the marriage to be real. That's jumping in."

True. But it didn't resolve other issues. How did he feel about me? He still hadn't told me, and I'd been clear on that. I'd specifically said I had no idea how he felt about me. "Okay, you did. But I didn't know why. That's kind of important, don't you think?"

"Very," he agreed. "But how could you not know why?" Now he sounded baffled. "We connected the first time we met, Daisy. Are you going to sit there and say we didn't?"

"I never said that." Flustered, I lifted my hands. "I was never opposed to marrying you, okay?"

"Me either, Daisy."

I caught a sharp breath and the heat left my voice. "So that's good. We understand each other then." I still didn't have a clue if he loved me or he just didn't want to die alone or be alone when he tackled his fresh start. Or if he wanted family and I was it.

"Yeah, I think we do." He spared her another glance. "Now tell me the truth. Why didn't you wear your wedding gown?"

Typical male. Push and push. And then push some more. "It's the most beautiful dress I've ever had. And I felt beautiful in it."

"You were. Stunningly beautiful. So why not wear it?"

Stunningly beautiful. I'd remember those words forever. He thought I was stunningly beautiful. And he knew there was more. He'd always known, and I suppose he always would. No holding back anything from this one. "I couldn't bear to get blood on it. I told Emily I wanted to wear it for the funeral instead."

"Closer to the whole truth, but that's not all of it, is it, Daisy?"

The lights from the car streaked across a wide ditch and beyond it, through the trees lining the road. "It's almost all." I read a *Dangerous Curve* sign and spotted a little cluster of white crosses just beyond the road's shoulder.

"You promised me honesty. The whole truth is honest."

I shook my head. "I'll tell you later." I felt

far too emotional to admit the truth. The look in Mark's eyes, that special twinkle that was just for me . . . I'd worn that dress and stood before the altar with him. I wanted to wear it always and feel as perfect as I felt in that moment.

"I knew you were holding out on me, Daisy Jensen."

Daisy Jensen. It sounded good. Right. "Just a little."

"And just so you know I know. That *later* meant really later not just a little later. I can tell the difference." He clasped my hand. "But one day you'll tell me."

Boy, could he tell the difference. That's exactly what she'd meant. Later as in a long, long time from now. "Maybe when we're old and gray and you've lost all your hair and teeth."

Mark laughed. "How charming a picture you paint of me in our future."

"Hey, I'm picturing us living long enough to get old and gray and you to get bald and toothless. In our situation, that's having a pretty vivid imagination, don't you think?"

"I think you're going to need that imagination — and I'm going to need to stay on my toes or you'll sidestep telling me anything, Daisy. You promised me no secrets and we're married — what? — half an hour, and already you're keeping secrets from me. That does not bode well."

"These kinds of secrets don't count. They're just thoughts, not real secrets. But I like it that you didn't complain about being bald and toothless."

"I noticed that I lost my hair *and* teeth and you lost nothing."

"Course not. I'll look then exactly as I do now." I laughed.

He did, too.

Laughing. We were about to die, and we were *laughing.* "You know, I think we have to be as certifiable as Lester and Em—"

Mark checked the rearview mirror, slammed on the brakes.

The car skidded. Fishtailed. Spun out of control then slid across the road.

Something thudded, crashed into the car. Debris flew. Smoke from the tires clouded around us, and we tumbled, slamming into the ditch. My body jerked toward the door, my shoulder smacking against the side panel. Pain shot through my arm, up my neck. I grunted, gasped, trying to catch my breath. *What happened?* Mark . . . "Mark?"

"Daisy, hush." He splashed me with fake blood and doused himself, then crammed the bag into his left pocket. "They hear you, and it ruins everything."

261

"That was on purpose?" I couldn't believe it. "You knew that was going to happen and you didn't tell me?"

"Gripe later. Not now."

"Who is going to hear me?"

"The cop who's been following us and is running toward the car right now."

I dropped my voice. "You should have told me —"

"Sorry, but would you please hush? We're dead," he muttered. "Dead people don't talk."

"Or gripe."

"Shh!"

The officer opened Mark's door. "You folks all — oh, man."

"They all right, Kev?" A second man joined the cop outside Mark's door.

My eyes were closed so I couldn't see him, but he sounded like Barry.

"No. I'm afraid not, Barry."

"Man. I saw the deer run out in front of them. When they started spinning toward the ditch, I was scared it'd get 'em."

"This curve's notorious for taking people out."

"In the last ten years, at least a dozen's been called to heaven on it."

"At least." The cop sighed.

He hadn't checked us for a pulse. Or done

any of the things one would expect a cop to do in a situation like this. Why not?

"Who are they?" Barry asked. "Locals?"

"Don't think so. I hadn't seen either of them before."

"Lemme look." Shuffling noises sounded, as if they were switching places.

"Don't touch anything."

"I won't."

"Recognize either of them?"

"Yeah, I do. Oh, man," Barry said, clearly closer to the window. "Mr. Perini just married 'em a little while ago."

"Newlyweds." The cop let out a heartfelt sigh. "Sure hate to hear that."

"They seemed like nice people," Barry said. "Hate it that they got killed here."

"It's a bad curve," the cop said. "How's the deer?"

I wanted to know that, too. I'd heard the thump.

"DOA."

They'd killed a deer in this? Actually killed a deer? Inside, I felt sick.

"It didn't suffer. Was dead before it hit the ground."

"Mercy in that," the cop said. "Keep watch no one comes around that curve and disturbs the scene, will you? I'm going to run back to the cruiser and call it in, grab a few things."

"Sure thing."

The cop's footfalls retreated.

Barry came close to the window. "Don't freak out, Daisy. The deer was already dead. Lester told me to be sure to tell you. Pete Ladner got it hunting late yesterday. We . . . appropriated it — with permission."

Did everyone in Dixie owe Paul Perini favors? Regardless, I owed Lester another one. Knowing the deer was dead before the accident did make me feel better. And I had seen the sign about Pete Ladner going hunting at the funeral home, posted on the outside wall near Mr. Perini's front door.

The cop returned. "I'm going to drop some cones on the other side of the curve. Don't touch anything, Barry. The coroner's on his way and he's in a foul mood."

"Why's he in an uproar?"

"He and the chief were still playing cards and some Detective from out of state came in looking for somebody. He brought an FBI agent with him."

Oh, no. Keller and Johnson. Had to be Keller and Johnson.

"No kidding."

"It gets worse."

"Yeah?" Barry asked.

"Chief had to fold and he had a full house.

He's not happy."

"So why is the coroner in a foul mood?"

"He had four of a kind."

"That'd do it." Barry clicked his tongue. "I'm seeing lights. Must be him coming down the road."

"Looks like."

"I hope he don't keep us out here all night. I got to get home and let the dogs out."

"Won't take long. They're dead, we both saw what happened. Ain't much to investigate when you witness it. Half an hour, tops."

In Biloxi, it took hours to investigate an accident and take statements and do all that had to be done when an accident happened. Course, those people were alive and would be filing insurance claims and liability suits, maybe. The police had to be prepared. When you have two witnesses and one is a cop, and the people involved are dead, it kind of cuts back on possibilities — unless the victims have heirs. Heirs could . . . *well, spit.*

We'd been duped. The cop had to also be in on this with Mr. Perini.

The team is ready.

Barry and Kev, the cop — they *were* the team and Kev, being a cop, was wired. The whole thing had been recorded. Hard to fight that kind of evidence.

And in my mind I again heard Mr. Perini's, *Trust me . . .*

CHAPTER 14

Not one but two vehicles arrived within minutes.

My adrenalin shot through the roof. There was no way the coroner would examine us and pronounce us dead, especially not with additional unintended witnesses. Barry stayed close to the vehicle and relayed information to us. Obviously, though I couldn't open my eyes to see, he had been rigged with a two-way communications device.

"Detective Keller and Special Agent Johnson," Barry said, relaying the identity of the second vehicle's occupants. "Keep them behind the tape," he added to an unseen someone, probably on the radio.

After a little bit of a distant heated dispute, a man's voice sounded. "Let's get this done. I need photos, measurements — all the usual for the record."

"The coroner," Barry clarified. "Apparently the FBI and out-of-stater ain't taking kindly to being kept behind the tape."

My heart thudded so hard, the coroner wouldn't need to check it with a stethoscope to verify my death. He'd hear the beating, disputing my death — and Keller and Johnson stood close enough to see it happen.

"Two more cars?" Barry said aloud. A long pause later, he added, "Marcello and Adriano themselves?" Another pause, then a worried, "Oh, man."

That jacked up my concern and fear. The entire entourage was there. Could the local cops keep them far enough away to protect our secret? I sure hoped they could, but these weren't just your everyday-average citizens. These were men with the power of the federal government behind them and, worse, two heads of the strongest mob families in the world. *We are so nailed.* If one didn't get us, another of them would.

From the sounds, a multitude of people shuffled around doing what they do. Outside Mark's door, the coroner told Barry to step aside. A camera flash went off repeatedly. My door opened and, since I leaned against it, I feared falling out. It took everything in me not to brace myself and shift. But a strong hand shoved me back into the car, and more flashes from a camera followed.

A bag snapped open, rustling and sounds of the coroner withdrawing something filled the silence in the car. A full three minutes later, which seemed like a lifetime, the coroner placed something cold and metallic against my throat, then my chest.

Panic set in. He had to know we were alive. Had to know it. What would he do? Did Paul Perini have a stronger hold on the coroner than the FBI or the mob? Having no clue, I began to sweat.

Think ice! Think ice!

If anyone, not just coroner, saw me sweating, they'd all know I was alive.

He stepped back, and a crisp breeze filled the car. He left the door open.

"Well?"

Johnson's voice. Definitely Ted Johnson's voice.

"They're still dead," the coroner answered flippantly. "That's pretty normal here. Expect it's the same wherever you're from, Special Agent . . . what did you say your name was again?"

"Ted Johnson," the man said through his teeth.

Turf war. The locals never appreciated being invaded by the feds. And the feds never appreciated standing next to two rival mob leaders and having their hands tied on being able to do anything about it because their star witness was dead. That tension just might be the luckiest break I've ever gotten in my whole life.

"Tag 'em and bag 'em," the coroner said. "Kev, you got everything you need?"

"Yes, sir."

"Then let's get 'em to the morgue before morning traffic sets in. Otherwise, we'll have even more white crosses beside the road here."

A whistle sounded and a vehicle drove up and parked alongside the car. The next thing I knew, I was wearing a toe tag, zipped inside a body bag, then being moved.

Keller's muffled voice carried to me. "Daisy was married? When did that happen?"

"Just before the accident." Barry elevated his voice so Mark and I wouldn't miss what was said. Thoughtful of him, considering.

"You're sure the accident killed them both?"

"Yes, sir, I am. I saw them in the car, and saw the wreck. Sad, thing. But it's a bad curve. We've lost a lot of people here."

Agent Johnson interjected. "I saw all the crosses on the shoulder. Maybe you guys

should consider a flashing sign or something."

"The poor kid never stood a chance." Keller sounded genuinely regretful. "What
caused the wreck?"

"The man was driving. A deer bolted out
of the woods and into the street. The guy
swerved to miss it. Didn't, but at least the
poor thing didn't suffer. I saw it all happen."

Johnson asked, "Anyone else around?"

"Just me and Kev — that's him right
there."

"The police officer?"

"Yes, sir."

Johnson persisted. "And you didn't see
anything unusual? No erratic driving, no
significant variations in speed — no anything that might lead you to think something
more than swerving to miss a deer happened here tonight?"

"Not a thing," Barry said. "If that's all
your questions, I really need to get going.
Hope my dog ain't busted a bladder. If not,
he's close. I'm never this late getting home."

"That's it. Thanks for talking with us,
Barry."

"No problem," he said. "You've got my
number if you need anything." His footfalls
grew weaker — walking away.

Engines roared to life and several cars departed.

"I guess that's it, then, Ted." Keller sounded disappointed.

"Yeah. Without her, we've got nothing." The frustration of not being able to make his case came through in Johnson's voice. "Hard to believe that with two mob families after her, it's wildlife that killed her."

"When it's your time, it's your time." Keller paused, then added, "If it had to happen, I'm glad it happened the way it did. She was a nice kid. Let's close it out and go home."

"Don't you want to investigate further?"

"No, I really don't," Keller said. "Daisy Grant is dead. We saw her. A cop witnessed the accident. What's to investigate?"

"Maybe she left something behind that'll help us . . ."

"Ha. You'd have better odds, going to heaven to get her to testify." Keller grunted. "Give it up, Ted. It's over."

"You're right." Johnson sounded irritated. "You're right. I just . . . we were so close."

"Close doesn't cut it," Keller told him. "This isn't horseshoes."

Car doors opened and closed and the vehicle, I presumed, that carried Keller and Johnson to the scene, departed. Where the

Marcellos and Adrianos were, I had no idea. Perhaps they had left earlier. Someone had. Not knowing their whereabouts had me jittery inside, and the body bag had me hot and itching. *Think ice.*

Finally someone approached the vehicle in which Mark and I lay stretched out side-by-side. I held my breath and prayed harder than I've ever in my life prayed.

Other footsteps approached.

"I want to see the bodies," a man said.

"Sure thing," a second man said. "Coroner sealed 'em. I can't break the seals. But follow me to the morgue. My boss will let you can take a look as soon as he logs 'em in."

"No," the man said. "I want to see them now."

My fear doubled. I resisted the urge to fist my hands. Was it Marcello or Adriano? Marcello wanted me to live, but on sight, Adriano would shoot me dead.

A third man piped in. "Sorry," he said. "He's a little emotional — friend of the victims. We'll follow you to the morgue."

"No problem." The backend of our vehicle slammed shut.

The air stilled and silence fell. Footfalls rounded to the driver's door, and then someone got inside. The engine started, and finally . . . *finally* . . . the vehicle moved.

I took my first easy breath since our deaths.

CHAPTER 15

When I next opened my eyes, I lay flat on my back on a slab covered with a sheet. Mark lay toes up on a gurney beside me. Did I dare to move more than the edge of the sheet to see more? *Trust me.* I shouldn't. But the temptation burned strong.

"Daisy?"

Someone called my name in a stage whisper. Unable to identify the voice, and fearing someone might be trying to trick me, I didn't move.

"Daisy? Mark? Ouch. Blast it all." He'd stubbed his toe. "Where are you?"

Sweeps of light from a flashlight crisscrossed the room. Why didn't he turn the light on? *Definitely Paul Perini.* I sat up. "Over here."

Mark sat up, too.

Mr. Perini smiled and walked across the long room full of gurneys. More than half were draped with sheets. "Place is busier than usual. I couldn't spot you."

"Might be easier if you turned that flashlight off," Mark sat up, "and the overhead on."

"It would," he continued to speak softly, "but we're being watched, so I'll pass on that. No sense telegraphing ahead exactly when I walked in the room."

I counted the occupied gurneys. At least a dozen of them. The room was cold, dim, and utilitarian. Chills rippled up my backbone. "Seems like a lot of bodies for a small town."

"For some towns, but not for Dixie. Mine's the only funeral home for miles." Paul's smile broadened. "Well, dying wasn't so bad, now was it?"

It hadn't been. "Not really, though I would have appreciated knowing it was about to happen."

"Sorry. That was my call," Mr. Perini said. "If you'd seen the deer, I figured you would tense up and maybe grab the wheel and you two would really get hurt." He glanced at Mark. "For the record, your husband opposed you not being forewarned. I insisted."

I appreciated knowing that, and relented because Mr. Perini had a point. I probably would have grabbed the wheel to keep from hitting the deer. But equally distracting was that this was the first time anyone had called Mark my husband. I liked it. A lot. "Someone at the scene demanded to see our bodies — a man — but another one with him said they'd follow us to the morgue. I've been laying here dreading the coroner coming to show us to them."

"That was two family goons."

"Which family?" Mark asked.

"Adrianos." Mr. Perini sighed. "Not an issue. Without a court order, no one will be coming in to see you. But they are both watching the morgue, the funeral home and half the businesses in town."

"Is that a problem?" Mark asked.

"Hasn't been yet." He tugged at his red cap. "Try not to worry. We try to prepare for all eventualities and we're pretty nimble at improvising."

That relieved and worried me. Oddities happened or they wouldn't prepare for anything and the unexpected did crop up or they wouldn't be good at improvising. "Now what happens?"

"We wait three days for Jackson to get here, and then we have the funerals," Mr. Perini said. "I know you wanted to avoid that, in this case, but if Adriano and Marcello don't see you up close and personal themselves and watch the grand finale firsthand, they're never going to believe you're dead." Paul lifted his hands. "It's necessary. Essential to the success of our plans."

"That's it, then," Mark said, dragging a hand through his hair. "So we have to stay in here for three days?"

Three days in the morgue didn't appeal at all. It was dark, gloomy, smelled strongly of antiseptic, and being surrounded by dead people who might or might not really be dead felt spooky. It was cold, too, and frankly, a little creepy. Most morgues kept bodies in mini-vaults or drawers, not in one large room, and on the far wall, there were silver-handled, mini-vaults that could be sliding drawers. Did that mean all the bodies on gurneys in here were like us and not real bodies?

I wondered. But I didn't dare ask. Surely if that were the case, Mr. Perini wouldn't be so loose with using names and talking specifics. Then again, if the people on those gurneys weren't dead, they had as much to lose as we did, so did what he said really matter? To utter anything overheard would expose them, too, and they had just as much to lose.

"You won't be staying here, no. You'll be leaving with me."

Mark had been speaking softly, but dropped his voice even lower. "Is it safe to talk openly in here?"

Clearly his mind had gone exactly where mine had been. Were these people all dead? Or were they like us?

Mr. Perini answered, but my specific question remained a mystery. "It's safe."

"We'll be at the funeral home, then?" Mark asked.

"Not exactly." Now Mr. Perini lowered his voice. Why? Only he knew. "You'll be at a special place — one where you'll be safe."

That he'd whispered had me second-guessing the alive-and-breathing-and-faking-their-death corpses versus the really-dead-and-faking-nothing corpses present in the morgue. *Trust me.* Mr. Perini had said it was safe to talk, so I trusted him. Still, I took my cue from him and whispered close to his ear. "Has Jackson been told?"

"Dexter is handling that — hopefully before Keller phones your brother. I have to say, the detective seemed genuinely upset at your death."

He had. "I'm not sure it was personal. I was his star witness."

"I think it was personal," Mr. Perini said. "Barry radioed in that, when the photographer opened your door, you were falling out

279

and flinched. Keller jumped the crime-scene line and shoved you back in the car. He probably saw the flinch."

That surprised me. "But he told Johnson I was dead and it was over. It was time to close the case."

"Yeah, he did." Mr. Perini looked me right in the eye. "He can't protect you, and he knows it."

I slanted a glance at Mark.

"We got lucky." He cocked his head. "Keller made his choice — to protect you."

"That's how I see it . . . maybe. Maybe not," Mr. Perini said. "With both families at the scene, Keller didn't have a lot of wiggle room. If he'd pushed, odds are good the situation would have disintegrated into gunplay. That Johnson showed up looking for a fight. If he found one, Keller might well have been caught in the cross-fire."

"That makes more sense to me." I didn't doubt Keller cared, but let's face it, I'm nothing to him. Saving his own skin likely mattered more than me or his case.

Mark shifted the topic. "What about Rachel and Chris?"

"Dexter is also handling them," Mr. Perini said. "Don't expect much. He'll deliver the news that you've revoked the power of attorney and they're not inheriting and then notify them of your untimely demise. They won't likely be focused on your death and those emotions, if you know what I mean."

"I know what you mean," Mark said, his voice world-weary in a way that proved he'd been used and discarded before, where another thought more about what he or she wouldn't gain than about what Mark lost. I hated it for him.

"You won't be at the funeral home until just before time for the service."

"Where will we be?" I asked.

"I have a friend with a place. You'll like it. It's isolated. Quiet. Peaceful." He lowered his voice yet again, to just a whisper of sound to be certain no one else heard. "Sampson Park. No phones. No computers. No modern conveniences, but special. Most importantly, you'll be safe there."

Mark raised a question that niggled at me, too. "Why not just hold us at the funeral home?"

Paul leveled his gaze. "Because Marcello and/or Adriano are going to demand to see you and I'm going to refuse, and when I do, I expect they'll insist. They can't find you if you aren't there, which they won't know, of course, but you'll be safe and Barry and I will deal with them."

Paul was sending us to Sampson Park to

keep us out of the line of fire . . .

"Barry or Lester will bring you back on Monday. Funeral's at two o'clock, so we'll retrieve you that morning." He touched our shoulders. "Now, no more talk. Lay down and play dead so we can get you out of here." He tossed them each a body bag. "But first, crawl into your traveling apparel."

Mark slid in and pulled the bag up to his waist but, still seated, he paused and looked at me then at Mr. Perini. "Wait."

"What is it?"

The worry on Mark's face concerned me, too. Had he seen or heard something?

"Daisy and Mark are dead. They aren't married anymore."

True, but nothing new. We'd discussed that several times. My stomach fluttered a protest. Just as we'd discussed that Rose and Matthew Green wouldn't be married at all.

"Well, yes." Mr. Perini seemed baffled. "Marriage is 'til death."

Mark looked away, then at me. "I don't want to start this new life without you. Will you marry me — again?"

I didn't stop to think, just reacted. "Yes."

Mark smiled and turned to Mr. Perini. "Could you marry us again, please?"

"Well, yeah, I can. But I won't." A little flustered, he frowned. "Not in a morgue. You're sitting in body bags on gurneys. What kind of memory of your wedding is that?"

"We want to be married, Mr. Perini," Mark said.

Getting a little tense. Before it got any more so, I interceded. "You married us in a funeral home the first time," I reminded Mr. Perini. "Funeral home. Morgue. Bridging that gap isn't a big leap."

"What about the license? I don't carry one around in my pocket, you know."

"We'll sign it when we get to the funeral home," I said.

"We can have a ceremony as soon as we get there."

"No," I said. "Now." What if we didn't get there? He said everyone is watching.

"You're sure this is what you want?" he asked Mark, who nodded, then looked to me. "Absolutely sure?"

"Absolutely," I said. And I meant it. Maybe it wasn't the best choice I'd ever made in my life but, right then, it felt like the very best. My gut alarm sent up a *go* signal, and I heeded it. "Life can change in an instant. We don't want to risk it."

"Understandable, considering. Lester

283

won't like it much, not being here to witness it but, well, all right." Mr. Perini took in a breath that hiked his shoulders. "Where you're going is a nice place for a honeymoon . . ."

And so Paul Perini, funeral home director and justice of the peace — and live bait retailer — married Mark and me for the second time. Me, sitting in my body bag on my gurney, and Mark, sitting in his body bag on his gurney.

When Mr. Perini pronounced us husband and wife, we managed a peck of a kiss, then settled back and readied to depart. I could have sworn I'd heard a sniff, but it was probably just my imagination. It bends toward vivid anyway, and in a morgue . . . well, one's apt to think one sees and hears all kinds of things. And that's all I dared to think or speculate on that.

Mr. Perini zipped our bags then wheeled us outside. From the voice, it was Barry who assisted him in transferring us from the gurneys to the hearse.

Brief as it was, the sun on the bag felt good. It hadn't been cool in the morgue, it'd been cold. And the diffused heat seeping through the bag warmed my flesh and bones and felt wonderful.

It seemed odd even to me, but I lay inside

that hot, itchy bag smiling. We were safe for now, and Mark had married me not once but twice.

I had a husband. A family beyond Jackson. And while we were homeless, we were not hopeless. We had friends and money and something many would forfeit their eye teeth — both of them — to have: A chance to start a new life together with a sparkling clean, blank slate.

The magnitude of that gift hit me hard and, at that second in time, I believed with everything inside me I was the luckiest woman in the world.

CHAPTER 16

Barry drove the hearse straight from the morgue to Paul's funeral home. When he unzipped the body bags, the high ceiling and bright fluorescent lights confirmed that we were in the huge metal building behind the funeral home proper. The large, heavy door had been closed behind us.

The still air felt cool and refreshing on my face. I crawled out of the back of the hearse. My Cinderella dress looked a lot worse for the wear. "Whew, I'm glad that's over."

Barry laughed. "I'll bet."

Mark came out behind me. "Where's Mr. Perini?"

Seeing even fake dried blood splattering his white shirt flipped my stomach.

"He went to do the paperwork for your wedding — the one at the morgue, I mean." Barry's bushy beard parted and a flash of white teeth appeared in the mouth-gap. "Now that's a story worth passing on.

Shame you won't be able to tell it." He checked his watch. "Stay put in here for another thirty minutes. I'll be back to drive you to Sampson Park."

"Okay." I said, looking around at a multitude of equipment and vehicles.

Barry went through a door that opened into an internal breezeway to the funeral home.

The garage looked like any other only on a much larger scale, except for the three hearses parked inside and two long rows of medical-type equipment I didn't recognize. Two normal vehicles and a workbench, stacks of a menagerie of furniture, odds-and-ends and lawn equipment, and shovels and hoes lined the west wall. A tall stack of new boxes not yet put together that had to be seven-feet long lay flat on a wooden platform. "Wonder what he does with those?"

"Not a clue, and I wouldn't hazard a guess." Mark sat down on the edge of the workbench.

"Me either." A body would fit inside, but cardboard? I shuddered and took a few steps so the boxes fell out of my line of sight. Why wasn't it hot and stuffy in here? The air smelled fresh and clean — ah, a filtration system. I visually followed the ducts. "Mr. Perini's interests are diverse. I wouldn't be surprised to see anything stored in here."

"Isn't that the truth?"

We chatted about the wreck and the worries that all our enemies being in Dixie created. We didn't talk about our second marriage. Despite the abnormality of it, we both seemed pretty relaxed. That's hard to imagine in our circumstance, and I can't say I understand it totally myself, but like Lester says, *what is, is. Ain't no help for it.* Weary to the bone, I decided not to look at any of it any closer. There would be time for that. For now, I chose to accept the good and be grateful for it. That included Mark.

"Daisy?"

"Mmm?" A pair of yellow gardening gloves too small for any man I'd seen here lay on the end of the workbench. Mark sat on the other end of it.

"Thanks for marrying me again."

Uncertain but happy. I felt both more than heard either in his voice. He craved a little assurance, and remembering my honesty pact, I gave it to him. "I want to be married to you, Mark."

"Why?"

Too tender. "Later. I'm not keeping a secret. I'd just rather talk about this later.

I'm punch-drunk tired and so are you. When we have this conversation, we need to be alert and fully awake."

"But you agree that we do need to have this conversation."

"Definitely." I turned and looked at him. "We made a commitment to each other. Not once, but twice. Before and after." I paused, trying to gauge his reaction, but it seemed as if a mask had slid down over his face. His expression told her nothing, and his body language hadn't changed. "I intend to keep it. Do you?"

"I do." He didn't hesitate. "Which kind of makes the conversation we need to have moot, doesn't it?"

"I guess it does." I smiled.

He smiled back, and something cold inside me melted. I'd felt that feeling before, but not to this degree. It'd been honest then, but not strong and solid. More wispy and mingled with hope. This was much different. More potent, more fixed. This warmth was meant to stay with me the rest of my life.

The door leading inside opened and Mr. Perini and Barry walked out. "I've got your papers ready to sign."

We stepped over to the work bench and affixed our names in the appropriate places, making our marriage legal. Inside, I felt almost giddy, and from his smile, Matthew did, too.

"Congratulations Rose and Matthew." Paul passed over a miniature copy the size of a business card. "I'll hold the originals for you for . . . after."

"Thanks," Mark said. "So what's next?"

"It's Barry's regular quitting time, so he'll be taking you to Sampson Park now. We need to stick to regular schedules around here, especially since we're being watched every second."

That worried me. "Where are Lester and Emily?"

"They left right after the wreck. But they're close, and they'll be here for the funeral."

"Okay." I supposed that was wise. I mean, why would they hang around a funeral home because someone they knew died? Anyone would consider that odd, much less our crew of suspicious enemies.

"You'll need to both scoot down on the floorboard, so it looks like Barry's leaving alone." Paul walked us to an old red truck. "We'll see you on Sunday at one."

"Okay." I looked at Mark. "Front or back?"

"Back. I'm a little bigger than you are.

More of me to scrunch down."

I stepped back and he climbed in and curled up on the floorboard. "Ready?"

"Yes."

"Thank you, Mr. Perini." When he nodded, I got in and slid down to the floor, curling my legs under me, then leaned my head forward to be sure it was a safe distance below the dash.

Barry got in, tossed a towel over Mark, a jacket half on the seat and half over me, then cranked the engine. The garage door opened and then he drove out. "Man, those people are everywhere."

"Watch for cameras," Mark said in a muffled voice.

Barry inched down the long gravel driveway and then pulled out onto the less bumpy and smoother asphalt road. "I gotta go by the house and let the dog out. Then we can get on the road. I do the same thing every day. If I skip it —"

"Don't skip it." Mark and I both said.

"It means you'll be down there another fifteen minutes."

"That's fine," I said. What choice did we have? Cramped muscles or bullets in the head, I'm going to pick cramped muscles every time.

"They following us?" Mark asked.

"Oh, yeah."

Ten minutes later, Barry braked to a stop. "We're there. They're still on us, so it'll be a bit." He parked, let out his dog, then whistled to call it, and seemingly settled in for the night. Fifteen minutes passed, then thirty.

An hour later, I asked, "What's taking him so long?" My legs had given up on feeling needles and had gone numb.

"Something's spooked him," Mark whispered.

"What do we do?"

"Nothing."

"Nothing?" That troubled me.

"Nothing."

It made sense. Obviously, they were still watching or Barry would have come back. Since he hadn't, anything we did would be a mistake. "Okay."

In the quiet that followed resignation, I gave in. Worn out, I closed my eyes and drifted off.

The click and creak of the car door opening awakened me. It had gotten dark outside. The interior of the truck lit up.

"It's me. We're okay now." Barry started the truck, put it in gear and took off. "Sorry about that. We had two separate cars on us.

292

No choice but to wait them out."

"Good that you did," Mark said, but I sensed his relief that we were back on the road.

"Can we get up yet?" I think I'd lost all blood flow from the waist down. It felt as if I had.

"Best give it a few more miles to be sure."

I accepted Barry's edict without complaint. After all, the man was putting his life on the line for us. We knew it. He knew it. So with no other options, I rested my head against the seat and again closed my eyes.

When on the run and unable to act, sleep. Odds are good, you're gonna need it.

The world according to Lester . . .

CHAPTER 17

"Rose? Rose, we're here."

Mark — Matthew. Mark and Daisy were dead. Matthew and Rose were who we were now. I had to remember that even if just awakening and stumbling in the fog of sleep.

The door to the truck stood open behind me, and Matthew waited on the pavement. He reached in. "Let me help you out."

On unfolding, pins and needles pricked my legs and had me wishing they were still numb. Pain spiked through my back from a catch in my side. "Yeow." I grabbed a hold of Matthew and scooted out of the truck. When my feet hit the pavement, that pain shot up my legs through my whole being. My left arm was stiff. I rubbed it, paused and shook one leg, rotating the foot, then rotated the other and looked around.

A broad arched sign rose above a wrought-iron gate. "Sampson Park."

Though it was dark, the parking lot was

well lighted. From what I could see in the diffused light, the grounds beyond the gate looked lush: tall oaks, leaves sprinkling the ground, and islands of thick green bushes. On the right, an armed guard stepped out of the tower-like arch that swept skyward and across the road.

"Evening." The guard dipped his chin. In his sixties, I guessed, and not a crease in sight in his prim blue uniform.

"Mr. and Mrs. Green." Barry stepped forward. "Darby is expecting them."

"Just a moment, please." The guard stepped back into the arch and pressed something on the far wall. "Mr. and Mrs. Green have arrived."

"Please deliver them to the Village, cottage number seven."

"Right away." The guard stepped out. "Any cell phones, iPods, iPads or tablets, laptops, or other electronic devices?"

"No."

"Any cameras, recorders, other communications equipment or devices?"

"No."

"Good. All are barred from the park. If you're caught with any of those things, you'll be arrested."

"Arrested?" Mark couldn't or chose not to retain his surprise.

"It's essential to the guests, sir."

When it became obvious that's all the explanation he'd be getting, Mark said, "I see."

"Your luggage will be delivered to you after it's processed."

We had luggage? I hadn't even thought about luggage? Emily. She'd thought of it. Only God and she knew what would be in it. The wedding gown had been gorgeous, but I couldn't forget that ski-mask.

The guard looked from me to Mark. "You'll need to remove your watch, Mr. Green. There are lockers available for your use. Watches are not allowed in the park."

"No watches?" Matthew removed his watch and passed it to Barry. "Hang onto that for me, will you?"

"Sure thing." He stuffed it in his pocket without looking at it. Not once had his gaze left the guard.

"No, sir. No watches." The guard said. "There's a clock on Main Street in the village if you need to know the time for something. Most don't."

I slid Matthew a *what kind of place is this* look. He returned it seeming just as befuddled as me. "Anything else we need to know?" I asked.

The guard cleared his throat and answered

by rote. "Before you engage in conversation with any other guest, be sure to walk from your cottage to the bridge and read the message posted there. You'll pass the bridge on the way in, and that's not a suggestion. It's an important rule."

Extremely odd. "What's the sign posted on?"

"You'll see it. It's huge, bronze. Can't miss it at the foot of the bridge."

"What if we need something?" I asked.

"Oh, you can summon any member of the staff," he assured us. "It's just the other guests you can't interact with until after you read the sign."

"Okay." I didn't understand any of this, but hey, there were no mob thugs after us here and not interacting with anyone except Matthew suited me just fine. A couple days of isolation and maybe, just maybe I would think of him as Matthew and not Mark and of myself as Rose and not Daisy. That'd be a huge leap, but we both had to try hard to make it. A slip could wreck our deaths, and while Mr. Perini had managed them with an enviable flair, I sincerely doubt either of us were eager to go through it all again.

Barry cleared his throat. "I can't go into the park, so I'll leave you here. If you need anything, let the owners know."

"Who are the owners?" Mark asked.

"Darby and Miss Emily," Barry said. "One of them will contact us." He lifted a hand. "See you Sunday."

"Thanks." *Our Emily?* Couldn't be, could it? I had an uneasy feeling in the pit of my stomach, but I made myself turn and walk through the gate. Had we found sanctuary or entered the twilight zone?

As if mocking me for calling the question in my own mind, a horse-drawn carriage pulled forward and a jaunty little man with a white shock of hair and shiny brass buttons on his uniform stepped down to open its door. "Good evening, Mr. and Mrs. Green. I'm Speckles, your coachman." He gave us a wild-eyed, bizarre grin that proved impossible to interpret. "Welcome to Sampson Park."

CHAPTER 18

"What an odd place," Matthew said. "And coming from New Orleans, that's saying something."

New Orleans thrived on odd. It embraced it. I looked out the carriage window. "Sampson Park might be charming. We'll have to see it in the daylight." At night, the tree branches made for hovering, menacing silhouettes.

Matthew dropped his voice. "Are they bent on keeping people out, or us in?"

I'd wondered the same thing. "Either way works for me. We need the reprieve, and I intend to enjoy it."

The horse's hooves made little clopping noises on the compacted dirt. Speckles didn't seem to have any problem traveling the dark roads by the lantern-light. I wished the moon were brighter so I could see more of the area. What I could see was the silhouette of a huge old Victorian he'd pointed out as the "main house" and a lovely little gazebo near a lake. Beyond it we reached a fork in the road. The horse veered left.

"The village is beyond that rise," Speckles said. "The cottages are just north of it, near that copse of trees." He pointed to a cluster of lights shining through windows of small cottages. Candles or electricity? I had no idea. We drew closer, and the cottages came into a tighter view. They were painted pastel colors — green, pink, blue and yellow — and framed by lush foliage that separated all but two. Numbers six and five, if I'd counted correctly.

At number five, a man a few years younger than Matthew sat outside on the front porch steps. Behind him, two rockers stood empty and still. A little girl I nearly missed sat in the shadows under a huge oak tree, a pink teddy bear beside her on a colorful quilt. Odd time of night for a small child's pretend picnic. Even more odd, she didn't so much as glance our way as we passed by. "Is that child all right?" I asked Speckles.

"Ain't nobody here all right, Mrs. Green, but Gracie isn't in any danger."

His response should have comforted me. Instead, it made me edgy.

"Whoa." Speckles instructed the horse to stop.

It did with a little whinny, outside an arbored opening in a white picket fence. Climbing baby roses clung to the structure. Whether it was wood or wire, I couldn't tell.

"Here you are." Speckles jumped down. "Miss Sinclair manages the village. Anything you need, ask her."

"How?" Did every cottage have a telegraph? "There are no phones, right?"

"Absolutely not." He seemed affronted that she'd even ask. "The cottage has a bell pull, if you're desperate. If not, walk to the village. Clock's at center-square. Miss Sinclair's office is at ten o'clock, right between the jewelry store and the candle shop. There's a general store across the street at four o'clock." He climbed down to the ground. "Miss Darby thought you might be hungry. A late supper is warming in the oven. After this, you'll tend yourselves unless you'd rather not. Then just tell Miss Sinclair and meals will be delivered to you."

"That's thoughtful." And appreciated. My stomach had been growling since awakening the first time in the truck.

Speckles escorted Matthew and me through the gate and up a brick sidewalk to the wide front porch. We too had two white rockers and a swing, perfect for just being still. I'm ashamed to admit just how much that appealed. "Nice."

"Better all the time," Matthew agreed.

Speckles unlocked the door and passed Matthew the key. "Remember, no talking with any other guest before you read the sign at the bridge."

"Of course." Matthew nodded.

Speckles smiled, revealing a broad gap between his front teeth. "Congratulations on your marriage. Hope you two have lots of good years together."

Mr. Perini had told them we were newlyweds. "Thank you," Matthew said. I mimicked him, uncertain if sharing that tidbit of personal information was a good idea. Then again, at this point, I second-guessed everything. Except for Matthew. I didn't once second-guess him, which some would say made me crazy. But he'd passed the gut alarm and that twinkle was still in his eye. I trusted the gut alarm and that twinkle.

Speckles made his way back to the gated arbor. Just before reaching it, he paused on the brick sidewalk and looked back at us. "Oh, if you see a man shuffling around, pay him no mind. It's Mr. Nelson from two cottages down. He don't much like being around other people, so he usually only comes out at night."

"Thank you, Speckles." Considering our situation, anyone skulking around was not a pleasing thing, but it helped to know Mr. Nelson belonged here.

"And if there's any kind of trouble — likely won't be — yank your pull bell twice. That's the distress signal to alert our security force."

Security *force*? "That sounds a lot more serious than a single guard or two."

"We have a substantial security force, Mrs. Green. Miss Emily and Miss Darby take privacy seriously — and they take protecting guests even more seriously. Locals are aware of it, and even the kids don't mess around with the park. But every now and then we get a stray tourist. They tend to learn quick, though, so don't you worry about a thing. You're safe here."

"That's good to know," I said, clasping a hand at Matthew's wrist to prevent him from asking any questions. How I knew he was about to surprised us both.

I turned to walk inside.

"Wait!" Matthew scooped me into his arms. "I have to carry you, Rose. It's tradition."

I laughed and looped my arms around his neck.

We crossed the threshold, kissed, and the bedtime nerves began to set in. It wasn't that I was opposed to sleeping with Matthew. The idea actually appealed immensely. He was my husband, after all. I guess I just hadn't thought we would actually have the opportunity to sleep together for a while, and now that we did, I wasn't quite sure how to handle it. From the heat in his eyes, he had no such qualms.

I think I loved that.

Inside the cottage, he kissed me again. The heat between us threatened to consume, and I didn't feel exactly steady by the time his lips left mine. "I'm starving," I said the first coherent thought that raced through my mind.

"Me, too." Matthew smiled. "Let's check out the place, then eat."

Clearly his protective instincts had kicked in and to relax, he needed to assure himself the cottage was empty and get familiar with the lay of the land.

The cottage was charming. One bedroom, one bath, a kitchen and living room. It was about the size of my apartment in Biloxi, but so much lovelier. The furniture was gleaming cherry wood and it all matched, whereas mine was early garage sale and *a la carte* Good Will. The sofa and two chairs were oversized with thick, plump cushions that looked inviting, and would have been inviting even if I weren't exhausted. The entire cottage was decorated in a warm peach and soft cream. Soothing and calm colors, with splashes of bright blue and lime green to keep it interesting and still cozy.

Mark pulled two plates of food out of the oven and flipped it off. "There's a decent kitchen in here," he said.

From a chef, that rated as high praise. "Good." I opened the fridge and spotted a fresh pitcher of iced-tea and a bottle of wine. "Tea or wine?"

"Tea, I think," he said, putting the hot places on mats on the table. "Best to stay alert, just in case . . ."

I fixed the tea and Mark located the silverware, then we sat down to eat.

"This is nice," he said, looking a little sheepish. "After the storm, one of the things I hated most was eating alone."

"Mmm." I'd eaten alone most of my life; all of it, since Jackson had moved to Dallas. But I can't say I didn't like having company better, and I wish I could say, I didn't skip meals or eat in front of the TV just to avoid staring at empty chairs across the table. But I did. "I've done a lot of it, but I don't care for eating alone either."

He reached across the table and took my hand. "Another reason us marrying was a good idea."

I grunted and lifted my fork. The roast and parsley potatoes and candied carrots smelled wonderful and my stomach was in full "feed me" revolt. "I'm not so sure wanting someone to eat with should be a criteria for marrying, hon."

"I didn't say it was." Matthew speared a baby carrot. "I said it was another reason it was a good idea."

Another reason. "You have a list or something?"

"Not really." He bit into the carrot and slowly chewed. "Though I have thought about us a lot."

"Me, too." That seemed nothing short of a miracle considering everything else going on in their lives — and their deaths. "Do you think we're really safe from Marcello and Adriano out here?"

"Probably safer than anywhere else." Matthew sliced a bite of roast, chewed and a look of surprise flashed across his face.

"What?"

"It's good!" He frowned. "Melts in your mouth."

"You didn't expect that."

"Well, frankly, no. I didn't. But someone

here knows their way around the kitchen."

"It sure isn't me." I chuckled. "I promise I'll never make you eat anything I cook. Your stomach is definitely thanking me for that."

"Baby," he dropped his voice and added a throaty growl, "I'll cook for you anytime."

I smiled, flirted back, and we worked our way through an entirely pleasant meal.

"Full yet?"

"I need to grow half a foot to have more space." I pushed back my chair, took my dishes to the sink.

Mark brought his. "I'll wash and you dry."

"Okay." I stepped aside and grabbed a cloth. The sexual tension between us ramped up through our meal. I played as much a part in that as Matthew. It might sound silly, but every move he made, every tilt of his head, expression that crossed his face fascinated me. I've been in lust before, and I recognize it. But this was . . . different. More. Somehow . . . more.

"There's a loft upstairs with a second bed." He passed me a plate he'd rinsed of soap. "So are we going to use both or sleep together, Rose?"

I hadn't expected him to be that blunt. "What do you want to do?"

"You don't get to answer my question with a question. You get to be honest. Do you want to sleep with me?"

"Well, yeah. I assumed we would, since we married each other twice."

"That was different. You married me so I wouldn't be alone. You knew how much that bothers me." He looked me right in the eye. "Isn't that true?"

"Well, it is . . . and it isn't."

He paused washing the glasses. "I'm pretty good at interpreting, but you're going to have to explain that one to me."

I sucked in a deep breath, hoping some courage came with it — he might not want to sleep with me — but found I really didn't need extra courage. There was power in this honesty thing we had going on between us, and I felt confident no matter what I said, it'd work out fine. That was such a heady feeling for someone who'd worked to please people to stay put in good private homes and not be sent back to the group home. Deep inside, I knew Matthew wouldn't dump me, no matter what. That was priceless. "The first time, I married you because I knew you didn't want to be alone. At least, partly. The other part was that I didn't want to be alone either. All that's happened — is happening — it's unnerving, scary stuff."

"Can't argue with that. People out to kill

you and blowing up your business is pretty scary."

I bit back yet another apology, knowing he didn't want to hear one. "I figured anything to make it all easier for either of us was good. I mean, we were going to be dead within hours, so what could it hurt? And there is something special between us — at least, there is for me. And honestly, there's one more thing. If I had to die never realizing my dream —"

"You're talking about a home of your own, right?" he asked. "I just want to make sure I'm perfectly clear on all this."

I nodded. "If I wasn't going to realize that dream, I didn't want to die with nothing. You're a long way from nothing — this isn't coming out right." Why couldn't I adequately verbalize all this? It'd been so clear in my mind. "Marrying you was a good thing to do. It made me happy, it made you happy. That's two unhappy people happy and that's enough."

He leaned back against the kitchen counter and folded the dishcloth. "That was the first time. What about the second time?"

"I wasn't finished." Flustered, I paused to get a grip on myself. This was hard. Putting all these feelings I've either never had or buried so deep I was ignorant of them into words. The fact is you can speculate on what you're missing. You can dream about it, fantasize it, and let your imagination go wild with the possibilities. But you can't miss the reality you've never had. What you have had is your normal. But now reality was normal, and I couldn't be ignorant anymore. I knew exactly what I was missing — and reality held the promise of so much more. I had to be out of my mind because I wanted more. I wanted it all. Every single atom. Never, not once in my whole life, had I dared to want it all. Not until now. And to want it now terrified me. To rely on someone else for anything . . . ? Definitely out of my mind.

But was I? I didn't want it all with anyone. I wanted it all with Matthew. My Matthew. And that didn't seem a bit crazy. It seemed . . . right.

"I'm sorry I interrupted," he said, clearly concerned about my long silence. "Just tell me you don't regret marrying me the first or the second time. I see you're wrestling with something in there." He tapped the side of his head.

"I don't regret marrying you either time," I choked out. "But my reasons for marrying you the second time were different." I pushed myself to reveal my thoughts, bent on keeping my no-secret policy intact. "The second time, I married you because —"

"You didn't want to start over alone either. Or to try to keep an eye out for danger without backup."

"No, not exactly," I said. "Well, maybe in part, but . . . not really. I have to say though, that's all logical. It just didn't occur to me at the time."

That remark engaged his curiosity. "So what did occur to you at the time?"

"Not one logical thing." Even to her that sounded strange.

"Rose." He crossed his arms. "You're evading. Don't do that to me, or to us. Not on this."

It mattered to him. Really mattered. I stilled and turned to him. "I was, and I'm sorry. I'm, um, not used to talking to anyone about things that cut close to the bone."

"I cut close to your bones?"

He didn't seem unhappy about that. "Yes, I find that you do. Well, my feelings for you do." He smiled, and that melted something inside me. He wouldn't use my vulnerability as a weapon against me. That, I realized, had been my real fear. It had happened before, and it hadn't been an easy lesson. "The fact is, I didn't want to lose you." I let him see the truth in my eyes. "I just . . . I didn't want to lose you."

He stepped closer and wrapped me in his arms. His breath warmed my face. "I didn't want to lose you, either, Rose. Not then, and not now." He nuzzled my neck. "Not ever."

It wasn't anything as fickle as love, but it was a loving thing for a husband to say to his wife. And the orphan inside the wife who had been forced to stand alone for a lifetime clung to it. Clung to him. Little shivers danced on my skin. "I guess that means we're sleeping in one bed."

"I vote yes." He looked down at me, let me see the desire in his eyes. "You okay with it?"

I smiled and curled my arms around his neck. "Saves me a midnight trip to join you in the loft . . ."

CHAPTER 19

By the next morning, everything had changed. Okay, so call me naïve. I thought things would be, you know, normal, between Matthew and me in bed, but there was nothing normal or typical or whatever else you want to call it about any of it. Relations between a woman and her husband are private, of course, but I'll tell you this much: If ever again, someone tells me that sex is purely physical and there's no difference between having sex and making love, I'm telling you from firsthand experience that they're either ignorant or lying or they have the soul of a dead stump. The two aren't even in the same stratosphere — and that's all I have to say about that specifically.

It's enough to say openly that I had an amazing night with an amazing man, and that I have a lifetime of more amazing nights with that amazing man to look forward to . . . well, pardon me while pinch myself.

Let's just say that this morning, I am certain Matthew didn't marry me to be doubly sure the legalities of his assets were secure. I'm also certain he didn't marry me to avoid starting over alone. And I'm totally and completely confident that he married me because . . . well, I'm not sure why exactly, but so far, I sure like being married to him. Today, I am one happy bride.

It's more than I've had before, and considering our situation, it's important to be happy when an opportunity arises. Who knows if another will come along? Or when that might be?

Embrace the moment.

That's the thing. I've never lived like that. By necessity, I've rolled with the flow. But embracing the moment and reveling in it, just loving it? That's new to me.

Loving it.

Was this love?

I wonder. It's possible. Is it probable? Who knows? I sure don't. I have absolutely no frame of reference outside of loving Jackson and Lester, but that's totally different. Maybe this is love . . . or something like it.

I don't know. And this morning, I don't care. Matthew hasn't stopped smiling. He's thoughtful and tender and, when he looks at me, that twinkle in his eye swears there's no one else he'd rather be with and nowhere else he'd rather be. Given the baggage I brought with me, by anyone's standards, that's nothing short of a miracle.

After breakfast, we walked down to the bridge, and Speckles hadn't been kidding. It was impossible to miss the bronze. Rather than a sign, it was a monument that stood over eight feet tall and stretched at least an arm-span wide.

"Boy, they don't want you to miss it." Matthew craned back his neck and stared up to its top.

I stopped beside him, and he reached for my hand. Standing linked together before the bronze, I read the words chiseled into its flat face:

Life shapes and defines us. When experiences are positive, we embrace them. When they are not, we bury them, shutter, and become whole. But little shuttered remains shuttered. Past secrets surface and torment us. We try but fail to break free, and being imprisoned steals our present and future.

Some so tortured seek traditional help, gain new insights and wisdom, and successfully put the past to rest. Some die never realizing their potential, robbed of their destinies and peace. Others cobble together a life, but remain haunted by their pasts and their unrealized dreams.

And still there are others. Those deemed helpless and hopeless, condemned to stumble forever through their darkest night.

These are the lost souls. Abandoned and forgotten, they are left by all to remain lost with their misery. Or so it was . . .

But it is no more. An ordinary woman refused to forget the Lost. Though it cost her mightily, she welcomed them here, met their challenges and her own, and she discovered an extraordinary thing:

Pasts may be horrific. Trials may be incredibly risky and dangerous and outcomes riddled with uncertainties, but with faith all things are possible, and with God no one is ever truly lost, without hope or help, or forgotten.

Embracing that discovery, she became the bridge between the Lost and these truths. That revealed another truth.

We are all someone's bridge.

And that is the secret of secrets at Sampson Park.

"Powerful." Matthew covered our clasped hands with his free one. "But what exactly does it mean?" He looked from the bronze to me. "Are they saying that everyone here is beyond conventional help, so they're all mental cases but someone else here can still be their bridge?" He glanced at me. "I'm not clear."

Standing there with our hands linked, I felt clear, but not on the bronze. On my deep connection with him. My heart seemed full. Content. It wasn't that I was unhappy alone. Being alone was . . . normal. I didn't know anything different. Now I would, so I paused and whispered a little prayer. Down to the marrow of my bones, I felt certain that this special connection was the fruition of the bond I'd sensed on meeting him for the first time in his office. It strengthened when he awakened me on the bench outside the cathedral, and strengthened again many times in the weeks after, but last night . . . Lying in his arms, replete and awed and humbled and deeply touched by our love-making, I knew that bond would not be breached. It was more than I'd known, and my heart promised I'd feel it far longer than a season. This man would be with me for life.

If Mr. Perini sent us here because he thought we were crazy, fine. I want more crazy. I think I need more of it. Desperately. For the first time in my life, when I look into a man's face, I know I matter. I count. I am special. Significant. Important. Me, the unwanted orphan left at the curb like waste. The disposable one no one cared if lived or died.

That aroused strong emotions and nothing in them ranked as crazy. The success of Sampson Park evidenced throughout the village had nothing to do with magic and everything to do with reaching out, having faith in people, and in never giving up. There's a special power in faith and compassion, in caring and refusing to allow anyone to feel forgotten or disconnected from everyone else. I'd felt forgotten, but I think now, I hadn't been. I just had to grow into the knowing I'd been remembered all along.

"Have you puzzled through it yet?" Mark asked.

"Working on it." Sunlight slanted across the monument and reflected with shiny sparkles. "I think it means everyone here *isn't* crazy. They're somehow . . . broken. Wounded works better. Yeah, wounded." I looked from the huge bronze to Matthew. "For whatever reason, they haven't been able to work through their problems in the usual ways, so people have given up on them. But the people at Sampson Park don't give up and they help them in other ways."

"By being their bridge."

I nodded.

"Admirable, but there's also a warning in this message."

"What warning?" I didn't track a warning.

"If someone acts unstable, it's because they probably are." He shrugged. "Just so we know — though it seems odd to put a monument to it at the foot of the bridge."

I toed the soft gravel and looked at the bright pink blossoms clustered on the other side of the wooden bridge. "Maybe the people who read it assume that because they're reading it, they're not lost and it applies to everyone else here, but not to them."

"Could be." Matthew studied my eyes. "You're not saying we're lost, are you?"

I smiled. "Actually, I think I've spent a lot of my life lost, but I'm not lost now."

He dragged a fingertip along my jaw. "I hope I have something to do with that."

"You have a lot to do with that."

He paused a moment and let my admission sink in and then let his gaze roam the words on the bronze, as if somehow seeing them differently. "I've been more content since you walked into my restaurant than I've been since Hurricane Katrina, Rose."

I squeezed his hand. He too had trouble defining us. I wish I could say our relationship was simple. That it could be simple.

But in a way, we were wounded. Oh, not like the people here, but wounded by life all the same. Wounds made simple things complex, but not hopeless. And, to be honest, this morning I felt more hopeful than I had since my stint outside the Piggly Wiggly. That these people, according to the monument, were hopeless hurt my heart.

"You look so sad."

"It is sad. People being lost. Others giving up on them."

"The *she* in Sampson Park — whoever she is, or was — didn't give up on them," Matthew reminded me. "She fought for them. I think that's a hopeful thing, and I'll bet they do, too." He brushed a wisp of hair back from my face. "And just so you know, Rose. I'll never give up on you."

My heart felt squeezed, and tears I didn't expect burned my eyes. I blinked them back, looked up at him, and smiled. Someone believing in you . . . what a potent thing. What an amazing and powerful, potent thing. Breathless, I said, "You are so good for me."

He kissed me. "You're good for me, too."

That night, I lay beside Matthew certain the words on the bronze had been etched not only into my mind but also into my heart.

Long before we were ready for it, Saturday night came, and when Matthew and I settled in to sleep, that we'd be returning to the funeral home for our services tomorrow weighed heavy on my mind. I would miss Sampson Park. In just days, it had become a special place that I would cherish forever.

The absence of modern conveniences like phones and computers hadn't bothered us a bit. Instead we'd had a picnic by the lake, walked for hours and hours through the woods and talked endlessly about everything and nothing. A little girl living two cottages down, Gracie, seemed to always be watching for someone, but she refused to say for whom. Matthew and I speculated on that a bit, and on the man in the cottage beyond who seemed to watch over her, but truthfully, Matthew and I were so caught up in each other, we didn't worry overly about anything, though I suspect whoever it is Gracie waits for is someone very important to her. I freely admit I have issues with kids left waiting, so I'd spoken to Gracie's aunt Jenny. She assured me that Gracie was fine. Since Jenny designs jewelry and is well-respected in the Park, I let my mind rest easy on Gracie and her waiting.

Matthew and I had visited the village and its shops several times. We bought hand-cranked home-made ice-cream and funnel cakes, watched old-timers teach young ones how to play horseshoes, and attended a floral show where a ten-year-old boy escorted by Speckles, won Best in Show for his *Darby* Rose, named after the youngest owner of Sampson Park. Over cherry snow-cones, I had a confusing but compelling conversation with Gracie and her favorite teddy bear, Miss Dixie. The bear spoke more than the child.

She and her aunt had definitely come to Sampson Park for the child. I had no doubt about that.

Scooting over the sheets, I snuggled the already sleeping Matthew. When his arm came up to embrace me and he pulled me to him, I sighed, content. Even asleep, he wanted me close.

Sometimes life is good. So sweet and so good . . .

Sometimes life is sweet and good . . . and then reality crashes down around your ears.

Reality struck us at exactly three in the morning. It took the form of someone banging on the cottage door.

Matthew dragged on his pants and went

to answer it. "Lester? Emily?"

His surprise carried to me in the bedroom. What were they doing here? My shock fell to fear. Whatever the reason, it couldn't be good. I jumped up and slipped into a t-shirt and jeans, then joined them all in the living room.

Matthew stood in the kitchen, putting on a pot of coffee, and Lester and Emily were settling into seats at the kitchen table.

"Hey." I walked in. "Is everything all right?"

Lester motioned for me to sit down.

I pulled out an empty seat at the table, and Matthew sat down in the fourth chair. We didn't ask again, just waited.

Lester looked at me and then at Matthew. "Married life's agreeing with you two."

"Of course," Matthew said.

I smiled. "Very much so, Lester. You can stop your worrying."

"Sampson Park's a good choice. Emily and me always stay here whenever we can."

"You've been here the whole time?"

He nodded. "We got here before you two but stayed out of the way, what with it being your honeymoon and all." He grunted. "Figured you two wanted to be married bad to get hitched in the morgue."

"Funeral home. Morgue," I said. "When

you get down to it, what's the difference? We wanted to marry and seized the moment. That's all that matters."

"I wanted to be sure she didn't bolt on me, Lester. Couldn't let a gem like her get away." Matthew winked at me, then poured coffee and set a cup before me and Emily, and then put one on the table before Lester. "If you've been here the whole time we have, then why are you dropping in on us at three in the morning?" Matthew retrieved his own cup, then returned to his seat.

"Sorry as I am to say it," his worry came through in his shuddery voice, "there's been a development."

That disclosure sent a chill up my backbone I wouldn't soon be forgetting. "What kind of development?" With Lester, one never safely assumed anything.

"It ain't just the minions coming after you two," Emily said. "That's a big development."

"What is she talking about, Lester?" Matthew asked.

"Marcello *and* Adriano — not just their goons, but them. They showed up at Dixie General Hospital, demanding to see your bodies."

"Paul expected that." I finger tapped my cup. "He told us he did."

"Well, he was right." Lester bristled. "The hospital told them the bodies had already been moved to the funeral home."

My heart thundered and fear slithered through my whole body. "They went to Mr. Perini's?" He suspected they would and sent us here. He said he and Barry could handle them. Had they? "Was he hurt?"

"If you'll hush a minute, I'll tell you, Dais— Rose Matthews." Lester took a swallow of coffee and his cup hit the table with a healthy *thunk*. "They went to Paul's *together* — Marcello and Adriano's men, I mean." Lester looked from me to Matthew. "*Together,* if you can believe it. Rival families at war, and they're working together to find you two." Lester was stunned, pure and simple. "They insisted on seeing Daisy's body. Actually, the Adrianos insisted on seeing Daisy's body. The Marcellos insisted on seeing both your bodies."

"Figures," Matthew said. "I — um, Mark went to school with Edward."

"Well, that makes sense, then," Lester said. "Paul refused, of course. Told 'em he would lose his license if he did it without next-of-kin permission."

"So Mr. Perini wasn't hurt, then?" I asked specifically, anxious and needing to be sure.

If he'd been hurt, I'd never forgive myself. Never.

"Nope, not then."

"He was hurt later?" I couldn't keep the squeal out of my voice.

Mark reached over and covered my hand on the table with his. "Calm down, Rose. Mr. Perini's fine or we'd already be moving."

Lester looked happy with that deduction, and at seeing Matthew being protective of me. "Matthew's right. Paul ain't hurt, but we got plenty trouble. Plenty *other* trouble." He looked from Emily to me.

"For pity's sake, Lester, spit it out. My pet's about to hyperventilate."

"I'm getting there, Em. Give a man a minute." He looked to me. "Detective Keller and Special Agent Johnson are trying to get court orders."

"For what?" Matthew asked.

"To take possession of the bodies."

"Why?" I asked, getting a grip on my breathing. "Can they do that?"

"Dexter Devlin says no. But they can cause complications, tying things up and slowing them down," Emily interjected. "Annoying men. Why they can't just leave the dead alone to rest in peace, I have no idea."

Lester calmed her, too, with a gentle hand. "Point is, we can't stall the court orders long. They're wanting their own ME to examine the bodies since Dixie's ME is also its Coroner. They took exception to that, though it's the case in most small towns around. I don't get it."

"It doesn't have anything to do with the ME," Matthew said. "They want leverage with Marcello and Adriano. That's what they're after — and them using the dead to get it really bothers me."

Lester leaned forward at the table, circling his hands on his cup. "Well, Paul ain't too happy about it, but Dexter says he's got the authorities under control. What he can't control is Marcello and Adriano. They make their own laws and rules."

"Them teaming up doesn't make sense to me," I said. "If my enemy killed my son, I sure wouldn't be buddying up with him on anything."

"That's the development — or the start of it," Lester said. "After Paul refused to let them see your bodies, they left peaceable enough. That happened yesterday morning."

"They came back earlier tonight," Matthew speculated. His hand stilled on his spoon. "Is that what's happened?"

"They came back last night." Lester confirmed it.

I couldn't stand it another second. "Lester, did they or did they not hurt Mr. Perini?"

"Or Barry?" Matthew added.

Heaven help me, I'd forgotten all about Barry! How could I do that? My stomach roiled and I pressed a hand to it to calm it down.

Emily stiffened and that worried me more.

"They ain't hurt." Lester grunted. "Paul and Barry had a trap waiting for 'em." A light of pure excitement burned in Lester's eyes. "Soon as they tried busting into the funeral home, Barry snagged 'em up in a net and hoisted 'em twenty feet straight up in the air." He swung a hand skyward.

"Oh, my gosh. You're kidding me." The image of those two cutthroats dangling in a net from a tree . . . "They must have been furious."

"Oh, they're furious all right, but it wasn't Marcello and Adriano what got snagged, Rose. One of the men, we didn't know. But the other one was Lou Boudin."

Edward's shooter. "He's here, too?" I couldn't believe it.

"Paul left 'em hanging until the sheriff arrived. He didn't insist they be arrested. Ain't sure I agree with that, but when a bear's snarling ain't no time to stick a thorn in his paw. We figured since Boudin's with Adriano then the other one's gotta be working for Marcello. Paul told the sheriff he could let 'em go, provided they kept their distance 'til the funerals. They could all see you both then with their own eyes."

My shock doubled. Tripled. And then shot straight off the chart. "He told them, *what?*"

"I can't believe Paul invited them to our funerals to see our bodies." Matthew groaned. "How does he plan to pull that off?"

"Beats me. Truly does," Lester said with a shrug. "But the man said to trust him, and we all agreed, so I guess we gotta do it."

I looked around the table from one nervous face to another. "So if we're trusting him on that and on his handling of this crisis, then why are you here at three in the morning?"

Lester gave me an owl-eyed look, then snapped to on the matter. "They've got folks watching the funeral home. All of 'em, on both sides of the law. Paul says I gotta get you two back there right now, if not sooner."

"Lester," I softened my voice and tried to calm down. "If all of them have spies watching the funeral home, then how are we supposed to get back there?"

"Emily got herself killed last night — like you did."

"Same curve," Emily said. "People die out there all the time, so no one thought a thing of it."

"Why did you have to die?" I asked.

Her cheeks flushed and she dropped her gaze. "I went back to Dixie to take care of a little business and I made a mistake. I got spotted." She lifted her hands. "Had no choice but to die so Paul took care of it."

"That's some mistake," Matthew said.

"Sure was." Her face brightened. "But at least now they think I'm cooling my heels at the morgue, so all is well again."

"They?" I asked. Who spotted Emily, and why was that a bad thing?

"Actually, he." Emily frowned. "Victor Marcello."

My jaw went lax. "You know him, too?"

"I did at one time." She looked away. "A long, long time ago."

"Then why is him spotting you now worrisome enough that you had to die?"

She cocked her head. "Time don't change some things, pet. That's just the truth of it."

Clearly, she didn't want to get specific or even to discuss it. I didn't like it, but I liked the sadness in her eyes even less, so I respected her choice and didn't ask the questions rapid-firing through my mind. "Well, if Mr. Perini wants us back in a hurry, we'd better go." I stood up. "Wait." The logistics hit me. "How are we all supposed to get where we're supposed to be?" Us to Mr. Perini's, Emily to the morgue, and Lester at only heaven knows where and none of us had transportation.

Lester hiked a bony shoulder and pushed out of his chair. "All I can tell you is I'm to take you to a drop-off point," he said to Emily, "and the two of you to another one." His chair's legs lightly scraped the floor. "When Paul's moving Emily from the morgue to the funeral home, you two will be hooking up with the hearse."

Matthew rolled his gaze ceiling-ward. "I can't believe the coroner goes along with all this."

"Course you can." Lester gathered the cups and washed them at the sink. "You seen it happen yourself."

The lilt in his voice caught my ear. Pure mischief. "Wrong question, Matthew."

"What's the right question?"

I tilted my head. "*Why* does the Coroner put up with all this?"

Lester smiled.

"What?" Mark asked, clearly still not following.

I touched Mark's arm. "I suspect he's been dead before too, and I also suspect Mr. Perini helped him start over in Dixie."

"Ah . . ." Matthew nodded. "That would make sense then, wouldn't it?"

"It would." Lester checked his watch. "Hate it for you kids, but the honeymoon's over. We got less than sixty minutes to get out to the drop-off point."

"What if Mr. Perini's being watched, too?" Matthew hitched his jeans.

"Beats me." Lester shrugged. "Trust he's got it all worked out."

"But what if —"

"Rose, Lester knows what we know. We have to trust the man," Matthew said. "Mr. Perini's gotten us this far. Let's have a little faith."

"All right. But this trusting business is new to me, you know?"

"I know, and you're doing better at it than I expected." Matthew clasped my arm, gave it a little squeeze.

"You really think so?" I looked up at him. "I'm trying, but it's hard. I've been alone and in control for a long time."

"Spitwads and fudgesicles," Lester fussed. "Emily, grab Rose's stuff. She's of a mind to jaw a while and we gotta hurry."

I frowned at Lester and gathered my own things.

Within minutes, we headed out the door and toward a waiting carriage. Looking smart in his uniform, Speckles stood holding its door.

He smiled as broadly as if it were mid-afternoon. "Watch your step, please."

When we were seated in the carriage, Speckles cracked the reins, and the familiar clopping of horse's hooves moved us away from the village and toward the bridge to the main gate.

"So what did you think of Sampson Park?" Lester asked me.

I loved it here. Simple, peaceful. Interesting. "It's a wonderful place."

"Some say it's magical, though I ain't seen that side of it myself."

"In a way, maybe it is, Lester." I looked to a house where a single light burned. "Broken people heal here. I met a little girl in the woods, and she told me fascinating stories. I just wish . . ."

"What?" he asked.

"She lives in a cottage a couple doors down, and she carries this teddy bear, Miss Dixie, all the time."

"Ah," Lester said. "Miss Dixie is sad, eh?"

"The little girl is sad. Miss Dixie is a well-adjusted chatterbox."

Matthew added his perspective. "The child's father died, but she's not accepting it. That's why she's here."

Her father. That's who she watched for all the time. My heart shattered and crumbled. "How'd you know that?" I asked Mark. Neither Gracie nor Miss Dixie had said anything about Gracie's dad.

"The gardener guy in the cottage on the other side of them told me."

"Brad Nelson," I supplied his name.

"Seems you two met a lot of people here." Lester looked at Emily, then at Mark. "I'm not sure that's wise."

"Rose and Matthew met a lot of people here. Ones who are staying here. We avoided Outsiders."

"Glad to hear that." Lester nodded.

"So where do you two stay when you're here?"

Emily put a staying hand on Lester's thigh. "At the Main House."

In minutes, we passed that Main House, and Speckles halted the horses at the gate. I had mixed emotions about leaving. Our time here had been carefree. I wasn't eager to step back into the chaos.

The guard appeared and asked about

lockers and cell phones or any other contraband we had placed in storage, we declared we had none and he nodded, giving us permission to exit.

Mark reached for my hand, seemingly as reluctant as me to leave our idyllic time behind.

"I loved it here, too," I said. "With you."

"You always know exactly what's on my mind."

I wished that were true. If I did, I'd know whether or not my husband loved me. Oh, he respected me, cared for me, was protective of me. But none of that meant he loved me now, or that he would ever love me. Sooner or later, I'd work up the guts to just ask him, but it wouldn't be now. Not because I'd be scared of him saying he didn't. Because if he turned around and asked the same question of me, I wouldn't be able to answer him. What I think and what I know are two different things.

What most worried me was that, being clueless about love, how could I ever know with certainty if I was in it?

Having no answer to that generational question, I watched Emily step away from us. "I'll see you soon."

She walked back through the gate and Speckles helped her into the carriage. I slid into Lester's black Lexus and buckled up, confused that she wouldn't be riding along at least on this part of the return trip. "Why isn't she coming with us?"

"She needs to get back sooner."

"So she's taking a carriage?" Lester logic strikes again.

"Yep." He grinned. "To the helicopter, waiting for her."

I grunted. "Not inside Sampson Park it isn't."

"No, not inside Sampson Park."

Lester seemed fine with whatever was going on, so I took my cue from him and hushed. It wasn't as if I needed to borrow trouble to find any. We had plenty. With all the players gathered in Dixie, this was not going to be a pleasant funeral — if we lived long enough to make it to it.

At the moment, it seemed impossible that Mr. Perini would be able to pull off getting us back into the funeral home and that, in my book, made our survival odds pretty iffy . . .

The bronze monument at the foot of the bridge flashed through my mind. Its words replayed in my mind.

With faith, all things are possible.

I don't know how Mr. Perini will do this, but I decided to believe he will.

And again I heard the secret of secrets of Sampson Park.

We're all someone's bridge.

Chapter 20

We arrived in Dixie before sunrise.

Lester pulled into a service station, then drove around back. What was he doing? "Lester, that's a car wash. You're getting your car washed at four-thirty in the morning?"

"Yep." He drove in. The washing and drying began, thumping those heavy ragged strips against the car. It inched forward and a healthy spray started. Wax. "Get out."

"What?" Matthew and I asked simultaneously.

Lester looked back at Matthew and me. "Get out. Walk straight through that door and get into the hearse. Move it now, or we'll be too late."

"The machine is still spraying hot wax, Lester." I stated the obvious.

"Rose Green, move it!"

We stepped into the spray, got soaked with hot wax, then angled through the side door.

On the other side, the hearse door stood open. Its lights were on and its engine running. I guess not that many people want to steal a hearse.

Jumping inside, I rolled toward the center and bumped a half-zipped body bag. "Sorry, Emily."

"No problem. Zip me up, will you?" she asked. I did, and felt Matthew graze my back. He pulled the door shut.

Barry came out of the little store to the right with a fountain drink in his hand. He got in and closed his door, then buckled his safety belt. "Everybody here?"

"We're here," Emily said.

"You okay, Miss Emily?" Barry asked her, plopping his cup into a holder.

"Fine," she said. "Dying's a snap, hon. It's living that's hard."

"Amen, ma'am." He hit the gas and pulled the hearse into the street. "You two get into the bags back there, just in case."

We helped each other, and Matthew zipped me in. "How will you get yours zipped?"

"I'm fine, Rose. Don't worry."

Minutes later, Barry asked, "You watching, Matthew?"

"Oh, yeah."

"We being followed?" Emily asked.

Barry responded before Matthew could. "Three cars full of them, best I can tell."

"Three?" I lay stunned. "What if they saw —"

"They didn't." Matthew patted my thigh. "They would've stopped us already."

How could he be sure of that?

"They can't see through brick walls, honey," he added, obviously sensing my skepticism. "For the moment, we're fine. Just relax and remember you're dead . . ."

By the time we reached the funeral home, I was having muscle spasms all over my body. I'd gotten used to being relaxed at Sampson Park and somehow I'd forgotten about these enemies, but now we were back and so were they. With a vengeance.

Pulling around to the back of Mr. Perini's funeral home, Barry stopped on the crunchy gravel. Soon the sounds of the broad door opening on the huge metal building filled the vehicle. When the sound stopped, Barry pulled inside and cut the engine. The big door came down again. "Stay put, until I'm sure we're clear."

A door sounded — likely the one from the breezeway between the funeral home and the metal building — and then footfalls. "Barry, you have them all?"

"Yes, sir, Mr. Perini." Barry unzipped our bags.

"Ah, good. All will soon be well," Mr. Perini said, a body bag in his hand.

"That it?" Barry asked nodding toward that body bag.

"Yep." He passed it over to Barry.

"Good. It's the only one that stands a chance of being big enough for all three of them."

Now I understood. We were going to be packed into one bag like sardines for transport. Grateful it was just for the short ride, I bit my tongue, hoping it wouldn't be hard on Emily.

Barry and Mr. Perini spread the bag on a gurney. Lester held the foot of it.

Matthew climbed on and lay flat on his back. "Come on, Rose."

I climbed up and took my place and motioned to Emily. "Ready."

"Oh, Lester, there's no dignity in a woman my age crawling around like this."

He chuckled. "There's dignity in life, Em. Come on now. You can do it."

Her elbow smacked me in the ribs. I let out a heartfelt "Oomph."

"You okay, pet? I'm so sorry."

"I'm fine."

Behind me, I felt Matthew grinning.

"She's sliding!"

Matthew's arms shot up and wrapped my sides. He grabbed fists full of the back of Emily's blouse. Lester, Barry and Mr. Perini stepped closer and helped Emily get balanced. It took us all but soon we lay stacked like a sandwich on the gurney.

"I think I got the best of this," Emily said. "Am I squashing you, pet?"

"No, I'm fine. Matthew, you okay?"

"Great."

I smiled. "This is as good as it's going to get, Mr. Perini."

Emily swayed. "Oh, dear. Don't let me fall off here."

Barry stepped to the other side of the gurney. "I've got you, Miss Emily."

"I've got you, too," I told her, feeling like the stuffing of an Oreo cookie. "I'm going to hold tight until we're off this thing. We're not going to fall."

"You could slide, too."

"Matthew can't slide, and he's got me." I tightened my grip on her. "And I've got you. We're going to be fine." *We're all someone's bridge.*

"Mr. Perini, if you've got a compassionate bone in your body . . ." Matthew didn't finish.

"I know, son. I'm hurrying." He worked

up the zipper. "It's tight, but we made it. Barry, let's roll."

The gurney wheels began moving and before the guy's voices stopped echoing to signal they'd entered the breezeway, Barry uttered a deep, "Uh-oh."

I stiffened. So did Matthew and Emily. The wheels kept rolling so I had no idea what that "Uh-oh" meant, but I didn't like it.

The floor surface changed and the ride smoothed out and then changed again. We were inside the funeral home.

"What are you doing back here?" Mr. Perini asked someone not yet identified.

"There was no one at the desk," a man said. "Is that Emily?"

Emily turned wooden and Matthew tensed all over. "Marcello," he whispered at my ear.

"It is," Mr. Perini told Marcello. "And like I told your men, you can't see her without a next-of-kin permission."

"You know I can't get one," Marcello grumbled. "Darby won't let me anywhere near Sampson Park, and she never sticks her head out of that no-man's land she's built."

Emily was the same Emily who owned Sampson Park? I couldn't believe it. But she needed cataract surgery. She had no money. Whoever owned Sampson Park clearly had bucketsful of money.

"I'm truly sorry, Mr. Marcello," Paul said. "Our families go back a long way."

"To Sicily."

"Yes, and you know for that reason, I would help you if I could. I do understand your issue, and I offer my condolences on the loss of your son."

"Edward was a good boy."

"I'm sure he was."

"He loved to eat. Good food, not trash. Good food." Victor Marcello's voice cracked. "Too many young people today don't appreciate good food."

"You're welcome to come back for the service."

"I'll be here for Daisy and Mark. My Edward was fond of Mark Jensen. He didn't know Daisy."

"She had no family," Mr. Perini said, knowing full well about Jackson.

"She had a brother," Marcello corrected him. "Just the two of them. No mama or papa. Had to be hard for them, growing up with nobody."

"I'm sure it was," Mr. Perini said. "Well, we'll see you at the service. I have to get the last preparations done." He gave the gurney a little push and the wheels began rolling.

"Of course." A pause, then Marcello added, "I'm buying this funeral home, Paul."

"It's not for sale."

"Oh, you'll sell it to me."

"No, Victor, I won't." The gurney stopped rolling. "I'm going to have to ask you to leave now so I can get on with my work."

"Name your price."

"You can't afford it." Mr. Perini paused, "Barry, get Emily into the prep room, will you?"

Barry rolled us inside and closed the door. We could still hear every word spoken in the hallway.

"Don't ignore me, Paul."

"I'm not ignoring you, I'm simply not interested in selling my funeral home."

"I want to see her body."

"Emily's?"

"If that's what it takes to see Daisy Grant's. She's the only witness to my son's murder."

"She was the only witness. She's dead, Victor. You can see her body at the funeral. It's only hours away."

"No," he insisted. "I want to see it now."

"I can't do that."

"You can and will."

"Mr. Marcello," Mr. Perini clipped his

tone, chilled it to icy chips of sound that sent chills up and down my spine. "I know you're upset at your loss, and I've been patient with you because of it. I could have had your men arrested and didn't do it out of respect. But my patience is wearing thin and —"

"Your patience is of no consequence to me." Marcello softened his tone. "You know my family, Paul, but I wonder, do you know me, and who I am?"

"I do."

Marcello's tone deepened, harsh and unrelenting and rife with a lethal warning. "Then you know I can crush you — and unless you let me see Daisy Grant's body now, I will."

"Go ahead," Mr. Perini told him. "But before you do, let me ask you a question."

"What?"

"Do you know me, and who I am?"

Marcello hesitated. "No, I guess not."

"I advise you to find out before you threaten me again," Mr. Perini warned him, sounding even more deadly than Marcello. "Fair notice. As a professional courtesy and out of respect for your family and your grief, I let you and your men off easy. But if you persist being disrespectful to me, I'll take off the gloves. If I do, Mr. Marcello, it will not end well for you or your family."

"Don't you dare talk to me like that."

"I dare," Mr. Perini said. "And I have the family to back it up." He dropped his voice, cooled the heat from it. "Now, I'd prefer to remain on a friendly footing with you and yours, but if you insist on hostility, well, I'm prepared to deal with that, too."

"Who is your family?" Marcello asked.

Barry coughed, blocking us from hearing Mr. Perini's answer. He spoke it, but the sound came through the closed door garbled and muffled.

I wasn't sorry about that. Their entire conversation struck me as menacing, and I really didn't need more menacing, though I did wonder how was Emily connected to Victor Marcello? I couldn't figure that out. He definitely knew her and he had strong feelings for her; that was evident in what he said and she'd had to die because he'd spotted her.

The outer door closed and soon Mr. Perini came into the prep room then unzipped the bag. "I'm sorry for the delay. Is everyone all right?" He reached for Emily and helped her to the floor.

"I'm fine." She shuddered, stood and smoothed her skirt. "That man totally creeps me out. He didn't give Darby a hard time, did he?"

"No. He never got past the gate guard."

Relief washed her face. "Thank goodness."

I slid down and then Matthew stood up. "Emily, do you have anything to do with Sampson Park?"

Silence.

"You own it. She owns it," Matthew told me. "She's the *she* in the bronze."

I glanced over at her. "Is that the truth?"

No answer.

"Emily, how can you own all of Sampson Park and not be able to afford cataract surgery?" I asked, totally bewildered. I shot a charged look at Lester. "I don't understand."

"I never said that," Emily insisted. "I never said I couldn't afford surgery."

"Lester did. Several times."

"Well, there you have it, then." Emily dismissed that as if it meant nothing.

"Wait a minute." I looked at Lester, then back at Emily. "Are you saying Lester lied to me?"

"Absolutely not." She straightened her shoulders and hiked her chin. "He told you exactly what he was supposed to tell you. We all have wounds, Pet. Mine just walked out of here a few minutes ago."

"Victor Marcello." I still didn't get their

connection, and staring straight at two brass trimmed, glass coffins for a long minute didn't make it a bit more clear.

"We were married . . . in another life." That sadness I'd seen earlier returned to her eyes. "He's having a hard time accepting I would rather live in a guarded fortress — Sampson Park — than be married to him." She sniffed. "Imagine what he'd be like if he knew I'd rather be dead than to return to him."

It took me a long moment to process and recover from that bit of news. "You were married to Victor Marcello . . . ?"

"Were you Edward's mother?" Matthew got the words out before I could.

"No. She was Victor's second — or maybe his third — wife's child. Not mine. I was his first wife. It was a very long time ago."

"Too much information!" Mr. Perini interrupted then cleared his throat. "Let it go, Rose, please. It upsets Emily and there's nothing to be gained from discussing it."

"I'm sorry. I just . . ."

"You were confused and afraid," Emily said. "I was, too. All these years, and he still frightens me." She shot Mr. Perini a let-us-be look, signaling she had something she wanted to share.

Tears burned the back of my nose, threatened my eyes. "Did he hurt you?"

"Terribly, but not as you think, pet." She reached for my hand, clasped it and gently squeezed. A whisper of a smile curved her lips. "I decided to leave him and to counter his evil with good. I was terrified, but I did it. I'm still doing it."

The truth settled in. "Matthew is right. You are the she in the bronze monument. You bridge the gap."

The fear and sadness fell under dignity. She lifted her chin. "We all do, dear. Each and every one of us."

I remembered holding on to her on the gurney, promising her she wouldn't fall, and I smiled with her. "Yes, I guess we do."

Mr. Perini cleared his throat. "Rose, someone is waiting to see you."

From his smile, I had a strong suspicion my brother had arrived, and I dared to hope. "Jackson?"

Mr. Perini nodded. "He's in the upstairs parlor."

I ran for the steps.

Matthew's footfalls echoed on the treads, right behind me.

"Jackson." Breathless, I rushed from the doorway of the interior, upstairs apartment across the carpeted floor then embraced my baby brother, who stood a head and a half taller than me. "Oh, Jackson, I'm sorry to have put you through all this."

He hugged me so tight I couldn't breathe. "Daisy, I was terrified that I'd lost you forever."

I reared back and studied his face, saw the ravages of fear and grief in his weariness. His dark brown hair was shorter, his face leaner, and he'd filled out. Still working out every day, gauging by the bulk of muscle, and carrying the world's weight on his shoulders. Still I couldn't relieve him but had to warn him for his own sake as well as mine and Matthew's. "Daisy is dead, Jackson. You're here to bury her." Overwhelmed at seeing him when I'd thought I'd never be able to do so again, I felt hot tears roll down my face — and I pretended I didn't see the ones rolling down his. "I'm Rose Matthews, and this is my husband, Matthew Green." I leaned back further to bring Mark into the circle.

Matthew smiled. "It's good to see you, Jackson." He extended his hand.

Jackson grabbed it, pulled him into a fierce hug. "Matthew." Jackson smiled through the tears now. "Are you two really married?"

"Yes, we are." I smiled from ear to ear,

signaling my brother I was not only married but elated to be married to his old friend.

"I knew it." Jackson released me. "Craig and I both did. We were positive if we could just get you two together, it'd be kismet."

"Well," Matthew said, "I've married her twice, so you guys were definitely right." He laughed and pulled me to him.

"The lawyer told me you'd gotten married before you died, but I thought you did that for legal reasons. I didn't realize . . . He didn't say . . ." Jackson went silent. "Wow. Love looks really good on you two."

Love? Was it love? I avoided Matthew's eyes. If it wasn't and he looked shocked . . . Call me a coward. I just couldn't deal with that and our funerals in the same day.

"You got married *twice*?" Jackson repeated.

I nodded. "Once before we died, then again after we were reborn."

"Wow. I'm thrilled. Seriously. Congratulations." Jackson shook his head. "I'm glad something good came out of all this. Really glad."

"So are we," Matthew told his brother-in-law. "Come and sit down. We need to catch up."

Jackson looked at his watch. "We don't have a lot of time before your funerals."

"Then we'll make the best of what time we do have," I said, feeling almost giddy. There was something special about having two of the men I most love in the same room with me. If Lester were here, I think it'd be one of my life's most perfect moments. That struck me as bizarre, considering I was about to be buried. Guess you never know when life's going to toss you a juicy bone.

"We need to talk a bit about assets, too, Jackson," Matthew said.

"Better see to essentials first." He again checked his watch.

"You can rebuild Jameson Court or not, your call," Matthew said. "But Rose and I need at least a million of the money to start over."

At least a million? My ears had to be off. Just how wealthy was he?

"Whatever you want. It's yours. I'm just caretaking."

"You use what you need to have the life you want."

Jackson looked stunned. "You're serious."

Matthew nodded. "You're my family, Jackson."

A hard lump rose and fell in Jackson's neck, and his voice turned husky. I was overwhelmed. Never had he had anyone but me. Now he had Matthew. And that Matthew loved him, called him family . . . I couldn't process all those feelings. I'd never allowed myself to dream all those feelings.

"You're my family, too," Jackson said. "Anything, anytime, anywhere. Long as I live."

Matthew clapped Jackson's shoulder. "Honored."

"Me, too." He smiled at me and then looked back at Matthew. "I'm happy being a pastry chef and Dallas suits me so, no, I'm not into rebuilding Jameson Court. I'd think of the jerks that made you two die every time I walked in the door." Brutally honest, Jackson turned back to specifics. "How do I get what you want to you?" He sat back in a chair near the sofa.

We sat down on it, and Matthew shared our plan. "We've got it all worked out," he said. "We'll funnel everything through Mr. Perini. Messages, money, whatever. He'll get it to us and there'll be no added jeopardy to you. We want you safe."

Surprise flitted across Jackson's face. "You're not going to even tell me where you're going?"

Everything in me rebelled. "We'll be in touch as soon as it's safe." I licked my dry lips. "Jackson, there are a lot of people who want us dead. They'll harm anyone in order to make it happen. If any of us, you included, are going to have a life, then we've got to be careful." I pressed a hand to his knee. "You understand?"

He nodded. "I hate this." Venom filled his voice. "But I understand."

"When we settle and don't think it'll endanger you, you'll get postcards. They won't be signed, but you'll know they're from us."

"I'll miss you, Daisy."

"I'll miss talking to you, too, but I'll keep watch so I know you're safe. I'm not sure how yet, but I'll find a way."

Too soon came a knock on the apartment door.

It opened, and Mr. Perini came in, wearing a stern expression full of worry. "Jackson, you have to go. We're being watched by everybody and his brother. They're not even trying to be subtle." He lifted a hand, his disbelief in his razor's edged tone. "Remember, you're in mourning, and you've just seen your sister dead for the first time." Mr. Perini's expression turned more grim. "Convince them, son. Lives depend on it."

Jackson stood up, smoothed his slacks at his thighs then tugged at his waistband. "I'll give it all I've got." He leaned forward.

"Make this hug a good one, sis. It's got to last me a long, long time."

I held him hard and whispered close, "I love you, Jackson. I've always loved you and I always will." Tears threatened. I blinked hard, holding them back. The last thing either of us needed were the waterworks. This was a time for strength, and as always, he looked to me for his cue on how to behave. If I cried, he'd be upset too. I pulled back. "How's that for a hug?"

"Perfect." He held me by the upper arms. "I love you, Daisy."

"I know." Though I feared my face would crack from the effort, I smiled.

He cleared his throat, then reached for Matthew. "You take care of her."

"With all I've got, Jackson."

I watched the second peacock strut, and felt incredibly moved. Most women had one. I feared having none, once I learned what it was, and now had two. Incredibly special moment, this.

"I'll be back just before two." Jackson stopped at the door, took one last hungry look at me, and then headed down the stairs.

"You raised a fine man, Rose." Mr. Perini grunted. "We'd better watch, just to see how he handles his performance firsthand."

"The window?" I asked.

"Absolutely not. I wasn't kidding about everybody being out there. Keller, Johnson and men from the Marcello and Adriano families are on the street — and some guy in a cop's uniform from NOPD. I'm not sure who he is. Barry's running a check on him."

Matthew frowned, but I sensed more than saw he was pleased. "Probably Tank. I can't imagine any other cop from New Orleans coming to send me off."

"Big guy, broad shoulders and a thick neck?" Mr. Perini asked.

Matthew nodded. "Definitely Tank."

"Is he a friend or foe?" Mr. Perini walked to the other side of the living room then paused, waiting for Matthew's answer.

"Friend." Matthew shrugged but looked Mr. Perini right in the eye. "Probably the only real one I have left from my life at home."

A look of understanding passed between the men. "Something my father passed to me, I'll share with you. He said, if a man lives a long life, he'll be lucky to count his real friends on the fingers of one hand. Nobody gets two hand's worth, and if on the one, you have a couple fingers left, you've been a lucky man."

"One real friend is worth more than two

hands of others." Matthew nodded. "Thank you for reminding me of that."

"One of your real friends just left this room," Mr. Perini said. "You've one in this room still, and if you've another outside . . ."

"I'm blessed three times over."

"All that, and a good wife? More than three times over." Mr. Perini pressed a button behind a shelving unit full of colorful knickknacks that probably were art and cost a fortune. They had that look. The unit slid away from the wall and exposed a doorway opening.

We followed him through it, into a small room filled with dozens of monitors. Every inch of the interior and exterior of the funeral home was on one screen or another. No wonder Mr. Perini had been so confident of stopping the families from breaking in. They hadn't stood a chance.

I spotted Jackson in the parking lot. He stood outside his car, his head hung, his shoulders stooped. So still. So very still. I couldn't see the tears running down his face, but I felt them, and a moment later he buried his face in his hands and openly wept. Sobs wracked his body, heaving his shoulders and rippling his shuddering muscles. I knew him better than anyone else in the world, and I believed he was grieving.

"Looks convincing to me," Matthew said from beside me.

"He is convincing — and truly grieving." Aching and relieved, I nodded. "For the first time in his life, he can't pick up a phone and find me on the other end."

Something in my voice or what I said must have alerted Matthew that I felt fragile, because he wrapped his arm around my waist. "It's okay, honey. He knows he can get to us through Mr. Perini any time, and he knows you're fine."

"He's afraid for us. And he's worried about when he'll see us again."

"She's right." Mr. Perini told Matthew. "Most of my life, I've studied people at their most vulnerable — nothing kicks a soul to the knees like grief. Jackson's scared to death and he's genuinely grieving."

"Everything's changed forever, and he knows it." I swallowed hard.

Paul looked me right in the eye. "How lucky you are to be loved that much."

"It's always been just him and me," I said with a sniff. "He's feeling orphaned."

"He's been orphaned all his life," Mr. Perini said, clearly confused.

"Yes," Matthew said, "but Daisy made

sure Jackson didn't know it."

"Ah, and now he does." Mr. Perini grunted. "Poor guy."

"Will you help me watch over him, Mr. Perini? Please?"

"Of course." He clasped my hand and gave it a reassuring pat. "He's your family, Rose. We take care of family."

"Thank you." I sniffed and swiped at my eyes.

Jackson got into his rental car and drove out of the parking lot. I watched through the trees until I couldn't see him anymore. Craig Parker would help him through this, but I couldn't, and the weight of that bore down on me like a ton of bricks.

"Don't be sad," Mr. Perini said. "You have much to do and I've said we'll take care of this. Trust me."

I nodded, though I wasn't sure my heart was in it.

"Barry will be back for you in thirty minutes." Mr. Perini looked over at the clock on the monitor screen. "I guess now is the time to fill you two in on just how all this is going to work."

I'd been curious of course, but I didn't want to infer a lack of trust in Mr. Perini by asking questions. Dying and starting another life taught a woman a lot of things. Patience, and to reach out and be a bridge. And that forfeiting control didn't mean losing yourself. Sometimes it actually helped you find yourself and become a better person. I needed to think more on all this, but for the moment, knowing not asking how it would all work was a good thing. Mr. Perini had a thing about being quizzed, and Lester did, too.

Interesting for Lester in particular, considering he'd been under cover and dishonest with me from the start. But in spite of that, I had no doubt whatsoever that he loved me, and he'd gone to great lengths to do what he could to help me and keep me safe. *A bridge.*

A father.

"Let's sit at the table." Paul grabbed a cup. "I always think better with a mug of coffee in my hand."

CHAPTER 21

Rose and Matthew huddled at the surveillance screens and watched the dreaded arrivals.

The little chapel had seven rows of double pews flanking its center aisle. Two huge sprays of lilies lay atop wooden tables on either side of the narrow room. One bore a pink ribbon, the other a blue. And heavy silk drapes hung ceiling to floor behind them. Just in front of them, perched on a wooden easel, stood a photograph of a smiling Mark and Daisy in their wedding finery. They looked . . . happy.

Noises sounded from the apartment.

Matthew took a quick look. "Lester," he said.

"Here you are." His head and shoulders appeared at the doorway. "Paul says it's time for your coffin stint."

My tangled nerves sizzled. "I'm going to cough or sneeze or something and mess this up. I just know it."

"You won't," Matthew assured me. "Neither will I."

We couldn't. Our entire futures, our very lives depended on not messing this up.

"Just think of Jackson. We have to be perfect for his sake."

For Jackson. "Right." I took two steps, stopped and pecked a kiss to Matthew's lips. "You're playing me, and I know it. Using Jackson because you know there's nothing I won't do for him. I just wanted you to know that I know what you're doing."

He smiled. "Whatever works."

"Move it, you two," Lester interrupted. "It's time to work."

We went down the back stairs and into the prep room, where Barry stood waiting.

He did a double-take at seeing me in my wedding dress and Matthew in his wedding tux. "Best move it. People are starting to arrive." He stepped aside.

The two glass coffins I'd seen earlier stood waiting. That was both a blessing and a curse. They'd see us, be convinced we were dead. But if we so much as flinched, they'd see that too. So the exposure was both a blessing and an added danger.

In short order, we lay inside our coffins. Lester adjusted the skirt of my gown. "You okay, Daisy girl?"

No sense in lying about it. He'd know the truth anyway. "Scared stiff."

"I expect so, but there ain't no help for it. This'll be over soon enough and you can start your new life. Make it a good one, you hear me?"

"I will." Near tears again, I swallowed hard. "Lester, I — I love you." No way could I tell him how much he meant to me and all that was in my heart.

"Love you, too, Daisy girl." He patted my hand, then crossed on top of me in the standard funeral pose. "I'm gonna miss you."

"I'll miss you, too," I whispered. "You'll keep an eye on Jackson?"

"Yep, I surely will."

"Thank you."

"No need, darlin'. He's mine, too. Taught him to fish, if you recall."

"And so much more." I swallowed a lump in my throat. "What he knows about being a man, he learned from you. Have I ever thanked you for that?"

"A thousand times, Daisy girl. Bailing me outta jail, eating peanut butter for a week time and again. Oh, you've thanked me plenty." He sniffled. "Now hush yourself and be still so I don't have to kill nobody today, eh?"

That widened my eyes. But I knew in a blink he wasn't exaggerating, he was dead serious. "I won't mess up. I promise."

He winked. "Now that's the kind of talk I like to hear."

"Where's Emily?"

"Dead, remember?"

"I know that. I meant right now."

"Watching from above, like the angel she is," he said, his gaze rolling toward the ceiling. "Too risky, her being down here."

Watching from the surveillance room and, with Victor Marcello in the building, it was way too risky for her anywhere else in the building.

"You've got plenty of air and we'll get you out as soon as we can. Whatever you do, don't move." Barry started to lower the lid.

"Wait!" I looked over at Matthew. I wanted to tell him that I loved him, but I couldn't. Not for the first time here, not like this. "See you in just a bit."

He smiled. "In just a bit."

Mr. Perini walked in, ending the moment. "Jackson's arrived. They're all here. It's time."

Barry closed the lid on Matthew's coffin.

Lester closed the lid on mine.

"Blink if you can hear me." Mr. Perini

stepped between their coffins. "Okay, good. Lester, you go join Jackson. You two," he said to Matthew and me, "no moving at all. No breathing deeply, or through your mouths. Here's how it's going to happen. We'll wheel you into the chapel. I'll open the curtain, announce that both of you requested there be no service or viewing, then Barry will close the curtain. They'll all see you, but that won't be enough."

It wouldn't. I mouthed a question, hoping he'd understand. "Did Keller and Johnson get the court order to take possession of our bodies?"

"No judge would grant any of them possession."

I innately knew there was a "without my approval" attached to that. Between Mr. Perini and Dexter Devlin, I felt confident that was the case. "Are you going to bury us?"

"No, not bury." He moved into position at the head of her coffin, motioned to Barry to move to the foot. "Burn."

Mr. Perini and Barry positioned the coffins at the front of the chapel, opened the drapes, and then placed the sprays of flowers atop our coffins, their movements methodical. I could see each step playing out in my head.

"Okay," he told Barry. "Let them in. Jackson first, then when he's seated, the others can enter."

Barry had been with Mr. Perini a long time, which meant his words were for Matthew and me and not for Barry.

Rustling sounds soon penetrated the glass surrounding me. The creak of wood — Jackson sitting down on the wooden pew — and then the low-key din of others shuffling into the chapel. Inside my mind, I saw them. Detective Keller and Special Agent Johnson entering and sitting on the right, near my coffin. Victor Marcello choosing to sit in the last pew on the left. For Edward, he would sit on Matthew's side, and he'd surely be flanked by two of his well-dressed thugs. The stocky man with dark hair and eyes and heavy jowls Matthew described as Adriano would sit in the back near the entrance, fearful of being too close to Marcello and unable to exit. He too would be escorted by his men. Tank, I imagined, seating himself in a front-row pew close to Matthew, his expression set in stone, his gaze never wandering. He had to be on edge, sitting this close to Marcello and Adriano, knowing they bombed Jameson Court and prompted events that led to Matthew's death, and still he remained helpless to do anything to them.

Mr. Perini quickly did what he said he was going to do, then the sounds of the curtain drawing closed filled the air.

Marcello's voice echoed through the chapel, confirming Mr. Perini's supposition that seeing their bodies wouldn't satisfy these men. "This isn't over until I see them put in the ground."

Johnson agreed.

"I'm afraid that's impossible." Mr. Perini sounded calm but firm.

"Why?" Keller asked.

"They aren't being buried," Mr. Perini said. "The bodies are being taken directly to the crematorium."

"Then we want to see them cremated," Victor Marcello insisted.

"Mr. Grant," Mr. Perini said to Jackson. "As next of kin, we have to have your permission for anyone else to view the cremation — unless you all have court orders."

Not one of them uttered a sound.

"Why is that necessary?" Jackson asked. "We all just saw them both. Why do these people have to intrude there, too?"

Adriano gave the only answer they'd be getting. "We want to be there."

Mr. Perini interceded. "Mr. Grant . . . Jackson, we have a viewing room at the crematorium. They will be sequestered there and not intrude on you or the process in any way."

Jackson would understand that Mr. Perini wanted them sequestered. He wanted them pinned in place as long as possible. It afforded Rose and Matthew time they sorely needed to come out of this alive. *Get it, Jackson. Come on. Get it.*

"All right." Jackson said. "If they stay in the viewing room and don't try to intrude, I'll permit them to attend.

"That's for the best," Mr. Perini said. "Gentlemen, if you'll exit the chapel, we'll prepare the bodies for transfer."

Victor Marcello called out. "We need directions."

"Of course," Mr. Perini said. "Barry, pass the gentlemen the printed directions to the facility, please. Mr. Grant, your limo is curbside out front."

Printed directions. Clearly Mr. Perini had been prepared for exactly this.

And just as clearly, he had prepared Jackson.

The Dixie crematorium was a red-brick, six-story building two blocks behind Paul Perini's funeral home. On each end, tall spires stretched into the sky, and a square emissions system stood like a spike near the rear of the building. At the other end of that tower, deep inside the building was a flue. One that would be important to us.

The building looked exactly as Mr. Perini had described it when briefing us on this finale to our deaths and what we must do to finish this. While we lay in the hearse in our coffins, we heard the men gather near the building's entrance.

Mr. Perini spoke. "Mr. Grant, I'll escort you. The rest of you may follow at a respectful distance. Detective Keller and Special Agent Johnson, if you'll join Barry when you see him, he'll have your authorization badges for entrance into the viewing room. Mr. Adriano and Mr. Marcello, you and your associates join Barry also, please, and keep your badge affixed to your lapels and in plain sight at all times. You all must stay with Barry the entire time you're in the facility. No exceptions. I'm sure you understand, for safety reasons, they can't have people in here, wandering at will." He paused, and when no one objected or commented, he continued. "Mr. Tank, if you wouldn't mind accompanying Mr. Grant, that would be helpful."

"Yes, sir." Tank readily agreed.

"Thank you," Mr. Perini said. "I have duties, you see, and I'd rather Mr. Grant not endure this alone."

"Of course."

Mr. Perini seemed formal but compassionate and made it clear to everyone in the group that he was in total control and intended to fully exercise it. I didn't have to see it to respect and admire his savvy. So much came through in his voice and in their reactions to it.

All of the men had to be bristly at being in such close proximity to one another. There were histories here. Bad blood, too.

Mr. Perini fell silent and in my mind, I imagined them crossing the white marble floor to the elevator he had described to Matthew and me. Them riding it down to the lowest level, two stories below ground. The doors would open and they'd file out.

Barry opened the hearse and two men assisted him in moving our bodies inside, taking a different elevator and bringing us down to the bottom floor. Our elevator doors opened and we were wheeled into place in a cavernous, well-lighted room. The viewing room would be to the left, the furnace, as Mr. Perini called it, straight ahead, and his warning replayed in my mind. *Don't breathe deeply. Don't move. No twitching or scratching — not now. You'll be in full view of everyone until you're transferred. There's nothing to hide even the smallest of movements.*

"Here we are." Mr. Perini said. "Mr. Grant and Mr. Tank, if you will please come with me. You have to identify the bodies."

"I just saw them at the funeral home," Jackson said.

"I apologize, Mr. Grant. But it's state law. Before we can actually perform this service, we must have the next of kin personally identify the bodies."

"All right." Jackson's voice stiffened in what must be a common reaction. People did tend to get wired around dead bodies.

Barry moved the forty feet to Mr. Perini's side. "We're ready to transfer them, sir."

"Excellent. Kindly escort these gentlemen to the viewing chamber." He looked to Jackson and Tank. "It's insulated so it'll be cooler and more comfortable for you. Typically, we try to shield the loved ones from this part of the process, but in this case, that isn't possible. Everyone will have a clear view of the bodies entering the primary chamber."

"The primary chamber?" Jackson asked.

"Follow the conveyer belt. On the other

side of the main door is the primary chamber. Beyond it is a secondary chamber for the actual fire. We seal the bodies in the primary chamber — see that metal door?" Jackson must have nodded because Mr. Perini went on. "The bodies will enter the secondary chamber on the conveyer and then that inner door will seal off the primary chamber. It isn't —"

"Do you use wood, or what?" Marcello asked.

"Mr. Marcello," Mr. Perini admonished him. "I can appreciate your curiosity, but we must respect the sensitivity of the situation. Now isn't the time."

Jackson interjected, "I'm curious, too."

"In that case, some use wood. We do not. Natural gas." Mr. Perini sniffed. "Ours is the latest technology, of course."

The men's voices muffled. Apparently, they'd entered the glass-wall viewing room. Mr. Perini had said there were two rows of six blue padded seats. In my mind, I saw the men walk in and sit down, their gazes trained on the unobstructed view of the flames inside the outer door. It would be opened. Mr. Perini wanted the men to see the fire and flames, to assure them in their own minds, anything going inside would not survive. Their perception, while a bit macabre, was essential to our fresh-start success.

Keller asked, "Did you check the credentials on this place?"

"Yeah." Johnson answered him. "It's clean."

That seemed to satisfy Keller; he didn't ask anything else. And Marcello and Adriano would have had to be deaf not to hear the exchange in the silent little room.

Jackson stood near the two glass coffins. Barry and Mr. Perini, aided by the same two men who'd wheeled us down here, transferred our bodies from the coffins to white combustible boxes. He waited until the boxes were closed, then pressed a hand to each one and paused.

Mr. Perini, from the rustle of fabric, clasped Jackson's upper arm then their footfalls faded; leading him to, I supposed, the viewing room. I didn't have to see Jackson to imagine his face. It would be pain-ravaged by grief; his eyes red, his cheeks flushed and tear-stained. He'd sit down in the first available seat in the nearest row.

A door closed.

My heart rate kicked up. The viewing room door closing, locking them inside.

Now, I dared to squint to see, terrified because even Mr. Perini had deemed this the most dangerous part of the entire operation.

Two thick stone-looking slabs on wheeled metal frames stood waiting. On them rested single stones. Our boxes would be placed atop those single stones. The wheels rolled forward across the concrete slab floor, backed up and then rolled forward again. A metal clacking sounded — the conveyer belt had been turned on.

My heart thundered. If not for the roar of the fire, closed door or not between us, the men watching would have heard. It hurt, as if it banged against my ribs, my chest wall. Suddenly, I was hot all over, pouring sweat. Mr. Perini had warned us about the heat and not to fear it. But with every pore in my body wide open and sweat drenched, I did fear I'd vaporize before the sweat soiled the cloth of my wedding dress and it burned to ash. *Don't worry, Daisy. Rose. Don't be afraid, Rose. It's going to be all right. Just for a few more seconds. No, don't break out of here, don't try to run. That's certain death. Just try to breathe.*

My gut alarm said to escape. Every instinct in my body warned me to move, to run, to get away from the fire. It roared in my ears, burned in my nose, and I wanted to heed the warnings. Wanted to, but couldn't. Lester and Emily and Mr. Perini's images filled my mind.

The battle raged fierce. *Trust them. Trust them.*

The heat inside the box grew hotter. "Trust them," I whispered. Hotter and then hotter. *I can't stand this. I can't do it!*

The outer door slammed shut.

Don't panic. Don't panic. A few more seconds and it's going to be okay. You're going to be okay. Oh, God, let me be okay!

A gear ground and suddenly we were moving, but not forward — upward. Upward, just as Mr. Perini had said. I began counting, as instructed. "One, one thousand. Two, one thousand . . . And on I went until I reached Twenty, one thousand.

I waited.

Nothing happened.

My heart stilled, hung suspended in my chest. Had something gone wrong? *Oh, no — we weren't going to be okay!* Terror paralyzed me.

My box opened. Matthew grabbed me by the arms, lifted me up and out of the box onto a narrow ledge. "Hurry. We've got thirty seconds to make it to the door."

He half-pulled, I half-scrambled, nearly tripping.

"Lift your skirt. It's going to get caught in

the belt or the barrier walls."

I gathered and scooped it up, crushed the delicate fabric to me, wishing I hadn't gotten sappy and sentimental and had settled on jeans. But I hadn't realized the handicap . . .

The primary chamber floor gapped opened and steel walls slid up between us and the flames. "Matthew . . . ?" We should be off the conveyer by now. Would we be trapped on the fireside of the door? Why didn't he say to get off?

The walls clicked, locking into place. "Now, Rose!"

Hands linked, the walls seeping intense heat, we jumped, landed on a broad ledge and watched the belt continue to move. When our boxes passed, Matthew squatted then lifted a trap door. He checked it, then looked at me. "Go on, Rose. Just slide down the chute."

Knowing the fire was beneath me *somewhere,* I told myself it wasn't down the chute and I tried to move, but I couldn't. My feet wouldn't listen to my brain. They seemed fused to the metal ledge. I stared at Matthew in horror.

He grabbed me by the arms. "You're safe, Rose. I've got you. I've got you."

The fear drained from my body. I looked

up at him — and he dropped me down the chute.

I hit the slick metal slide with a healthy thump that stole my breath and slid through the darkness. *Down . . . Down . . . Down . . .*

Above me, a low grinding noise sounded. It grew loud, then louder until it hurt my ears and jarred my teeth. Backlit by fire, I saw Matthew's silhouette. He jumped into the chute.

I hit the dirt with a hard thump and an unintended grunt. Pain shot through my arm, my back. Knowing Matthew was right behind me, I rolled aside and then just stopped.

He landed beside me with a healthy "Humph!"

It took a long moment for us both to recover.

"You okay, honey?" he asked.

"I'm okay." I swallowed hard. "You okay?"

He laughed.

That should bother me. Him laughing at a moment like that. But it didn't. I swatted at him and planted a kiss to his cheek — it was the only thing I could reach.

He lifted me to him and kissed me hard.

"I never want to do anything like that again," I admitted. "I hope Mr. Perini isn't planning that for Emily tomorrow."

"He wouldn't do that. She's being buried at Sampson Park."

"Clever." I grinned. "The one place Victor Marcello can never go."

Matthew dusted the loose dirt from his hands. "We have to move."

"Paul said the process takes seventy minutes."

"Yes, and we need every one of them to get a head start. We don't want to leave here at the same time they do. Who knows if they're still here now? They might have left as soon as the oven door closed."

He had a point. "I'm all turned around. We went up, sideways, then down. Where are we?" I looked around. A dimly lit, barren dirt tunnel. "Underground?"

"We went up a secondary flue — not in use obviously — then sideways through a passage outside the crematory, and then down a chute from inside the building to below ground. We're at least three stories underground right now. At least, that's how I remember it being described."

"We knew about this chute thing? I don't remember it. Where was I went that happened?"

"In the bathroom, I suspect, crying about Jackson. Seeing him grieving in the parking lot was hard on you."

It had been. "Well, probably best I didn't know. Lord, I thought the heat would really kill me."

"The jeopardy was in getting out of the box and not falling off the ledge." He looked back at me. "We need to move faster. Can you run in that dress?"

The dirt was smooth, fine. I paused and removed my shoes then bunched up the skirt of my gown. "Ready."

"I do love a practical woman."

I smiled. "How long is it going to take us to get outside?"

"About twenty minutes, unless we pick up the pace."

"Run."

He reached for my hand, clasped it, and side-by-side, we ran through the dim tunnels. Long before seeing an exit, my leg muscles burned, my calves ached, my feet turned leaden, sliding in the smooth dirt, and my breathing grew ragged and rough.

"Need to slow down?"

"We don't dare." It was all I could manage.

It was more than enough.

We kept running. A stitch hitched in my side. I pressed the arm holding the bunched skirt of my gown tight to my body, hoping the pressure would help and deepened my breathing. Then muscle spasms set in.

"What's wrong?"

"Muscle spasms. The heat. I got dehydrated."

"I'll carry you."

"No. I can do it. I can."

"Rose, you don't have to do this alone now. We've got each other. It's okay to need me."

He knew exactly what troubled me. "I know. But I have to know I can help myself. I have to, Matthew." I licked my parched lips and admitted that which I most feared telling anyone, even myself. "It's about me not being afraid."

"I understand. Okay. Okay." He started running again, but slowed his pace.

I passed him, forcing him to run at the speed we had been running.

Finally, in front of us, light appeared. We neared the end of the tunnel.

Minutes later, we stepped outside, into the waning sun. Trees and hills of dirt surrounded us. The distant sound of cars on an asphalt road and a cool breeze blew across our skin. I let go of the skirt of my gown and listened to the birds, trilling a sweet tune. "What I wouldn't give for a bottle of water."

"I'm surprised Mr. Perini didn't stow

some in the tunnel."

"He probably did. We didn't check."

"True." Matthew slowed the pace to a brisk walk. "It won't be long and we'll be to the car. Do you have the keys?"

"Barry was afraid I'd lose them between there and the car, remember? Considering the chute, that was probably smart. He put them under the rear floor mat," I reminded Matthew.

Just short of a clearing in the woods, Matthew stopped. "You stay here. Let me circle around and make sure it's safe."

"No. We'll go together."

Whether that pleased or frustrated him, I couldn't tell. But we stepped out into the clearing and hastily made our way to the other side of it, then back into the wood, grateful for its cover. "I didn't expect this." Sunlight filtered through the trees, dappled the forest floor. "Where exactly are we?" I'd expected to come up from down under in the town not far from the crematorium, not out in the middle of nowhere.

"No idea, but it's not important." Matthew craned his neck, squinted his eyes, seeking. "Or it won't be, once we find the car."

I looked in earnest for it, and saw nothing. My stomach sank. "I don't see —"

"There it is." Matthew headed to the southeast, toward the green truck nearly obscured by small branches thick with leaves.

"I missed it twice, knowing right where Paul said it would be," Matthew complained.

"I didn't see it, either." I stepped on a crackling branch.

He opened the door. "There's a cooler." Bending, he pulled two bottles of water, twisted off the tops and then passed one to me.

I drank long and hard. The cold rushing down my throat was the best feeling. "Oh, that's good."

Matthew upended his bottle and rinsed his face. "Then polished off the rest and put the bottle back in the cooler."

I opened my door and saw changes of clothes on the seat. I passed his to him and switched from my gown into the jeans and blue top. "Ah, that's better."

"Definitely," he said, buttoning the last of the buttons on his shirt, then tossing the tux into the back seat. "Want more water?"

"Oh, yeah."

He grabbed two bottles, passed them to me, then slid into his seat and cranked the engine. The vent blew blessed cool air.

I took another drink of water.

Matthew stilled, then turned and looked at me. He seemed a little wonder-struck. "We did it, Rose."

"We did."

Laughing and crying at once, we hugged. "We did." I kissed Matthew soundly.

He kissed me back, then smiled. "What's that for?"

"Throwing me down the chute. I don't know what happened. My feet wouldn't work. I couldn't move."

"You did fine. Better than fine. We're finally free, Rose. Alive and free." He pulled me closer, then kissed me again. Longer. Deeper. Full of fierce adrenaline and pure passion. When he separated our mouths, I expelled an unsteady breath. "Wow. Maybe I should freeze up more often."

Oddly, Matthew didn't smile or whip out a snappy comeback. His laughter was gone and the man facing me was serious, somber. "Before we leave here, I need to know."

That he did need to know was clear. "What do you need to know?" That was not. But whatever it was, it really, *really* mattered to him.

He hesitated.

I pushed. "Just tell me, Matthew."

His knuckles knobbed on the steering

wheel. "Did you marry me out of pity?"

"Which time?"

That earned me a glare I won't soon be forgetting.

"Either."

"No, I didn't."

Relief replaced his uncertainty. "Why did you do it, then?"

"I told you at Sampson Park."

He dragged a hand through his still damp hair. "I remember everything you told me at Sampson Park. But none of it explains why you wanted to sleep with me. You said us sleeping together would save you a trip to the loft."

"I did."

"We both know, I'd have been up there sleeping, which means we'd be sleeping together regardless."

"I guess it does."

"Was it just sex, Rose?"

"No." How could he even think that? But that he did made her wonder. "Was it for you?"

Now he looked angry. "Of course not."

A burst of joy and pure relief washed through me. "That's good to know." I lifted my empty bottle. "Do we have more water. That fire was so hot. I thought I'd melt before that conveyer stopped. Or that it'd sear the flesh off my bones."

"Me, too. Rattled me a little, though I knew it was coming." Popping the top on the cooler, he then passed me two more fresh bottles of water, then turned back in his seat and cranked the air-conditioner up another notch.

"It was all I could do to make myself stay put." I opened the bottle and passed it to him, then opened the second and took a long swallow. The cool felt comforting, going down my throat. "It had to be even worse for you. You were closer to the secondary chamber."

He emptied the bottle and reached for yet another. "I have a confession to make." He motioned asking if I wanted another. When I refused, he closed the cooler and the lid snapped back into place. "Inside that box, I had one regret."

Maybe he was sorry he'd married me. If so, I didn't want to hear it. Not now. But apparently now he intended to say it — whatever it was. "I'm sorry to hear that." This couldn't be good news. Regret and good news just didn't travel together.

"It kind of surprised me." He glanced toward me. Well, out my side window.

"Want to share it?" I held up a hand. "I'm not pushing, and if it's awful, then actually,

I think you should wait to share it because, well, it's been an . . . emotional day. I've had about all I can take for today."

"It's not awful," he insisted, then thought again. "Well, it's not awful to me. Actually, it's pretty wonderful. But I don't know. You might not like it. You might think it's awful."

"Well, are you going to ponder all afternoon or tell me? What was your regret?"

He put his water bottle in the cup holder and turned to me. "That if something went wrong, I'd die and you'd never know . . ." His Adam's apple bobbed in his throat. "I love you, Rose."

The joy inside me ran so deep, filled me so full, I feared I couldn't hold it all. That I'd float right off the seat and into the sky. And yet I knew. I'd always known. I'd run from it, hid from it, denied understanding it, terrified if I admitted it, it'd be snatched away and lost forever, but I'd known. I cupped his face with my hands, too tender to speak. For a long second, I just stared into his eyes, let him see all I felt for him without shields or barriers or fear. Finally, I gathered myself enough to give him the words. Like me, he needed them, and heart wide open, I gave him what he needed most. "I love you, too."

We kissed. A kiss unlike any kiss we'd shared before. Passion and heat, but tempered by love. And secure in his arms, the truth that dawned settled in and wove itself into the fabric of my life. Of his life. We became one.

I couldn't stop smiling.

Even half an hour later, cruising east on Interstate 10, feeling like a fool, I still couldn't stop smiling. The only thing that saved a shred of my dignity was that Matthew was smiling, too.

He turned the radio down. "So about this dream home of yours. The one you've got all the pictures of —"

I dipped my sunglasses down to the tip of my nose. "We're not going to find my dream home with a funeral parlor attached to it, hon."

"I don't suppose we will." He rotated his shoulder. "Guess we'll have to build, then."

Oh, I loved him for that. He wanted me to have my dreams. I pinched myself. Felt the sting. Smiled again. "No, we really don't." I glanced at a white truck parked on the side of the road. Flat back tire. "The dream house doesn't matter much anymore, though I still want a home."

He eyed me warily. "You kept a book.

Nine hundred pictures. It does matter to you, which means it matters to me. I want you to have your dream home."

Bless his heart. I had fallen into a mess but I sure had ended up with a good man. "I already do."

That confused him. "Angel, I love your optimism, and I hate to wreck your good mood, but the moment, we're homeless." Worry lit in his eyes. "Did you hit your head when you fell down the chute?"

"No, my head is fine." I leaned deeply toward him. "But somewhere in all this, I discovered something."

He bent his head to mine. "What's that?"

"Home is not a house." I leaned back, tugged a lock of hair away from his ear. "You're my home, Matthew. And wherever we are, so long as we're together, I'm home."

The look in his eyes warmed. That beloved twinkle filled them, and they shone overly bright. "Thank you, Rose."

He knew exactly what home meant to me. What it represented in my heart. I didn't have to explain a thing. I kept the glasses down on the tip of my nose so I could see his eyes unfiltered. "It seems simple now, but it took me a while to figure it out."

"The important lessons in life always take time."

"Is that one from your mom?" He was full of little bits of wisdom his folks had passed down to him.

"Actually, that one was my dad's."

I wished again, as I had so many times at Sampson Park, I could have known Matthew's parents. But in a way, I was coming to know them through the son they had raised. "On the house."

"Uh-huh?" He passed a pink Mary Kay car and eased back into the right lane.

"I'm fine with one connected to a funeral home, though in all my dreams, that's one thing I never pictured."

"Can't say I expected one attached to my kitchen, either. I thought I'd be at Jameson Court until I died of old age."

"I hate it that Jameson Court is gone."

"It was a special place. But we'll make another special place that's ours," he promised, then chuckled. "I still can't believe we're going to run a funeral home."

"Me either." I grunted. "But Lester and Mr. Perini were right. It's a healthy thing for us to do — help people get out of situations like we were in. What would we have done without Mr. Perini and Barry?"

"We'd be wearing concrete shoes, sitting

on the muddy bottom of the Mississippi River."

"That or be drowned in some bayou or swamp, acting as gator bait." My skin crawled.

Find a town and buy a funeral home. Mr. Perini had told us. *Wire Dexter Devlin and we'll get you the money to buy it. Learn how to run it, then in six months, let me know where you are and I'll send you some customers. We'll start our own brand of underground franchise.*

A franchise?

Sure. Down & Dead, Inc. Dexter's working on the papers. Oh, and get your notary.

A franchise. I grinned. I couldn't help it. Our bleak future had taken on a life and shape all its own. Our own kind of Sampson Park.

We're all somebody's bridge.

The sun slanted in through the windshield. I adjusted the visor to block it, and out fell a coin. My Grant half-dollar. "Mark?"

"Yeah?"

"I think Jackson and Lester are tracking the truck." I held up the Grant.

"They'll come for a visit soon enough, then." He glanced over, seemingly unconcerned.

"You knew they were tracking us?"

"No, but come on, Rose. You can't be that surprised."

I guess I wasn't. They would come to visit. And likely Emily would be with them. Knowing it made me happy. "I still can't believe Rachel didn't come to the funeral. She would have, I'm sure, except —"

"She has to live with Chris. I understand that." He paused, then added, "I imagine their house hasn't exactly been peaceful since Dexter Devlin told her Chris had mob connections."

"She'll leave him," I predicted. I couldn't see their relationship working out any other way. "Rachel's a straight up kind of woman."

"We'll see–eventually."

We would. I thought back to everything that had happened from the moment I kissed the concrete and Detective Keller gave me the suck-lemon news about Edward Marcello. So much I could never have predicted or would ever have even considered possible. Now I knew there were people that specialized in the impossible, and it was pretty exciting to think we'd be among them. Giving people second chances, new starts where they didn't have to be afraid or hurt, being their bridge . . .

"I think I'm going to love our new lives,

Matthew."

"Of course we will." He clasped my hand and passed an enormous street sign. "Well, it appears we're at a fork in the road. Do we go to Georgia or south Florida? Where would you rather live?"

"Georgia, I think." I scooted closer and rested my head on Matthew's shoulder. "Lester says dead people can live a good life in Georgia . . ."

Author's Note: Sampson Park is fictional, but Shelter House, which is located in the general area of Sampson Park is real, and its services include a 24-hour hotline, crisis counseling, advocacy, outreach, primary prevention, transitional housing and confidential shelter in Okaloosa and Walton Counties in Florida. For specifics on services offered or how you can support Shelter House, please visit www.shelterhousenwfl .org.

ABOUT THE AUTHOR

Vicki Hinze is an award-winning, USA Today bestselling author. She's had over thirty novels, four nonfiction books and hundreds of articles published in as many as 63 countries. Vicki also writes a weekly column for the Social-In Global Network and is recognized by *Who's Who in the World* as an author and as an educator. To learn more, visit www.vickihinze.com.

The employees of Thorndike Press hope you have enjoyed this Large Print book. All our Thorndike, Wheeler, and Kennebec Large Print titles are designed for easy reading, and all our books are made to last. Other Thorndike Press Large Print books are available at your library, through selected bookstores, or directly from us.

For information about titles, please call:
(800) 223-1244

or visit our Web site at:
http://gale.cengage.com/thorndike

To share your comments, please write:
Publisher
Thorndike Press
10 Water St., Suite 310
Waterville, ME 04901